MANTRAP

MANTRAP

BY
SINCLAIR LEWIS

AUTHOR OF
**MAIN STREET,
ARROWSMITH,
BABBITT, ETC.**

GROSSET & DUNLAP
PUBLISHERS   NEW YORK

To
FRAZIER HUNT

MANTRAP

CHAPTER ONE

PRICKLY heat jabbed its claws into Ralph's sweaty neck as he staggered under the load. All through the long portage and the torture of paddling afterward, he had looked forward to the shooting of Ghost Rapids, as anxiously as he looked backward to the man who was in pursuit.

He was glad to get it done, to come at last to those notorious rapids and see Lawrence Jackfish leap up in the bow, pointing with his paddle toward the one safe passage through the frenzy of broken currents. The stream poured between gnarled rocks in a gush smooth as a sculpture of polished bronze. Ralph fancied that if he touched that swelling sleekness of water it would be hard and slippery to his hot fingers. But beyond the gate of danger the churning and frightened river spread into a hundred whirlpools among rocks half hidden in the foam.

As he bent over the paddle, bringing the canoe's head sharply to the right to follow the fantastic jagged course which Lawrence was choosing, the rocks ashore caught the tail of his eye and he realized that the canoe was going with aeroplane speed into the mael-strom.

Suddenly they were in the calm waters beyond the rapids, and in relief Ralph sobbed above his lifted paddle, so that the girl looked back in wonder, and the Indian snickered. There was a sacred moment of security. But always Ralph knew that they were flee-ing from the angry man who might be following them —angry and swift and menacing.

Ralph Prescott was perhaps the most conservative member of that extraordinarily conservative firm of New York lawyers, Beaseley, Prescott, Braun and Braun. He played law as he played chess. A squabble was as inconceivable to him as a fist-fight, and it was a shock to find himself twitchy, irritable, likely to quarrel with clients and waiters and taxi-drivers.

He muttered, "Overwork—must take it a little easy —too much strain in the hydro-electric negotiations— try a little golf." But the little golf, or even the un-precedented dissipation of going to the "Follies" in-stead of staying home working over the documents with which his sober brief-case was always crammed, was insufficient to lull his jangling nerves, and night by night he awoke to obscure panics, lay rigid with black and anonymous apprehensions.

At forty Ralph Prescott was more than ever a

bachelor. The explanation was a mother so much more serene and fine and instantly understanding than any girl he encountered that he had preferred her dear presence to insinuating romance. But she had been dead these two years, and where she had once coaxed him away from his desk at midnight for a chat and easy laughter and a glass of milk before she ordered him off to bed, he sought now to fill the vacuum of her absence by working till one—till two —till weary dawn.

A friendly, grave man was Ralph, quietly popular among his friends, the dozen lawyers, doctors, engineers, and brokers whom he had known in college and whom he met nightly at the Yale Club; a man slight and eyeglassed and perhaps a little naïve.

However sharp he was, and however formidably solid about following up a point of law, he was still as respectful toward all the Arts and all the Politenesses as he had been in college, when he had listened to Professor Phelps in literature classes and from afar, with a small flame of worship for sweetness and light, made his bow to Thoreau and Emerson and Ruskin. It was concentration, with a trick of being obligingly friendly to judges and juries, which had won his legal prestige, not that thrusting power to bully and bluff and dazzle which distinguishes more realistic attorneys.

On a May day in the nineteen-hundred-twenties

Ralph Prescott perceived how badly his nerves were frayed.

He was driving, this Saturday afternoon, to the Buckingham Moors Country Club, beyond White Plains, for eighteen holes. He was driving his own coupé, which, with its prim nickel bumpers, its windows of speckless plate-glass, its chaste seat-coverings of much-laundered crash, was as depressingly proper as an undertaking parlor.

It was the first brilliant Saturday of late spring, and every one in New York who could drag out any sort of motor vehicle, from a 1910 Ford to a new Rolls-Royce, from a limousine to a passionately trembling old motorcycle, had been seized by the same enthusiastic notion and had dashed out to view Westchester County. When Ralph carefully turned from East Thirty-seventh, where was his small restrained flat, to Fifth Avenue, he found himself too tired to cope with the cruel and unyielding mass of cars.

Only by acrobatics and the risk of death could he zigzag his way ahead of the others. For miles he crept behind a venerable sedan, stopping in a panic whenever it stopped, till he came to hate the refulgence of the sedan-driver's bald head. Always he had to be attentive to the opposing line of cars so close to his left fender; had to be conscious of the car just behind him, which was apparently ambitious to run him down.

"And I'm supposed to be having an afternoon holiday!" he groaned. "I've simply got to get away. This isn't living. I'd like to go some place where I can have elbow-room and breathe again."

Once, when a traffic policeman halted him just as he came to a crossing, once, when a small boy ran out into the street in front of him, his heart almost stopped, in a panic as grotesque and alarming as the shriek of a lunatic. Through all the drive he never relaxed but only waited desperately for the end of this ordeal.

He finally won past the distasteful litter of gas stations, hot-dog stands, ugly frame houses, and came into the spacious peace of the Buckingham Country Club grounds. He halted his car on the curving gravel road hedged with rhododendrons, and drooped flabbily over the wheel.

"Got to take more care of myself," he meditated. "Rotten shape. Smoking too much—"

In that limp mood he was more than usually depressed by the locker-room of the club.

Damp cement walls, gritty cement floor, odors of sweat and gin and ancient bath-towels, sight of paunchy middle-aged men trying to be boyish in athletic undershirts, sound of overconfident laughter and more or less humorous boasting about scores—he had always felt fastidious about this den, but today it was intolerable. It was a relief to be taken up, bolstered

up, by the compelling breeziness of Mr. E. Wesson
Woodbury.

Woodbury was the chairman of the greens com-
mittee, and vice-president and sales-manager of the
fabulously powerful Twinkletoe Stocking Company,
whose sleek wares are to be observed on the ankles of
half the girls in the country, from Japanese cannery
hands in Seattle to chorus ladies in New York. Mr.
Woodbury was a round, thick, self-satisfied man. He
gave the impression of a particularly large and juicy
drumstick from the fricasseed chicken at Sunday dinner, and his loud sudden laughter had all the horror
of gears jammed by an unskilled driver.

Woodbury was dressing at a locker only four removed from Ralph's. He was donning checked knick-
ers, and stockings with rings of crimson and yellow
and pea-soup green, diversified by a few pretty adorn-
ments in the way of diamond-shaped blotches. While
he dressed he shouted as though Ralph were a mile
away:

"Better come join us—got three of a foursome—
just got three—me and Judge Withers and Tom
Ebenauer—just got three, but some gang, boy, some
gang, great gang. Better join us—better come join
us—the Judge might let you off easy when you come
up for transporting liquor."

Usually Ralph avoided Woodbury. He preferred
men quieter and more deft and honest. But today,

in his alarming shakiness, he was buoyed up by Woodbury's pink, swelling, shining self-confidence. He felt like the small boy in prep school who may not esteem greatly the football captain's notion of Latin declensions but who is glowingly flattered by his friendliness.

"Well—" he said.

Somehow, Woodbury was the sort of chap who would take care of him. He needed some one to lift him out of his shaky depression.

Ralph played a precise and conscientious game of golf, and for all his recent quiverings he was easily the best of the foursome. Woodbury had faith that by bellowing, "Well, by golly, how'd I happen t' do that?" he could make up for any slicing. As the four of them trailed along the serene pastures of the elm-shadowed course, Ralph found peace again and strength, and a certain affection for his jesting companions.

Woodbury was not always jesting, however. He had a grievance:

"I've certainly been having tough luck. Been planning a great ol' fishing and canoeing hike in northern Canada—way up north of railhead, along the Manitoba-Saskatchewan border—the Mantrap River country. Great place—get entirely away from civilization; just forget there *are* any doggone desks and phonecalls and bad accounts. I was up there three years ago—didn't quite get to Mantrap but nearly there.

And *fishing?* Say! Muskalonge, pike (only they call
'em dorés in Canada), ten-pound, fifteen-pound lake
trout—boy! I had it all planned out to go up there
this summer with a friend of mine lives in Winnipeg—canoes bought, route picked, four corking Indians
hired for guides; and then Lou—my friend—he had
the rotten taste to up and get sick on me. Say, Prescott, you better think about coming along in his place.
You lawyers don't have anything important to do anyway. Why don't you let up on your poor old clients
for a while and give 'em a chance to grab a little
money that you can take away from 'em next fall!"

"I'd rather like a vacation," mumbled Ralph, more
attentive to the probable lie of his ball than to the
Great Open Spaces.

"Like it? Ma-an! Pulling in a fifteen-pounder!
Sitting by the camp-fire, listening to the Old Timers
pull the long bow about pioneering! Sleeping in a
tent, without any autos honking! And look, Prescott:
seriously now: an awful easy trip, the way I make it.
The Injuns do all the carrying on the portages; they
cook the chow and clean the fish and put up the tents.
And when we don't use the outboard motor, they do
the paddling, not us."

"Motors? On canoes? In northern Canada?"
gasped Ralph. It was sacrilegious.

Woodbury waved his midiron in an hysteria of
laughter.

"You poor old tenderfoot! You Manhattan back-woodsman! Every Cree chief in Canada— I suppose you expect 'em to wear buckskin and paddle birch-bark canoes! Why, there isn't hardly a chief there that hasn't got an outboard motor and a white man's canvas canoe. Lord, you fellows make me tired. You—why, you know all about London and Paris and the Riviera—I've heard you gassing about 'em with Eddie Leroy—and you don't know these here North America no more'n a rabbit. Gosh, you're ignorant! Better come along and meet some real folks for a change!"

Ralph was both nettled and conscience-ridden. It was true. He knew nothing, nothing whatever, of the trappers and prospectors who still guard the frontier. He had never slept on the ground. He was soft. He was soft and timorous—he with his pretty little vacations in Brittany and Devon and the Bavarian Oberland! But also he was irritated by Woodbury's superior manner as he explained, like a radio lecturer, that there were six methods of propelling the big cargo canoes used for the long northern hikes: paddling, poling, motoring, lining, sailing, and even, in high waves, oars.

Mr. Woodbury evidently viewed with scorn the dainty canoes with red cushions and fancy names which are to be found at summer resorts. Now as those were the only canoes Ralph had ever known, as he remembered with fondness a certain lake, a certain canoe, and a certain girl whom he had paddled as much as a whole mile in the golden days of twenty years ago, he felt that Woodbury was a boor. . . . Horrible sort of chap to have with you in the strained intimacies of a wilderness journey!

But at the end of the game, as they tramped back to the clubhouse and to the gin and ginger-ale for which a hard week of sentencing people for selling gin had made Judge Withers peculiarly thirsty, Woodbury flung his arm about Ralph's shoulder and cried in a boyish and fetching manner he had now and then:

"Don't mind my kidding you, Prescott. You're not used to the wilds, but you'd learn—you've got nerve and sense. If you could make it, I'd love to have you come along. Think of it! Up towards Hudson Bay, where you begin to get the Northern Lights streaking across the sky in August!"

Though he had not taken the proposal seriously, all the way home from the country club Ralph drove easily, unconscious now of the press of traffic, absorbed in visions of the North—visions derived from the yarns which he absorbed in bed, after midnight, when he was too twitchy to sleep. . . .

The long trail. A dim path among enormous spruces. Overhead, gold-green light slipping through the branches. Lost lakes, reflecting as ebony the silver of birch groves. The iron night, and in the vast silence more brilliant stars. Grim wordless Indians, tall and hawk-nosed, following for league on league the trail of a wounded moose. A log cabin, and at the door a lovely Indian princess. A trapper bearing a pack of furs—luxuriant ermine and cross-fox and beaver.

Dreaming thus, cheered by an excellent dinner at a Japanese restaurant on the Croton River, Ralph drove home and left his car in the huge humming garage where live like royalty the motors of corporation counsels and millionaire bootleggers and even movie actresses. He came whistling home to the old brownstone residence turned into flats, and he whistled as he opened his fantastic black and orange door.

He stopped short, gasping with terror, his heart somersaulting. Facing him was an intruder, his arm out, holding a revolver . . .

In two seconds he saw that the intruder was himself, imaged vaguely in the full-length mirror of the bathroom door; that the outstretched arm was his own, and the shining revolver his conservative doorkey. But the shock left him panting as he wabbled down the hall, into the heavily ornate and bookish living-room, and lay limp in a red leather chair.

"I've—I've got to do something, or it'll be a breakdown! I will go to Canada with Woodbury! After all, he's a mighty good fellow, despite his bellowing and his confounded pep and punch. I'll *go!*"

In all of his guarded and carefully planned existence he had never sounded so desperately resolute.

His voice seemed frightened as he gave Woodbury's number on the telephone and as he addressed that good man in his West End Avenue residence; it sounded but a little less frightened as he summoned a taxicab and said good night to the janitress, who leered from the vestibule at the spectacle of the well-behaved Mr. Prescott starting out at eleven P.M.

"You bet—you bet—come right up—don't matter how late, and I'll tell the wife to have the Jap stick some real genuwine beer on the ice," Woodbury had greeted him. As Ralph bounced northward in the taxi, his heart was warm with the friendliness of the quartermaster-colonel of progress.

"—quit all this cross-word-puzzle mongering of the law, and these concerts and highbrow English weeklies and cautious games of bridge. Get out among real men and eat real grub and sleep on Mother Earth," he murmured. "Good old Woodbury—what a generous fellow he is!"

Woodbury was waiting in the lower hall when Ralph arrived. He greeted him by thrice shaking hands, thrice pounding his shoulders, and led him up the highly carven black-walnut staircase to the Den, a room rich and slightly stuffy, profuse in mounted ducks, old pipes hanging on a pyrographed rack celebrating the valor of Colgate University, and the originals of those very paintings of girls with lovely silk-smooth legs whereby the good tidings about Twinkletoe Stockings had been made known to a yearning world.

He produced Mrs. Woodbury, a pretty woman of thirty, who gulped:

"Oh, Mr. Prescott, I do think it would be too delightful if you could go with Wesson. The old bear! He pretends to be such a husky man of the wilds, but he's as soft as a baby, and I do hope you'll go along with him and keep him in shape. You say you aren't used to roughing it, but honestly you look quite athletic—like a track-runner."

Her lord admitted: "Yes, I guess that's about right. I'm not so good as I let on. But I get along on bacon and bannock a lot better than the little woman here thinks, and it'd be just as well for you to make your first stab at the Big Woods with a man who wasn't too hard-boiled, and wouldn't keep you hiking maybe eighteen hours a day."

Their modesty about Woodbury's achievements as a Hardy Pioneer did more than hours of boasting to convince Ralph that it would be agreeable to accompany him; and as Woodbury, like a rather bloated but very jolly small boy, dragged all his beloved playthings out of closets and cedar chests, what won

Ralph's affection more than the beauties of a varnished fish (looking too disagreeably dead to suggest any joy in the catching), more than the cleverness of an agate-mounted reel, was a worn and wrinkled pair of laced boots.

"Now there's some real Ritzy dancing-pumps," yearned Woodbury. "Look at those spikes—like they'd been sprinkled on with a salt-shaker. Had 'em done specially. And that foot—soft as a moccasin. Those boots—why, say, they've been with me in Maine and Michigan and Canada. Many's the big ol' bass I've pulled out wearing them! Many's the hill I've climbed! And now let me show you something that *is* something!"

He flipped open a linen-backed map bearing the legend "Mantrap River and Vicinity." There was Winnipeg, at the lower right-hand edge; there was the Flambeau River; there were Lake Warwick and the Mantrap River, Mantrap Landing and Lac Qui Rêve, Ghost Squaw River and Ghost Rapids, Lost River and Weeping River and Lake Midnight.

Ralph could more or less picture Winnipeg, though he had never been west of Chicago; and he had heard of the Flambeau River. He imagined its sulky yellow flood, rolling for a thousand miles through a wilderness of pines and willow thicket and lone swamp melancholy at sunset. But most of the map, whether the Manitoba side or Saskatchewan, was as unfamiliar to him as central Tibet, and the names lured him: War Drum Rapids; Singing Rapids; Lake Nee-pegosis; Mudhen Creek; Thunderbird Lake; Jackpine Point. And settlements named Whitewater and Kittiko and Mantrap Landing—villages, no doubt, entrancing with swart Indians, papooses on the backs of squaws, the log cabins of Hudson's Bay Company posts, and trappers gay in checked shirts of red and black.

Before his usually shrewd and unromantic eye had half traced the map, he knew that he was going to break away from his neat little accustomed life and plunge into mystery; and before he had half finished the bottle of beer which Woodbury proudly opened for him (under the handle of a drawer in the kitchen cabinet, in the astounding but surely temporary absence of all openers), Ralph flung out what was for him an almost hysterically incautious statement:

"I really think I might try to see if I couldn't arrange to get away, and I'm most frightfully obliged to Mrs. Woodbury and you for welcoming me at this indecently late hour, and—"

That night, very late, he walked all the way back to Thirty-seventh Street. He felt brawny and tall and free, and as his trim feet, supercilious in black tie-shoes and linen spats, clacked on the pavement, to him they were padding in the mold and moss of far northern trails.

CHAPTER TWO

A MONG the Fifth Avenue windows given over
to silver cocktail-shakers, emerald bracelets, and
gowns direct from the Faubourg St. Honoré, is the
magnificent display of Messrs. Fulton & Hutchinson,
the great sports outfitters.

It is a camping scene. How green the cotton
grass, how aqueous the glass water, how affecting to
any exiled Dan'l Boone must be the stuffed blackbird
singing a soundless lyric on a lifeless reed. And how
necessary for hardy camp-life are the portable radio
set, the pneumatic cushion which becomes a life-belt,
and the four-burner gasoline stove.

Ralph Prescott stared at this realistic scene rever-
ently, marched into the store, and was directed to the
Outing Garments Department, on the seventh floor.

"I'm going to northern Canada, fishing, and I want
something durable and quite simple in the way of
clothes," he said modestly to the clerk who glided
up.

"Certainly, sir. The entire outfit? May I recom-
mend these whipcord riding-breeches, with laced boots,
a real Ouspewidgeon flannel shirt, and a waterproofed
canvas jacket with game pockets? Now these breeches,
for example, they'll last a lifetime, and they're a very

nice value at only sixty-eight dollars," beamed the clerk.

Ralph winced, and squeaked slightly, but let himself be led into them. He chose two pea-soup shirts— one of black and crimson checks, one of green and yellow plaid. He added a bold two-gallon Bill Hart hat with an ornamental leather band, and in a triple mirror he regarded himself in all his bravery.

To Ralph, as to most males, trying on clothes was ordinarily a torture, and the newness of a new suit made everything he had worn before seem frayed and shabby. But out of his camping armor he had all the pleasure of a masquerade. He looked very virile and competent, he told himself. He straightened up with ferocity, he put both fists on his hips with a swagger, then he removed the rimless eyeglasses which took away slightly from his appearance as a tough man of action. At that moment he had no doubt of his competence to shoot rapids, tote three hundred pounds on the portage, and whip the most aggressive Indian.

"I'll order some big round spectacles, like Wes Woodbury's—look more outdoorish," he determined.

The expert clerk, whose training in perilous exploration had not been entirely within the establishment of Messrs. Fulton & Hutchinson, but had included three weeks in a Y.M.C.A. camp on Lake Chautauqua, unloaded upon Ralph a few large red bandannas, coat and trousers and hat of oilskin, self-ventilating gloves, folding slippers, woolen socks especially made by some special firm for some special purpose about which the clerk was a little hazy, high laced boots, low laced boots, and shoes of canvas with rubber soles an inch thick.

By this time Ralph was recalling Wes Woodbury's tense prayer, "Whatever you do, for the love of Mike keep your outfit small!"

He escaped from the seventh floor after buying, under the clerk's ardent counsel, a duffle-bag so large that if it were entirely filled no Indian yet born could have carried it across a portage. It was a charming and tricky duffle-bag. It had inside pockets, outside pockets, and topside pockets, each with straps and flaps and delightful little padlocks. It had loops and whorls and thongs. There was only one trouble: the top flap was so ingenious that there was no way of fastening it to prevent its bulging open and admitting all the rains of heaven. Ralph did not discover this until he was in a canoe on Lake Warwick.

The rest of his outfit he purchased on the main floor.

Tents, blankets, canoes, and the like had been arranged for by Woodbury's friend in Winnipeg, and would be awaiting them at railhead, at Whitewater, so Ralph contented himself with not more than two or three times as many things as he needed.

The sports-specialists managed to unload upon him certain toys which were later to give his Indian guides unmitigated delight: a ball-bearing compass, mosquito dope which the grateful mosquitoes regarded as nectar, an emergency ration of highly condensed and entirely indigestible food-tablets, and an apparatus which was variously a knife, a nail-file, an auger, a corkscrew, a pair of pliers, and a screw-driver. But several objects really were more or less useful on the trail: a magnificent electric torch, a twenty-gauge shotgun, and some small part of the reels, rods, flies, trolling-hooks, and fish-nets which the tackle-expert assured him were necessary.

—For a first adventure in outfitting, Ralph had really been very self-denying, when it is considered with what dreadful hypnotized fascination he looked at tents with phonographs and folding ice-boxes and portraits of Roosevelt; at lovely duck-hunting suits of grass, like the costumes of Hawaiian dancers; and compellingly real wax models slumbering with every sign of comfort in eiderdown sleeping-bags.

It was done. Ralph shook hands with six several clerks and the concierge, and took proud leave. All his purchases went with him in the taxicab. They were too delightful to wait for, and in their knobby suggestive packages they surrounded him on the seat and the floor of the taxi.

At home he did on his armor and stood before the

long door-mirror which so recently had frightened him. He was a splendor of wide-brimmed hat, canvas jacket with huge pockets for game—yet uncaught —red and black checked shirt, whipcord breeches, boots, and the startling, the ferocious, spectacles which he had picked up at the oculist's on the way home.

"Heh! I don't look so bad! I look like the real thing! I—"

Inexplicably all the magic was shattered, and he was no longer a child playing at being a hero, at being free and swift and strong; he was only a tired scholar on the slope of middle age.

"Hell, I look like Ralph Prescott, dressed up in baggy clothes! I look like amateur theatricals! Those clerks at Fulton & Hutchinson's are probably laughing themselves sick at me!"

He was suddenly as deep in self-conscious doubt as he had been high in selfless joy. In his costume of the wilds, stained as yet by no streak of mold, no drop of blood, no blot of rain, he sat miserable again and doubtful in a humorless red leather chair.

But out of his melancholy came one fact: He had a friend!

All his life he had known tepid and cautious acquaintances; loyal enough and sufficiently charted, intelligent and easy, but afraid of life, sore afraid of the sacrifices and hot partisanship of veritable friends. And in the same E. Wesson Woodbury at whom he had often laughed as a noisy and shallow fool, he had found the one enduring friendship.

"We'll have a bully time in the wilds. Wes is a real he-man. He'll make me get over my confounded cautiousness."

With a pale reflection of his afternoon's ecstasy, Ralph began packing. But it had come to him that this expedition might be perilous, and as he fussily arranged his treasures in the vast duffle-bag, he thought of canoes smashed in rapids, of broken legs in the wilderness, of bears prowling about lonely tents, of city weaklings lost in pathless forests.

CHAPTER THREE

WHEN Ralph awoke and rolled up the blind, the train was steaming through the Manitoba prairie.

He had seen the immensity of the Alps, he had seen steamers dwarfed in the unending round of ocean, but he had never felt the boundlessness of the world so sharply as now, looking across these level acres broken only by distant farmhouses with scant cottonwood windbreaks. It was a land valiant and young. As he lay relaxed and expectant in his swaying berth, he wanted to ride on forever.

They saw the pleasant city of Winnipeg; they had

a night at Bearpaw Junction; then all day long they lumbered through swamp and jackpine forest on the mixed train to Whitewater, which is on the Flambeau River.

The train had a caboose and an aged passenger car behind the long brown creaking line of freight-cars. Trains had to Ralph been affairs of steel Pullmans, disdaining the country through which they dashed, and it had never occurred to him that it might be agreeable to talk with a trainman. Now he sat in the caboose, tilted back in a wooden chair, and listened to the aged conductor, who had woolly hair in his ears and a drawling endless wisdom in his gossip of weather and government and traveling-men and the reason why wives are, of many, accounted irritable.

It was Woodbury who had secured for them the chance to ride in the caboose, sacred to trainmen, instead of in the crammed passenger car. Woodbury was the sort of man who knew how to get passes to theaters, discounts on tires, and tables in restaurants on a holiday eve. By the time they had been aboard for five minutes, he knew that the conductor had a grandson in business college, he had advised the brakeman regarding his dyspepsia, and moved Ralph and himself into the caboose.

It was like the office of a lumber-camp, the interior of the little red car at the end of the train. There was a desk, a shelf-table which could be folded up against the wall, and hard-looking chairs. Here gathered the aristocracy of the train: the conductor, a traveling salesman for groceries who knew every person and every scandal from Bearpaw to Kittiko, and a real sergeant of the Royal Mounted Police, as good as a movie in his taut scarlet coat, his broad hat, his incredibly well-cut riding breeches.

The train jogged on so slowly, the earth, seen through the open rear door of the car, was so close, that Ralph felt identified with its drowsy strength. He no longer belonged to the hectic city. No, he was one with these brown swamps stretching to a far horizon tragic with black skeletons of trees burned in forest fires. He liked the roughness of the caboose; he was released by it—released from all the stuffy neatness of offices and polite flats. He was strong and serene and ungarrulous; he was—

Then he was highly uncomfortable, jarred out of his reverie by the talk of the policeman.

"Terrible thing—never found his body—must have smashed all to pieces among the rocks—found part of his canoe and a paddle—never could understand how as good a waterman as he was ever tried to shoot Singing Rapids," the policeman was fretting.

"Wh-what rapids are those?" Ralph mumbled to Woodbury.

"Singing Rapids, on the Mantrap. The sergeant was just telling us about how a half-breed—corking good canoeman he was, too—how he got drowned in 'em."

Suddenly Ralph knew that he was a coward.

He knew that he was afraid, and deathly afraid, of rapids and of all the unknown risks of the wilderness. And because he was afraid he sought to sound careless as he chuckled:

"Hum. Really? Well, then, I hope we won't shoot 'em, Wes!"

"No. We go up 'em. Our route is up river."

"I see. But would, uh— What do you think about that sort of thing? Would you take a chance and try to shoot 'em if they were so kind as to be going our way? And what do you do? Line up 'em, or what?"

"Prob'ly portage around 'em. Time enough to think of that when we come to 'em. . . . They getting much moonshine up here now, sergeant?" said Woodbury, with booming amiability.

"Time enough to think of them. . . ."

Ralph's time to think of them, he shuddered, began right now.

"Am I going to be afraid all the while?" he agonized. His joy in adventure had dimmed; it almost vanished as he listened to the chatter, as he heard of wolves, of forest fires, of canoes capsized while sailing on lakes ten miles wide, of canoes sinking in a storm when they struck hidden snags.

And with his dreary apprehensions was a certain boredom.

For nearly four days he had been constantly with E. Wesson Woodbury, and he was a shade weary of that barking laugh, that loud patronage, that story about monkey glands which he had heard now seven times.

"Just as well we'll have separate canoes. Wes is a prince, but he's never learned to be quiet," Ralph sighed; and, "Now if we were in the rapids—if the canoe struck a rock and you had to swim— What if the current banged your head against a rock?"

Thus afraid of being afraid, which is of all fears the most unmanning and pitiful, Ralph sat paralyzed; and hour by tedious hour, as they crept through the dusty jackpines, as the train stopped at every lone wheat-elevator, and switched box-cars for interminable vacuities, his torpor was broken only by irritation at Woodbury's manly laughter.

It was a relief when the train reluctantly staggered into Whitewater, on the Flambeau River—end of rail, jumping-off place, end of what is called civilization—and it was a relief to see his first rapids and get it over.

The Flambeau crawls like a bloated boa constrictor through the shaggy woods. At the edge of town, beside the railroad, it breaks into the Whitewater Rapids. The whole stream is flung between two black granite bastions, gushing as smoothly as though it were poured from a million-gallon bottle. But below, among the slippery boulders, it is broken up into a welter of milky foam. No canoe could live in that chaos, where the tortured water is dashed up in rainbow-streaked foam, to fall in a curdle of snowy whirlpools.

Yet Ralph was comforted.

Like most silent and too-imaginative men, he was chiefly afraid of what he could not see. He had pictured all rapids as cloaked in menacing darkness, and however turbulent this cataract, it was something real and conquerable, under the light of the tardy northern sun. Swim it?—certainly he could swim it—well, perhaps he could—if he had to!

With a renewed joy of adventure and, tangentially, a renewed liking for E. Wesson Woodbury, he climbed down from the train, his shotgun and fishing tackle clattering and his new boots making the most touching and satisfactory clump on the plank platform, and came to his first frontier town.

CHAPTER FOUR

WHITEWATER was once a sawmill town of fifteen hundred persons. But the patriotic lumber company has slashed away all the timber, that is, all the timber that was not carelessly burned, and the place has dwindled to a hundred souls—a cluster of tumbling shanties in a prickly wilderness of stumps and bogs.

The chief adornment is a tall iron sawmill chimney, covered with a dome of wire netting to keep in the sparks. But the chimney is ruined now and likely to collapse in the next storm. The secondary pride of Whitewater, rising loftily among the tar-paper shanties, is the Bunger House: Meals and Lodging.

It rises three whole stories. It has never been painted, and the dinginess of its gray clapboards is broken only by the clean yellowness of such new boards as Mr. Bert Bunger has been compelled to tack on to keep out the rain. Most of its windows are broken. Where once the lumber kings, or at least lumber knights, had suites of two rooms (both without bath—one room to sleep in and one to play poker), where once the dining-hall banged to the tread of lumberjacks' clogs, now Mr. Bunger is lucky if he has a single roomer, and six mealers festive over the pork and beans.

But Mr. Bunger in poverty cannot forget that once he was powerful. It hurts him to have to do anything for guests. It disturbs his games of solitaire and his sense of seigniory to receive perfect strangers.

Ralph and Woodbury were to spend the night here before taking the river steamer *Emily C. Just* up the Flambeau River to Kittiko, where they would finally

embark in canoes. They came mildly into the office
of the Bunger House. Behind them was the sergeant
of Mounted Police, as respectful as they. The Royal
Mounted are not noted for timidity, but Mr. Bert
Bunger was the only person in Whitewater who could
provide food and lodging.

The office was rather like a pigsty. Then again it
was like an attic filled with furniture of 1870. It was
a largish room. On one side was a pile of rickety
chairs and warped tables. Beside them was a por-
celain bathtub, indecently public. Probably somebody
had intended to install it in a room upstairs and connect it with water-pipes sometime; probably nobody
ever would connect it with anything any time. (It
must not be supposed that it was the only bathtub in
the house. There was one other, in a room the key
of which Mr. Bunger had chronically lost. But this
was a scaly structure of tin with peeling paint, an
extraordinarily rough object for plump and meditative
persons to sit in.)

The rest of the office was agreeably filled with a
pool-table of torn green cloth, a round pine table on
which rested, for hotel library, a copy of the *Montreal
Star* of six weeks ago, and the grained pine counter
behind which Mr. Bunger played solitaire with cards
over which soup—at least—must have been spilled.

Of the dust in corners, of the spider-webs in electroliers without electricity, of the general mixture of red mud, sawdust, and cigarette butts, it would not be refined to speak.

As Woodbury and Ralph and the sergeant filed up to the desk, Mr. Bunger raised his head in irritation.

"Could we get a couple of rooms for tonight, and supper?" inquired Woodbury, in his most flamboyant good-fellowship.

Mr. Bunger (and a skinny little man he was) carefully placed the nine of spades upon the eight thereof, dusted his hands, looked learned, placed the ten upon the nine, looked up again, and groaned, "Huh?"

"We'd like two rooms, and I guess the sergeant wants one. Be all right, eh, all right?"

"Oh, I suppose so," sighed Mr. Bunger. "Will you guys register? Now who the hell has taken that register away? Somebody always monkeying with things here! I'm getting good and tired of it!"

Ralph, genially permitted by Mr. Bunger to carry his own bag and find his own room, discovered that it had most of the legal equipment of hotel rooms, namely a bed, a bureau, and a chair, though the bed was of so sensitive a nature that it squeaked when he merely looked at it, the bureau drawers would not open, and the lone chair had been unsuccessfully repaired with fence-wire. But one thing generally found in hotel rooms it did vigorously lack: breathable air.

He found that the window had been nailed down. As a substitute for air there was an ancient scent of pink soap, crushed insects, and moldy linen.

He dumped his duffle-bag on the floor, took out only a handkerchief or two, and fled into the corridor.

Woodbury was fleeing with him. They met at the stairs.

"Fierce place! I think I'll tell Brother Bunger how much I love him before we leave here," growled Woodbury, and Ralph admired him again for that surly hardihood.

It was half-past five now, and the Bunger supper was at six. But they had to see that their Indian guides, their canoes and tents, had arrived. Ralph lost the feeling of desolation which had oppressed him, as they passed through the street of rotting log cabins and crazy shacks and came to a camp of white tents and wigwams in the shadow of jackpines.

"I really am in the North, among Indians!" he exulted.

Their Indian guides, who had come on by themselves from Bearpaw, escorting the supplies, were encamped with a band of Crees. When Woodbury inquired for them, they came filing out of their tent.

Ralph Prescott had been brought up on the Fenimore Cooper tradition of Indians. He expected all of them to look like the chieftain on the buffalo nickel, like the statue which in all proper parks stands between Goethe in marble and General Sherman in bronze—a sachem eagle-nosed, tall, magnificently grave. His heart was pinched as he saw shambling toward them four swart and runty loafers, introduced as Jesse, Louey, Charley, and Nick.

They did not look in the least like lords of the wilderness engaged in watching, under lean shadowing hands, the flight of a distant eagle. They looked like undersized Sicilians who had been digging a sewer, and their only human expression was their supercilious, self-conscious grins. Feathers and blankets they wore not, but rusty black suits from the cheaper kind of white man's back-street shops. The one sign of Indian art was their moccasins and one hectic bead belt displaying the Union Jack. They spoke only Cree, except for Charley, an older Indian who could do well enough with English when he was not too bored.

Ralph was regretful that Woodbury had taken Charley for his own canoe, leaving himself in the hands of two smoky men whose language was as intelligible as that of a woodchuck. Still, Woodbury was the captain of the fleet; he would have to take the lead—

Woodbury was greeting the Indians with boisterousness: "Well, well, well, boys! Here we are! Ready to pull out tomorrow! Got all our stuff on the steamer?"

Charley grunted, "No, not yet."

"Then what are you doing hanging around your tent? Got most of it aboard?"

"No-uh."

"Got *any* of it?"

"Not ye-et."

"Not yet! Not yet! Not yet! What do you think this is? Why didn't you— What's your explanation?"

Charley exchanged with the others a glance half sheepish, half amused at the rage of the tenderfoot over the insignificant matter of catching a steamer this week or next or a month after. Crees were not made for clocks. When Woodbury had finished his raving, ending with a powerful "And you get busy right now," Charley pacifically answered, "All right." He lounged toward the pile of supplies, contentedly followed by the others.

Charley was a moral man and a great canoe-steerer, but he was only fifty, he had only thirty-five years of experience in guiding white men. He was perfectly willing to do anything he was asked, but he never, by any chance, remembered to perform such duties as pitching tents or preparing meals or bailing out a canoe with three inches of frigid water gurgling about the miserable feet of his employer until he was reminded.

Woodbury's rage made him take the longer in checking up their supplies, heaped under a tarpaulin: tent, blankets, canoes, paddles, sails, motor, gasoline, food. It was nearly seven when he finished barking items for Ralph, who looked like a diffident bookkeeper, to mark off on the list, and they started back to the Bunger House. As they entered the disheveled lobby, Mr. Bert Bunger, in shirt-sleeves and sweat-stained suspenders, picking his teeth and scratching his head, was resting from innumerable labors, tilted in a chair with his feet on the decayed billiard table.

Woodbury was cheerful now, and he boomed fondly at Mr. Bunger, "Supper ready?"

"Yeh—and et!"

"We better wash and skip in."

"Wash all you want to, and skip all you want to, but you don't get no supper here, not *this* time o' night! Supper's over."

"Supper's ov-er—at six-forty?"

"Supper's *ov*-er!"

"Then have the cook shake us up something."

"I will not have the cook shake you up nothing! The cook's had all the work he wanted, feeding these hogs of railwaymen and teamsters, without working till midnight for a bunch of galoots that haven't got the savvy to come to their meals on time. I'm the cook!"

"Then why didn't you call us? We were at the Indian camp, not a hundred yards—"

"I've got enough to do, without going out and hunting for folks that're too lazy to come to meals."

"Then where can we get something to eat?"

With delicious enjoyment, punctuating his drawl by sucking his toothpick, Mr. Bunger drawled, "No place a-tall!"

"Then by thunder—"

Woodbury was off again. He shouted, he shook his fist; he would have the law on Bunger; if they didn't have supper at once, he would do something dreadful.

The dirty little man looked at him with contempt. Suddenly Ralph had enough of this dog-fight.

"Oh, don't make so much noise!" he snarled at Woodbury; then, apologetically, "I mean—there's no use talking to a swine like this."

"Who you calling a swine?" yapped Bunger. "You better be careful who you go calling names around here!"

As to the shooting of rapids, Ralph might be timorous enough, but he was accustomed to handling angry men and threatening men in courtrooms, and he ignored Bunger with a disdain more infuriating than words, as he continued to Woodbury:

"No use wasting time on this poor white trash. It's his inn—such as it is. Can't force him to cook after hours. Let's have our Indians prepare some bacon, and have 'em put up the tent. We'll take our stuff out of the rooms here and camp tonight."

"You can," bawled Mr. Bunger, "sleep in your tent

all you damn' want to, but you'll pay for your rooms!
You registered. It's the law!"

Woodbury emitted a portentous "Oh, it is, is it!"
but Ralph cut him off with a sharp, "And I'm a
lawyer! See here, my man!" (But that was a mistake. Bunger was so far down in the social scale that
he didn't even know he was being insulted by "my
man.") "The Mounted Police sergeant is over at the
railway station. Just go to the door and shout for
him, will you? Please ask him to arrest us for jumping our board-bill. Please! And then you listen while
I ask him a few things about the *lex talionis nisi sub
super cum poena,* code 47! Just call him, will you,
while we go up and pack!"

Woodbury was swelling with desire to spoil the
chill judicial effect by throwing another of his rotund
and pumpkin-like orations into the debate, but Ralph
held him with an unfriendly eye, with a sound halfway between a grunt and an exasperated sigh, and led
him to their sour-smelling rooms.

"That was a good bluff you threw," Woodbury
admitted. "By golly, I'd rather pay a hundred-dollar
fine and a lawyer's fee than give him the three dollars
for our rooms!"

"Yes. Lawyers love to hear people talk like that,"
said Ralph. "I wouldn't. And it isn't the principle
of the thing—it's the hundred dollars. But I'll do
that hog out of anything I can."

"You called him fine! Great stuff! He won't dare holler for the sergeant. That was a bully stunt of yours, to walk out on him. He won't do a thing."

Woodbury was for the first time adoring—and Ralph liked his pompous adoration as little as he had liked his undisciplined rage.

"Come in my room. Look," said Ralph. He pointed to the station platform a few yards away, where the sergeant of Mounted Police was talking to the local Provincial Policeman. In a moment he saw the raging Bert Bunger—but respectable now, with his coat on and even an aged tie—run across to the two functionaries.

"Bluff's called!" said Ralph. "Nothing we can do, I fancy. We registered, and got in too late for supper. Let's move anyway, and not let him make anything on our breakfasts. But we pay for the rooms."

Woodbury was instantly the oratorical business man, going-to-by-golly-*do*-something-about-it.

"We do not pay! If any man thinks he can get away with the stuff that fellow's trying to pull on us in this God-forsaken rat-hole, then let me tell you, let me tell *you*—"

Ralph left him abruptly, stalked downstairs, to meet Bunger and both the policemen as they entered the lobby.

Bunger shouted at him, "Now we'll see—" But Ralph ignored him, and of the Mounted Policeman, who looked sympathetic, he demanded, "From what I've heard of Canadian law, you have certain magisterial powers?"

"Yes."

"Then will you permit me to treat you as the court, and pay you the three dollars which we owe for the two rooms which we shall not occupy? You know the opinion that every decent person must have of this man. I hate to trouble you about this, but may I say, without libel, that he's so dirty that I'm really afraid to hand him the money myself."

The Mounted Policeman looked beatific. "So am I," he crooned—straight and formidable in his scarlet and blue, turning a razor glance on the infuriated Mr. Bunger. "I'm a little afraid of germs myself. I think we'll leave the job to the Provincial Policeman here. The Mounted are expected to get shot and frozen, but I don't believe they ought to take a chance on an infection like this."

Both policemen radiated delight. They knew that for a hundred miles about—gossip flying from frontiersman to frontiersman as though it were a boarding-house of old women—for a hundred miles and for ten years, every one who had suffered under Mr. Bert Bunger would yelp at the tale of the man who said Bunger was so dirty he would not hand money to him.

Their ecstasy was not lessened when, as the Provincial Policeman handed him the money, Bunger tore up the three bills and hysterically trampled on them.

But in Ralph there was no delight. His rage had gone dead. He left the lobby abruptly, clumped up to his room, and answered Woodbury's rumbling query with a curt "All settled. Let's pack and get out."

He sat on the edge of his frowsy bed, brooding.

It was his misfortune as a private citizen, and his blessing as a lawyer, that he could see both sides of any controversy, both of two conflicting personalities, even when one of them happened to be himself. Yet he was too thin-skinned for heroism—not so resolute as often to act on the knowledge when he saw that his opponent was right. It is such men who flee to monasteries, to narcotic reading, to a gregariousness hateful yet protective; unable either to tolerate or to change the childish hurts and squabbles with which we poison life.

He loathed himself, suddenly, for the cheapness of his triumph.

"Lord, how petty! So proud of myself for actually thinking up a way of insulting that mangy alley cat! Brought up in a log stable—how should he have courtesy? And is he any worse than the city lad who seems polite when he really hates you? And I so cocky! Oh, yes! 'Call the cop! I'll tell him something about *lex talionis sub nisi!*'

"The great I! The great lawyer! The clever city-man! Worse than Wes. He's simple and courageous. And he too—I've been feeling so superior to him, with his anecdotes—"

He perceived that much of his depression was due to the enfeeblement of his admiration for Woodbury. He perceived how necessary authentic friendship had become to him in a world left vacuous and bewildering by the death of his mother. In such circles of thought as had maddened him in his lonely flat, in black and sleepless reveries by night, he began to admire Woodbury again.

He did not veil the man's irritating qualities—his boasting, his noisiness, his fuss over inessentials, his pretentious ignorance—but he found assurance in that driving self-confidence, that cheerfulness which made Woodbury of good flavor between tantrums, that physical strength, gone flabby now.

He sprang up, flung into his duffle-bag the few things he had taken out, and closed it before Woodbury appeared at the door with his own luggage.

"Sorry I started all this scrapping, Wes. Do forget it. Let's get out of this absurd place and sleep on the decent honest ground."

Five minutes before, Ralph's hard fury had turned Woodbury into an anxious follower.

(You could see Wes as a boy, a puffy boy, the butt of his Gang, more ingenious than any of them at devising plans for stealing melons and torturing cats, but the first and only one to be, in a most unhygienic manner, initiated into the fraternities they founded and forgot within a vacation-time week; a wistful fat boy, complaining "Ah—gee—quit, can't yah?" and with drooping bulbous lips following a sharp-nosed little leader half his size; always longing for some one to bully as he had been bullied.)

Now, instantly, he bounded back into command with:

"I tell you, son, you got to learn to never fuss, up here in the woods. Take things the way they come, Ralph—take things the way they come—just the way they happen to come. No *sense* in cussing and discussing with that pup Bunger. I'd just have handed him one and walked out. This trip'll be a fine thing for you; teach you to pack all your troubles in your old kit bag and smile, smile, smile—that's the ticket— that's what we said at my officers' training-camp— that's the stunt up here, in the big outdoors—pack up your grouches and smile, smile, smile. Well, we'll forget it now. Tell you"—brightly—"what we'll do. We'll sleep on the ground. That'll make you husky."

Thus, wavering with his duffle-bag, Ralph followed the generalissimo who had thought up all these plans and beneficial ideas, and he had the manner of meek discipleship.

But he was again dreading a plunge into the wilds with no protection from Wes Woodbury's nobleness.

CHAPTER FIVE

THEIR tent, as the Indians set it up for them, was to Ralph not a mere shelter but a symbol of the wilds and of every gallant exploration. It was of balloon silk, with the bottom sewed to the sides, so that there was no crevice through which the man-eating mosquitoes of the North could creep. The five windows of netting were protected by silk flaps which in rain could be lowered by cords cunningly placed inside the tent.

There was a playhouse quality about these windows which roused in Ralph a gay childishness uncommon in that grave life of his. He chuckled as he lowered and raised the window-flaps, and Woodbury chuckled and exclaimed with him, and in wide good-humor they crawled out under the mosquito-netting to attack their first camp meal—the tea and bacon and bannock which old Charley, the chief guide, had prepared for them.

Now bannock is, technically, a variety of bread. But only among the copper-stomached Woods Crees is it considered to be an edible bread. It is well thought of as ballast, as a missile or an anchor, but for internal use it ranks with tripe and pemmican. Bannock is made without yeast. It is flour and water, caused to cleave together by boiling it in lard in a frying-pan over a maddened fire. Yet Ralph managed to swallow it, with liberal butter and marmalade; he found himself relishing the tea diluted with condensed milk; and he imitated the great Woodbury in eating the bacon with his fingers.

Woodbury was a zealot at showing how lusty and he-mannish he could be in the Great Open Spaces of which all city-dwellers speak so admiringly. He had as much pleasure now in acquiring grease as in New York he would have had in avoiding it. And he was mighty in discovering sportive events for the evening.

Now in June, in the far North, there was light until eleven, and they felt disinclined to go to bed, though they had to be up at five to catch the river steamer. The evening did rather drag. Ralph struggled to appreciate Woodbury's companionship, but he became a little melancholy over undiluted conversation about municipal bonds and the beauties of the stocking business.

Other entertainments were few in the hamlet of Whitewater. There had never yet been a movie in town; the last theatrical company had been the Lionel Lornton Big London Tent Show in "Little Lass o' Tennessee" and "The Perils of Limehouse," seven years before; and, even had Ralph particularly relished prayer-meetings, there was none tonight in the bleak frame chapel. Their friend the Mounted Policeman had driven into the country to examine a Swede who wanted to be naturalized. So the two explored the

place, craving excitement—and they discovered a
social gathering.

In front of the "British Jack General Supply Company: Hats and Caps, Boots and Shoes, Clothing and
Table Delicacies: Furs Bought at Best Prices and
Whitefish Forwarded: Our Motto a Fair Deal to All,"
which was a log cabin covered with tar-paper, the tin
discs holding the paper rusted by years of rain, sat
three men in overalls.

Ralph and Woodbury sat with them, greeted by not
unfriendly grunts of "Haaryuh."

For seventeen minutes the assembly argued as to
whether hay could be grown north of Reindeer Lake.
For nine minutes they discussed, with ardor, the reason why Pete Wrzska's outboard motor—the one on
his red rowboat, not the old motor Pete bought from
Harry Larssen, two years ago—had not started this
morning.

Ralph and Woodbury fled on to the next soirée;
the four men and a woman in an apron standing in
front of the doctor's cottage and listening to the doctor's account of the state of old Mrs. Bjone's rheumatism. But this seemed a choosey, private affair,
and they felt they could not intrude.

"Tell you what we'll do—tell you what we'll do!"
rejoiced Woodbury. "You know that Provincial Policeman stationed here. Well, they're always good
fellows—real hard-boiled birds. We'll rout him out

and get up a poker game! You've never seen any poker up here in the North. Boy, they're the boys can play! Trappers and traders and everybody, and some of the Injuns. Bluff on two deuces. Why, I've seen, I've seen a fur-buyer that was down to his last twenty dollars in the world—I've seen him bet every cent he had on the turn of one card. Great stuff! Playing up there in the woods, log cabin right among the thick pines, rough pine table, with one smoky ol' oil lamp, playing till dawn, then all of 'em jumping into the lake for a swim, just as the sun came up across the water. Boy, that's living!"

Ralph felt that to him it was a peculiarly painful way of living, but he warmed up his smile and, in as lively and anticipatory a way as possible, he followed as Woodbury galloped toward the Provincial Police-man's house, emitting poker enthusiasms punctuated with "You'll see—he'll be wild for a game—tickled to death—they always like to get us tenderfeet into a game and try to trim us—but not me they won't—you'll see!"

Ralph was appropriating thirty dollars as the amount he would lose, and framing a treacherous play for escaping from the game before midnight.

It was nine-thirty, and the sunset was still burning across the muddy current of the Flambeau, beyond the willows along the bank, beyond the gaunt sheet-iron chimney of the abandoned sawmill. At the shiny yellow and white cottage of the Provincial Policeman, there was silence, no answer to their knock.

"This is fierce," said Woodbury. "Nine-thirty is a little too early to go to bed in this metropolis—about a quarter of an hour too early—but it certainly is too blame' late to be out indulging in the giddy delights of visiting. Something gone wrong. Probably Bert Bunger's murdered the policeman in bed."

From the whitewashed log cabin next door, with its brave posy-bed of pansies and frail wild roses, a gaffer with silvery chin-whisker and spectacles half-way down his nose came crouching out to bawl:

"Looking for somebody?"

"For the policeman."

"For the policeman?"

"Yes."

"Somebody done something?"

"No."

"Well. *Well!* Strangers here, ain't yuh?"

"Yes. Say, has—"

"Going on the river steamer tomorrow?"

"Yes. Say, has the policeman gone to bed, or what—"

"Heh?"

"Has he gone to bed?"

"The policeman? Gone to bed?"

"*Yes!*"

"Why, no! Course not!"

The aged one felt wounded surprise. "Him and his missus have gone down to Milligan's, to do the cross-word puzzle in the Winnipeg paper that come today."

"Think he'd like a game of poker?"

"Him? The policeman? Why, he's a Seventh-Day Adventist! He ain't got a single vice, not one. Oh, maybe except chewing tobacco, and lapping up a little moonshine, just a little, when he pinches a still. No, sir. That's a good moral fellow. Now me, when I was a trapper, years ago, that was before I went with the trading company—I worked for them quite some time and then I come down with the rheumatism, but my daughter she married Ed Toggerman, a fine steady hard-working fellow he is, too, when he keeps off the booze, he sends me sixty dollars a month regular as a clock, he's got a new job over to Regina in a lumberyard, got a good thing of it. Zis saying, when I was a trapper I played some, but don't know's ever cared much for cards, always rather get in a little sleep. Still, guess if you gentlemen 'd like a game, try to oblige you. Guess I remember how to play all right, and maybe we could get my grand-daughter. She ain't only twelve, but she's smart 's a whip—she ain't Ed's daughter, she's my other daughter's daughter that works in the Bon Ton Store, and I don't know if she plays poker, but I know her and her ma play casino sometimes—"

They averted the calamity of family poker. They sat in front of their tent, on a bucket and a box of canned pears, and watched the river run.

It kept running.

Before eleven they were abed.

For Ralph, his bed-roll had something of the ingenious fascination of the tent. It was a sleeping-bag covered with festive green and brown canvas, lined with blankets filled with soft eiderdown. There were buttons, straps, snaps; there was a flap to cover his head in case of rain. It was in itself a little house and, feeling at once adventurous and secure in privacy, Ralph crawled into its cave.

He had started to undress, but Woodbury had snorted, "What do you think you're doing? All you take off in the North is your shoes and coat, you poor fish! And— You don't mean to tell me you've brought a *pillow* along?"

Ralph had, and a very nice little pillow it was, of the best down. To him a pillow was the noblest part of sleep. He liked to snuggle into it, to tuck it up about his sound-wearied ears as a protection from the intrusive world. He had felt proud of the practicality of his new traveling pillow. It was so conveniently small, and it was covered with gay dirt-proof calico in a pattern of parrakeets and orchids among which any one ought to be glad to sleep.

"Why not a pillow?" he squeaked.

"Good Lord! Takes up enough room for a three-days' ration! Besides, everybody will die laughing at you up here, if you're going to be such a mollycoddle. Roll up your coat and sleep on it, like a real man!"

Ralph rolled up his coat, but he was not so successful at sleeping on it like a real man.

For a second, weary with the day's cramped riding and the Bunger squabble, he stretched out luxuriously between his blankets. But this trodden ground beside the river was curiously hard. In ratio as he grew more drowsy, it thrust up the more viciously against him. It fought him. It heaved up and hit him. He discovered the importance of his shoulders and the points of his hips. They were sore with the incessant banging.

Woodbury had for a moment dropped snoringly into sleep, but he too was roused by the unyielding earth, and he stirred with the obscure cloudy sounds of night-time. The tent was not yet dark. Ralph lay studying the reënforced seams along the ridge; suffering with sleepiness and unable to sink into it— there was no sinking about this resolute ground.

And the manly rolled coat was like a pine board to his ear.

"Awake?" grunted Woodbury.

Ralph was silent.

"Awake?"

Still Ralph restrained himself. For no very defi-
nite reason he longed to hit Woodbury with something
—something heavy, but smooth to the clasping hand.

"Doggone earth's so doggone hard it makes every
bone in your doggone body ache. Well, gotta get used
to it," Woodbury said illuminatingly, then turned
again and apparently slept.

While Ralph lay in the clutch of creeping paralysis,
he remembered and tried to forget and remembered
again that he conceivably could desert Woodbury—
and that this was his last chance to leave him. He
pictured camp-hotels in Maine: the pines as gracious
as here, the lake as joyous, but with food meant for
self-respecting stomachs and reasonable beds in fra-
grant log-cabins. He recalled a friendly old inn on
a hilltop in New Hampshire. He saw a pension in
the Bavarian Oberland, with mountains beyond the
carved eaves of peasant houses; an inn on the Breton
coast; a path through Highland heather. In six days
he could be on a steamer, among civilized people who
would talk of something besides municipal bonds and
the stocking business; in twelve days he could be landing at Southampton—see again the chimney-pots and
the Bovril advertisements and sniff at the smoky ex-
hilarating odor which meant distant London.

To escape from this narrow companionship with
Woodbury, from this raw and traditionless land, from
this senseless discomfort . . .

"The most blatant of all our American myths: roughing it in the wilds!

"The virile open spaces—Wes Woodbury trying to play poker!"

Then he swore:

"No. I won't do it. I don't like this place. It occurs to me that I don't like this man Woodbury. But I've lived too soft. I must stick by it. Only—"

As though he were defying a throng of accusing sportsmen he clamored, and mighty was the noise, though it was entirely within his brain:

"Only let me tell you fellows right now that baseball bores me, and I think fishing is dull, and poker is duller, and even if it makes me lose my American citizenship, I maintain that sleeping on the ground is *rot!*"

Exhausted by this declaration of agnosticism, he slept for half an hour, and awoke to a further defiance so dreadful that his cloud of accusers gasped.

"And I'd just as soon shoot a duck sitting as on the wing. I don't know that it makes such a whale of a lot of difference to a duck whether he gets murdered sportingly or otherwise. Understand?

"And I *won't* throw away my little pillow! I'll sneak it along with me!"

CHAPTER SIX

THE steamer *Emily C. Just* crept down the yellow flood of the Flambeau River to Kittiko, where Ralph and Woodbury and their Indian guides would at last take to canoes.

As to the tonnage of the *Emily C. Just*—it hasn't any tonnage in particular; it has only pounds and ounces. Though it is sixty feet long, with no less than seven staterooms (including one cabin de luxe fitted with running water and a special china cuspidor, for such infrequent dignitaries as the Fishing Inspector), yet the superstructure is of inch pine, and the partitions of cardboard.

It has none of the regular habits of a liner. It runs each way twice a week—except when it is a day or two late, or when Captain Venner stops to look over the potato crop on his claim *en route,* or finds a poker game and gives up that particular trip entirely. It is a stern wheeler, and paddles contentedly through three feet of water or turns surprisingly from steamer into canoe and shoots a rapids, curveting among the rocks.

Once or twice it has sunk, and after such misfortunes the mud has been scraped off and the boat been repainted a pleasing robin's-egg blue with an orange smokestack.

There is an idle charm to river steamers. They are not forlorn in an alien expanse of waters. They run so close to one shore or the other as to share in its life, yet they are free from the cinders and stink of a train skirting tenements. The passengers leaning on the rail of the *Emily C. Just* and gravely spitting into the Flambeau can consider the family affairs of every chicken scratching in every runty clearing; and in luxurious scorn of hurry and ambition they can learnedly argue as to whether or no that ruined reed-mound of a muskrat nest was occupied last winter.

The *Emily C. Just* stops in at ports consisting of two log cabins and a wigwam; the captain, lordly in his pilot-house, is hailed by a half-breed trapper, with a face like bacon-rind, as "Cap," or "Billy," and that is all very pleasant and domestic. Sometimes the steamer makes a port that is not so populous, that is only a woodpile on the bank, and then the deck-gang, all three of them, pass the cordwood from hand to hand into the hold, which is a cross between a Vermont woodshed and an antiquated machine-shop.

The passengers may go ashore at any stop, with no formalities about passports, customs inspectors, jin-rikisha drivers, postcard vendors, bars, or the rules of the purser. If they do not return in time, the steamer whistles for them like a hen clucking to its young, then waits contentedly, while the captain plays crib-bage with the chief (and only) engineer, or shows the

missionary's children how to make birch-bark canoes
out of paper.

Ralph was relaxed in his raw-nerved and egotistic
resistance to the unknown land. He speculated on
ruined cabins of trappers along the shore, on clearings
wrung from the forest with such bitter grubbing of
stumps, such painful plowing of root-knotted fields,
but abandoned again, and tragic against the forbid-
ding and dusky spruce. He speculated on mink holes
and on mother black ducks, fearfully trying to save
their skittering brood by leading them right beside the
leisurely and chugging course of the steamer, in the
typically maternal impression that they were racing and
beating this monster of modernity, and that but for
their adult wisdom and clucking, the children would
instantly have been destroyed.

He went ashore (escaping Woodbury's company and
regretting such disloyalty and most vigorously keeping
it up), and he discovered a real Cree Indian encamp-
ment—birch-bark wigwams, young wives with babies
swinging on their backs, old women smoking pipes
while they cured moose-meat and whitefish on frames
over a sluggish fire, Indian men magnificently doing
nothing, thinking nothing, and wanting nothing. He
ambled into a forest of jackpine and poplar and occa-
sional clumps of birch silver as Diana; he was driven
out by an ambush of mosquitoes; he went aboard, and
cheerfully he sat on the deck floor of the *Emily C.*

Just, his back against the wall, smoking a pipe. . . . Wes Woodbury had explained to him that nothing was more necessary in the art of being virile than giving up cigarettes for a brave jimmy pipe.

He found in the steamer the same toy quality which had betrayed him into gayety in their tent. The dining-salon was a touchingly absurd closet in which a glazed-faced Chinaman served, he asserted, ham-neggscoffpie. The captain welcomed them in the tiny pilot-house, and showed them how to recognize the snags and ghostly sunken logs in the foam-streaked current ahead. And all day long the stern-paddles churned the yellow paint of the water into leaping foam through which, above that mossy mill-wheel, a rainbow burned.

If he could have gone on for a week, Ralph would have grown into serenity, have heard Woodbury's incessant heartiness through a veil of contentment. But next morning they landed at Kittiko—two log stores, two log boarding-houses, and the fish ware-house—for their embarkation in canoes.

Woodbury, in his zeal of being efficient and hardy, immediately blew up like a toy balloon.

Though they had two large freight-canoes, nineteen feet long, it seemed impossible that they should ever be able to stow away all this pile of tents, bedding, duffle-bags, boxes of food, sacks of flour and sides of bacon, sails and oars and gasoline-tins and frying-pans, which towered on the log wharf. And Woodbury's outboard motor had to be fitted to the forward canoe—Ralph's canoe he would tow, when smooth and open water permitted them to run on gasoline. A scratch or two had to be smeared with canoe-glue and paint. Saplings had to be cut as masts.

In all these tasks Ralph was sensationally useless.

Woodbury had at its highest the schoolmaster's art of making sport compulsory and laborious and pious and dreadful. He was a four-minute man, a suburban-development sales-manager, a lady chairman.

He rushed at the guides and agonized, "Now hurry up and get the stuff in—get it in—get it all aboard." He tried to fit the outboard motor to the rack on his canoe, and banged his finger nails, and swore, and glared at Ralph. He bellowed that the sapling masts were too large for the holes in the thwarts, and when they proved to be exactly right, he scowled, and announced, "Well, they don't look strong enough."

He shouted at Ralph: "Well, try to do *something,* anyway! Don't sit there admiring yourself!"

When Ralph ventured to lower a box of bacon into his canoe (riskily tilting on the gunwale, holding the rough edge of the wharf with one hand), Woodbury exploded, "Good Lord, don't put that box for'ard—gotta have the weight in the center."

Ralph felt meek, horribly useless, in everybody's way. He was tremulously polite to Louey, the

youngest and most bored guide, he was filial to
Charley, to Woodbury he was absolutely reverent;
and when the great white chief condescended to hear
his tribute, "You certainly do know this game, Wes,"
he was grateful.

For all of Woodbury's sales-manager efficiency, the
work did somehow get itself done.

The cargo seemed to condense as it slid into the
canoes. There had apparently been twice as much load
as they could carry, yet by magic the canoes seemed
only half full.

Amidships of each canoe was a nest for one of the
white men, his bed-roll as seat and his toys at hand—
fishing-tackle, gun, even a paddle (though Woodbury
had to sit in the stern when the motor was running).
The Indians didn't at all mind the tenderfeet pretending to help propel the unwieldy canoes now and then,
providing they were careful not to spatter water from
their paddles. Indeed they scarcely laughed at their
efforts, after the first few times.

Everything was complete except Woodbury's especial charge, the outboard motor, and that was clamped
in place, all pretty and shining, all ready save for one
thing—it would not start.

It would not give one sputter. Not after half an
hour of profane jerking at the starting-cord could
Woodbury get it to take hold.

Ralph looked wistfully from the log wharf down

on the raging Woodbury. He was alone. The population of Kittiko, five whites and nine Indians, had come to gape at the expedition, but in his present disillusionment about life Woodbury was not so cordial as usual, and they had drifted away. The Indian guides, their loading done, squatted on a pile of sawdust ashore and let the sun shine.

Whether they started this week or next year was the same to them, providing the bacon and cigarettes lasted.

Ralph knew as much about motors as the average man who has driven a car for only ten or twelve years. He knew a steering-wheel from a hand-brake, and he could pour water into a radiator. The outboard motor was a heathen mystery to him—a round something with a finned single cylinder, a long handle, and nothing else identifiable.

When Woodbury had for a moment given up, when he stood looking bitterly at the motor, as though he was wondering how he could best hurt its feelings, Ralph ventured:

"Do you suppose the feed-pipe might be plugged up?"

Woodbury, swaying in the canoe, raised his hands to heaven in the protest of a dying martyr, then patiently gave voice:

"It must take a great brain to think up suggestions like that! You're certainly helping me a lot! Of course I've only cleaned out the feed-pipe a couple of times now, while you've been looking on!"

Ralph retired to the end of the wharf; he considered two mud-hens and a clump of weeds, and longed for the Yale Club.

The Hudson's Bay factor ambled down the wharf. Woodbury could be seen stiffening, down in his canoe, ready to leap the five feet up on the wharf and choke the fellow at his very first suggestion. The factor, who looked like a preacher and who had a magnificent flow of divine language, squinted one eye, heaved with amusement, grunted "Vent choked in tank," and humped away with a scorn which reduced to pitiful greenness not only Ralph but the great E. Wesson Woodbury.

Ralph saw Woodbury swell like a pussy-cat's tail while he sought for proper language. But also he saw him examine and poke at the vent in the gasoline tank; seize the starting-cord and jerk it.

Instantly the motor spatted and ran clear, with the sound of a very tiny airplane.

Woodbury stood up in the canoe, his fists clenched, glaring at Ralph, daring him to say one word. Ralph looked as blank as possible. Then Woodbury glowered the other way, at the Indians on shore. They had gone to sleep. The cruelly used leader felt injured. He brooded for a time over all his unprecedented wrongs, then he roared, "Well, are you fellows going on a canoe trip or *not?*"

So the golden Argosy embarked; so the fabulous expedition started for the unknown heart of the North.

One Indian squaw came to her wigwam door and stared after them. Otherwise, the world seemed ignorant that Ralph Prescott and E. Wesson Woodbury were making history.

Then for two weeks all life was a routine of struggling on and stopping to catch muskalonge.

Sometimes they poled or paddled through shallow snaky creeks; sometimes Woodbury towed them, the motor's burr as hypnotizing as a humming bee. They came into Lake Warwick, a vast plate of water, island-spattered and stretching to a shore of black cliffs fantastic with orange lichens. On calm days the motor-driven canoe clove the polished water, but with a following wind they sailed.

There were only three or four inches of freeboard to the canoe, and often they took water. Ralph was tremulous as he considered their helplessness in sailing. They were miles from shore, in a shell which would go down instantly if they struck a submerged rock, and he could not have swum a quarter-mile.

He fought himself, he scorned his cowardice, he reproved himself by the spectacle of Woodbury relaxed in enjoyment of the sail, but he could not keep from speculating as to what chance he would have of drifting ashore if they sank.

Yet it was beautiful: waves glittering, triangular sails like curving wings of a gull till at evening the low sun turned the sails to gold, with that orange glory burning through them.

He hated the guides during sailing hours.

He had heard always of the "grim silent Indians." The Woods Crees, at least, exhibited a silence almost equal to their hatred of whisky. They kept quiet enough during the labor of paddling, and the motor drowned their clack when it was blessedly working, but in the stillness of sailing, when Ralph most longed to forget his detestable self-consciousness and timidity, to be absorbed in beauty, then his bow-man and stern-man babbled like washerwomen, giggled like little girls, shouted witticisms across to the Indians in the other canoe.

Some of their exasperatingly unending jabber was smutty stories, he concluded from their neighing; some of it, from their glances, certainly was poignant comment on Woodbury and himself. As his own Indians spoke only Cree, he could neither understand them nor tell them to shut up. And he wanted to be a "good sport," to keep from complaining. He listened, and suffered—and grew hourly more irritated.

They crossed from Lake Warwick to the wide Mantrap River, and headed toward Lac Qui Rêve, on which was a trading center where they could renew their food-supply and gasoline—a settlement called Mantrap Landing, with a Revillon Frères store, a Hudson's Bay post, and a free trader by the name of Joe Easter; a place with a vast population of perhaps a dozen whites and, in summer, when they loafed after the winter's trapping, fifty or sixty Indians.

Ralph felt hardened. He could sleep on the ground as in a four-poster, he could relish bacon, he was only a little apprehensive about sailing and rapids. He had watched his Indians zigzag their way down half a dozen smoking rapids now, and had come to see with indifference the rocks rushing up at them.

But he could no longer endure E. Wesson Woodbury.

Woodbury had developed from fussiness to nagging. He criticized Ralph's kit, his fly-casting, the amount he carried on portages, the way he strapped his bedroll, his shrinking before a swim in icy water, as though Ralph were his office boy and given to losing messages. Whatever his mood, Woodbury was unrestrained about it. His jovialities were as hard to endure as his bad tempers, and there were many of them to endure in the forced intimacy of tent and meals, and fishing from the same canoe. When he had a feeling for smoking-room stories, he shouted them and emphasized all the dirty words. But worst of all was his early-morning jokiness.

Before Ralph had even washed his sandy eyes, or
swallowed a drop of coffee to strengthen himself
against pleasantries, Woodbury would be bounding
with dreadful good spirits.

He would poke Ralph awake and yelp: "Going to
pound your ear all day? Well, there's one thing you
can do decently—you can sleep. Ha, ha, ha!" (But
the sound wasn't really a *ha;* it was a more gurgling
and complacent noise, and more enraging.)

As they went down to the water's edge, frowsy in
rumpled shirts, to wash their faces, Woodbury would
playfully splash a bit, and whoop, "All you need is a
little water on you to look like a drowned rat, dearie.
Didums got bad temper when ums wakes up?"

Of the matter of the odd slice of bacon when they
boiled the kettle at noon, "Oh, don't mind me, Ralphie
—just eat *all* the chow. I can live on air!"

And when Ralph spoke of anything more profound
than bonds, the stocking business, golf, or motors,
Woodbury croaked, "Great little talker, ain't you!
You'd make a fine college professor. Let's have a
lecture now on evolution!"

He was full of bright sayings and winning ways.

Ralph was not ridiculously meek. He snapped back
at Woodbury sometimes, but his effort was to endure
everything from cold to wittiness. And here, so
wholly submerged in a life new to him, he had almost
ceased to be the self-reliant Prescott who would never

have tolerated rudeness in a courtroom. In the arts of fishing and the canoe, in the strangeness of camp and portage, among the silent lakes and the noisy Indians, he could not predominate. These alien surroundings pointed by implication more strongly than Woodbury by derision his complete feebleness, and pointed it so strongly that he could not imagine any environment in which Ralph Prescott might perhaps be respected.

He had, for a time, no soul of his own. He became a serf to Crees and to Woodbury, with little thought, small feeling, and only a numb sense of his own stupidity—an insignificant figure crawling over the giant lakes, amid the engulfing gloom of forests.

"But how long can I stand being disciplined like this?" he wondered, when for a moment the breeze cleared away his torpor.

CHAPTER SEVEN

AT nightfall, after traveling too long in search of a good camping-ground, they came to the portage beside Wardrum Rapids, the most dangerous current on the Mantrap River. They heard rushing waters far off, and the unrelenting rumble disquieted their weary senses.

The beginning of the portage was a sloping bank

of clay, raddled and befouled by the feet of many canoe parties, no suitable place for their tents. But Woodbury said crossly: "Oh, let's camp here. We're too tired to make the portage and go on."

It was a lowering, unhappy dusk, the air wetly fresh. Ralph sat stiffly in his canoe, on his bed-roll, as the two canoes nosed up under the poplar shadows. Even in the looming distant growl of the rapids, he felt choked with stillness at the cessation of the motor's whir. The Indians crawled ashore, silent and morose, and morosely they lifted out the cargo, turned over the canoes on the muddy beach, pitched tents and made fire. No one spoke as they drank their evening tea. The bacon was burned. Wet clay seemed of itself to crawl over their boots, their cold hands.

And no one spoke as they crawled into blankets.

It was not till Ralph was half asleep that Woodbury grumbled: "I wish there was some way of getting you to remember not to leave your duds all over this tent. Here's your boots under my bed-roll. Even if you do want to lose 'em and go barefoot with your pretty tootsie-wootsies, you might show a little consideration for other people!"

Ralph's drawing of breath was audible as he started to snarl back, but he clenched his jaws and kept still.

He was awakened by the violence of rain on the tent. As he reached for his watch, with its radium-painted dial, he found the khaki ground-cloth of the tent soaking. Water was running down the slope on which they were pitched, flooding them. But there was nothing to do. There was probably no better site for miles, and the clouds had smothered the world with darkness.

Half an hour later Woodbury generously woke him to explain that it was raining.

They were both on edge when they crept out at five, in oilskins, to drink bitter coffee and gnaw wet bacon, but Ralph said with what he considered measured mildness, "Guess we'll have to stick here all day."

"Stick here, hell!" observed Woodbury. "On this slope? Sit in a puddle? We'll push right on till we find a camp with some shelter."

The rain promised to continue all day. Silently they began the portage, the Indians trotting with the inverted canoes on their shoulders. Ralph, as had always been his custom, and Woodbury's, prepared to carry only his own shotgun and fishing-tackle on the portage—a seeping mossy path, among dripping ferns, under poplars and birch beside the welter of the rapids. But this morning Woodbury chose to be zealous and generally disagreeable. He loaded himself with suitcases and food-boxes till he staggered and dropped a box or two. He tried to adjust a tumpline round his forehead to carry the boxes, and failed, while Ralph stared at him like a meditative calf.

Woodbury screamed, "If you can't help us by

portaging, day like this, you might at least give me a
hoist with my load and not stand there looking fool-
ish!"

"Oh, shut up!" Ralph heard himself say, with more
savagery than he had shown for years. But he re-
pented; he mumbled, "Be glad to," and loaded on
Woodbury's proudly athletic shoulders at least one-third
of the normal pack of an Indian on the portage.
Himself, he was shamed into carrying his own
duffle-bag as well as gun and tackle.

The strain of the weight on his back as they set
off was slightly less of a torture than being burned
at the stake.

While Woodbury wavered ahead, along the wet
path, in the green light through the showery trees, he
sonorously kept up his sermon:

"Of course the Indians are supposed to work for
us, but there comes a time when they can't do everything, and wet day like this, when we want to make
time and get on to a decent location where we can
camp comfortably, I should think even a tenderfoot
like you would want to pitch in and help 'em out.
Besides, they ain't dumb animals, you know! They're
human beings just 's much you are! They may not
belong to the Yale Club and wear lovely expensive
whipcord pants and be able to spiel about music like
you can, but, Gawd, they do have *some* rights! Matter of fact, don't see why you shouldn't do a little of

the work all the time, and not just sit around and think how doggone clever you are and—"

"I do as much as you do, Woodbury!"

"Oh, you do, do you! You do like hell! Say, can you beat it! And me with all the care of the motor on my hands—filling it, cleaning it, keeping it running all day long, so's I almost never get a chance to sit down and loaf the way you do— Can you beat it!"

That this was true did not soothe Ralph, but it did keep him silent.

He had been looking, always, for something useful which he could do, but he had neither the strength nor the training. What would to him have been an aching load on the portage was to the trained Indians but another insignificant ounce; what would have been an agony of paddling, to them was play. It had seemed absurd to kill himself on this "pleasure trip" without particularly relieving the guides.

As if they didn't have a beautiful loaf all the while the motor was in use . . .

And weren't they *paid* for it, and . . .

So he brooded, now miserably, now hotly, while they slushed along the path, dropped their loads, and went back for more. All the while Woodbury growled at him, at the Indians, at the rain, at the fish which, with a sudden feeling of injury and suspicion, he now remembered having lost off his hook day before yesterday.

The rain beat with gray resolute steadiness as they loaded the canoes and started up the river, motor-driven, at an unvarying pace, past an unbroken smear of rocky shores, of pines and poplars. The river banks were as lacking in human kindness as they were lacking in the bigness of mountains or open lake. Ralph's body was dry enough in oilskin coat and over-alls and fishing hat, but the canoe was soaked with a wetness which seemed to pierce through oilskins to his dreary heart. The Indians had covered the cargo with the heavy canvas of their tent, but the canvas was drenched. Greasy pools of water lay in its folds or leaked through. When Ralph drew it up about his chest, for a little warmth, the canvas was clammy to his hands. He envied, he respected, the Indians in their stolid patience. They were so wet now that they could be no wetter, and without even the nasty covering of the canvas to protect them, they sat unmoving, hunched over, expressionless.

But Ralph found himself creating a tolerable sort of shelter, crouched on the canoe bottom, his back against a bed-roll, the canvas making a doubtful roof. He had lost all feeling. They would go on forever, through eternal rain, joyless and with no destination, no hope; so why tear himself with desire? And as his body ceased demanding, his brain ran clear.

With all his stilled misery, he was rejoicing that for once the Indians were too soggy to chatter, and

that he was free of Woodbury's nagging. Ahead, in
the other canoe, partitioned off by the loud hum of
the outboard motor, the man was abolished, a nuisance
forgotten, so far back in history that now he seemed
almost diverting.

Ralph's mind began to tick as steadily as the motor.

"Even if I am a dub—yes, say it, a weakling!—
there are people who think I have certain qualities . . .

"Definitely, I've had enough of this—enough fishing—enough of the wilderness—it's all alike. And
more than enough of Woodbury.

"Blatant fool! Empty-headed buzz-saw! Hog!
Lord, if he were real—intelligent, solid, or even stupid
and kind—I'd stick by him through everything, no
matter how rough. I haven't complained once, have
I? But I'm through.

"I'd leave him here and now—if I could! Oh,
people would call me a quitter. Let 'em! I've gone
beyond the point where names matter—gone through
to reality.

"But how can I leave? How could I talk to my
Indians and tell 'em where I wanted to go? Charley's
the only one who understands English enough to
interpret, and naturally dear Wes would grab him.
Here I am, imprisoned. Have to stick till the trip's
over. With that blatting counter-jumper!

"No. Be fair. He's not to blame. I annoy him
equally. What he needs is a companion who likes

smutty stories and fishing. Nobody to *blame*. It would be just as silly to try to find out which of a divorced couple was to blame, when they just didn't get along together and that was all. Once I start really analyzing him I'll become desperate. Must keep cool. Either find some way to shut his mouth or get out of this.

"I wouldn't mind the rain, if there were some civilized people to laugh with after a day like this."

He was besieged by a vision of easy people, well-bred people, gracious people, talking on a sheltered porch facing the stormy sea, and all morning the thought of them tormented him as he crouched and waited.

For many miles there was no fit camping-place. The rocky cliffs rose too steeply, and so close did they come to the water that when the expedition reached a long shallow rapids, there was no path for portage. The water was not deep enough for motor or paddling, and Woodbury's Indians jerked their way up the pebbly current by poling.

But Ralph's bow-man, a reckless and fantastic youth named Jesse, who resembled a Chinaman, being now so cold and wet that coldness and wetness had ceased to be important, leaped out into the water and lined Ralph's canoe up the rapids, towing it in front while the Indian at the stern poled. Ralph crawled out as the canoe hung ashore for a moment, crept up the slippery rock face of the cliff above the river, and miserably made his way among the poplars, whose wet leaves slapped his face at every step.

Jesse was a slant-eyed genius at picking his track through rough currents, and a genius at Indian quadrilles in log cabins, but with his genius went a certain domestic undependability. He did not watch his footing as he trudged ahead through the shallow whirl —he had not troubled to remove his trousers or soaked moccasins. He hummed and regarded the heavens, pulling with stolid strength, the line over his shoulder.

He jested at Charley's poling in the canoe ahead. He remembered Red Wing, the belle at Mantrap Landing, and as he splashed on he bawled to the other Indians his highly colored opinion of her, all in firecracker Cree. Just then he slipped, sprawled under water, let go the line, and the canoe shot back.

Looking down from among the poplars on the high bank, Ralph saw his canoe turn broadside and bump a rock. The Indian at the stern, pushing with his pole, lost balance and tumbled out, while the other Indians cackled with delight. As Jesse splashed and galloped after it, the freed canoe gained speed, struck a fanged rock which slit its side, humped its shoulders once or twice in indignation, and peacefully sank.

Jesse reached it in time to rescue the bacon, but not Ralph's duffle-bag nor his bed-roll, which rested in a canoeful of water. Jesse shrugged, and began to line the water-logged craft up the rapids again. No beach here on which to make repairs. There was a wide enough beach beyond the rapids, and amiably, as part of the day's work, the four Indians made a fire by which to dry the soaked cargo a little, and began repairs, with new slats, new canvas, canoe-glue and paint, while even Jesse whooped and ceaselessly giggled about his disaster.

It was not till the Indians were already at work that Ralph, caught in a tangle of brush, sliding and bruising his shins on mossy rocks, made his way past the rapids and joined them.

He found Woodbury striding the shingle by the river as though it were the quarter-deck of a pirate craft. Before Ralph could let himself down the cliff, Woodbury was screaming at him:

"I might of known you'd do something like this! And in the rain! Ruin a good canoe! Ruin a sack of flour! All the—"

"Had nothing to do with it!" Ralph retorted. He spoiled his effect a little by sliding down the last four feet of the cliff and flaying his hands on the gravel, but he did not sound obedient now.

"Help it? Course you could help it! Letting Jesse play the fool with the tow-line!"

"How could I tell him? Charley's the only one here that understands English, and of course you hogged Charley!"

"Well, anyway, you—"

Woodbury's gust had blown itself calm, but Ralph's had begun. He faced the bigger man. He was no longer slightly absurd in his baggy oilskins, so hard was his thin face.

"You knew before I started that I wasn't used to this hiking, and yet you've done nothing but kick, the whole way. Let me congratulate you on one thing, my friend: you've managed to spoil the one long vacation I've taken in years!"

"Well, if you think it's been any picnic for me, Prescott, with your sulking and your would-be polite condescension and your would-be highbrow gassing and— And your inconceivable butter-fingered clumsiness! Things any real American boy of ten could do! When you said you weren't used to hiking, I didn't suppose you were a paralytic!"

. . . A crescent of gravel, five or six feet at its widest, under a dripping slope of rocks fleeced with wet lichens; on the other side, the river hastening down to a debauch of rapids, a stream black under black clouds, viciously glazed save for sinister little whirlpools and the pitting of ceaseless rain. On this crescent of gravel, a few forlorn and dirty men, two of them squabbling like old women over a back fence. All the glory of history and the human will choked and made futile by a rent in a canvas canoe, a clash of incompatible senses of humor. And round them a

million square miles of tangled forest and bleak lake
and dreary tundra, dwarfing their heroic contest to
the buzzing of flies in a spider-web.

Of this disproportion Mr. E. Wesson Woodbury
was probably not conscious. He went on with as
much joy in hurting his companion and hurting himself, and hurling out nastinesses which he would later
regret, as though he were a drunkard accused of being
a drunkard. But Ralph, with his years of legal controversy to weary him of all ugliness, was instantly
tired of the spat, and instantly aware of the snickers
of the Indians, who were listening to them with beautiful glee.

There was for once nothing of the Neat Little Man
about him, there was something stripped and formidably direct, as he stared down Woodbury's bumbling and stated: "Very well. I'm a burden. And
let me warn you that it'd be a pleasure to quit you."

"Don't be a fool! You can't!" chuckled Woodbury.

CHAPTER EIGHT

IT was toward evening when, with the canoe repaired, the motor drumming through the rain,
they came to the end of the poplar-crowned cliffs and
found an open camping-spot in an ancient clearing. It

was marked as an old Indian haunt by the staggering
poles of a one-time drying-rack for whitefish.

Neither Woodbury nor Ralph knew it, and if
Charley the guide had known he would not have
dreamed of telling, but here the first French mis-
sionary-explorers built wigwams in 1587; here ever
since had governor and bishop and lone trapper found
rest for a night, a week. Though the forest round
about is as unbroken as it was in 1492, the Mantrap
River is the royal highway, the Boston Post Road, the
Great North Road, of the wilderness.

It was a grassy and friendly place, well drained,
free of rocks, sheltered by a wall of rare white pine.
The Indians pitched the tents, and in five minutes
they had burning a vast bonfire which would have
taken a white man half an hour to set going. Soaked
of neck and wrist and hands, numb and stiff, Ralph
sat luxuriously on a food box under a canvas shelter
which was stretched over a bough lean-to before the
fire, his arms out toward the rejoicing flames.

For the first time Woodbury and he did not make
up their quarrel. There was tension, silence between
them and a sense of waiting, of listening for danger.

Woodbury sprang up. "Get a few fish," he belched.

Ralph saw him on the low rocks by the river, throwing out his trolling-line again and again, sometimes
pulling in a pickerel. It was presumably not at all dry,

down there on the rocks, and Woodbury looked infi-
nitely lonely and pathetic.   Ralph felt guilty.   He
buttoned the long oilskin coat, which with such delicious relief he had thrown open, he sighingly tugged
on his water-logged boots, and ambled to the shore.

"I say," he murmured, as Woodbury forlornly
dragged in his trolling-line, hand over hand, the water
dripping through his puffy fingers, "I do know I'm
not a very useful companion, and I do know you have
some reason for feeling sore at me just now, but I
hope I'm not keeping you from the fire."

"You? Keeping *me?* Don't be silly!" Woodbury
did not sound highly lovable.   (But, oh, all the time
you might have seen him as that fat little boy from
nowhere in particular, being so touchy because he
knew that he was nothing, being so offensive because
he was always being offended and hurt.   And a little
of this Ralph understood, but not much, for nowhere
here has it been stated that Ralph Prescott was a
greater or more tender soul than most of us.)

"I happen to enjoy fishing," said Woodbury.   "I
enjoy it enough so that after coming two thousand,
and maybe it's three thousand, miles for it, I like to
fish! The rain won't hurt my complexion, like apparently it does some people's!"

Ralph said slowly and carefully, but really without
much interest, "All right, you can go to hell!"

He returned to the canvas shelter and the enrobing

warmth; he stripped off his oilskins entirely. He wasn't quite sure how, but he felt that he was being defiant in thus settling down to effete comfort; and he considered that he was being absolutely mutinous when, without asking permission of Woodbury, whose stomach had been the only legal clock on the trip so far, he ordered Charley to break out a hunk of bannock for him and give him a cup of the tea which the Indians—sound fellows with no nonsense about the joys of fishing in the rain—were contentedly guzzling in a tent smoky with the steam from their wet clothes.

He watched Woodbury fish his way up the river, out of sight round a bend. He felt that the chieftain was being a martyr for his benefit. But he refused to be moved into obedience again, and he was beatifically dozing off when he was roused by the sound of another motor.

It was a sharper, more aggressive outboard motor than Woodbury's. Through the haze of rain Ralph watched a strange canoe fleeing up the river, heading toward their own camping-place. When it was come near he saw that there were two men in it: at the bow a young, unpleasant-looking Indian, at the stern a white man in an ancient black-rubber raincoat and canvas hunting-cap. Where Woodbury had backed and filled in making landing, had stood up and shaded his eyes and bellowed vague queries at Charley, the stranger shot up unquestioningly, in a wide curve, nothing of him moving save his hand on the tiller-throttle of the motor as he headed for exactly the right strip of sand.

He rose, took off his wet cap, wrung it out. Ralph saw that he was a gaunt, rusty-headed man of forty or forty-five, large-nosed, heavy-browed—a North-of-Boston Yankee perhaps, or a Cape Breton sailor.

He called out curtly, "Mind our camping here with you?"

"Why, no!" said Ralph.

He sounded independent enough, but he was quavering at making an arrangement without permission from the great E. Wesson Woodbury. And he did not like the stranger, who helped his Indian bow-man unload the canoe and turn it over, pitch their one low tent and put up mosquito bars inside it—theirs was no silken tent to keep out pests.

"Oh, Lord, this fellow is going to be more pestilentially virile than Wes!" Ralph groaned.

The man stooped under Ralph's shelter and without asking permission he sat on a low flat bacon box. He pulled out his pipe.

"Got any tobacco? My pouch is all soaked," he said.

His tone was mild enough, but he did not look at Ralph; he ignored him as a possibly knowable human being with an indifference worse than Woodbury's blowhardiness.

"Sorry," Ralph said curtly. "Have some cigarettes though. Don't suppose you smoke such effeminate things."

"Why! I'd be real glad to have one if you could spare it!"

The man spoke with surprise, and he turned full upon Ralph the blaze of astoundingly pale and innocent blue eyes.

For a second Ralph liked him, felt in him something simple and superbly genuine. But he smoked silently, and Ralph sank into discomfort again, feeling pitifully the tenderfoot as he watched those chapped, long-fingered hands, thin yet big-knuckled, apparently of steel.

In a puzzled way the newcomer pondered, after a time: "Say, I guess I made some break somehow, brother. You seemed kind of touchy about cigarette-smoking. Did I hit on a sore spot? Oh, Lordy, I'm always doing that! Haven't got much tact in my make-up, I guess. Or—say—gee—maybe you're almost out of cigarettes!"

He spoke with a grave gentleness, the rare gentleness of the man to whom it never occurs that any one could be such a fool as to take advantage of it, the man who never fights because he never has to.

Ralph urged: "No! Really! I have plenty, and they're in tin boxes—got soaked today, but thank Heaven the cigarettes are all right. It's just that the—well, the chap with me says that you must be a he-man if— You've probably guessed that I'm not the General Commanding in this party, but only the orphan tagging after it!"

Again the amazing light of those candid blue eyes, but this time with a worried query in them; and:

"No—no—hadn't figured out your party. Course before I landed I knew there was another white man—"

"How?"

"Why, I saw the footprints—city boots—where both of you jumped out of your canoes. But I didn't do any real sizing-up. By the way, I better introduce myself. My name's Joe Easter. I'm a free trader, at Mantrap Landing, on Lac Qui Rêve. I'm trying to run an opposition store to the H.B.C. and Revillon Frères, and one tough time I'm having of it, too— those big companies are pretty cute. The Hudson's Bay factor at Mantrap is a whiz—fine man, and his wife's an awfully nice lady, too. I've just been out-side—Brandon—buying supplies. Say, I guess you come from the East, don't you?"

"Yes."

"Chicago?"

"New York."

"Well, well! That a fact! Met a man from New York one time—going through here fishing—no, four years ago it was—fellow named Brown—in the wholesale grocery business he was—don't suppose you know him?"

"I—"

"Say!"

Joe Easter suddenly reared up his shoulders, astonishingly broad for so gaunt a man, and smiled, a rugged smile, unreserved, taking in his blue eyes, his wrinkling heavy brows, ugly mouth and rough red cheeks. It was as though sunshine had burst out on these soggy pines, this lugubrious river. "Say! I suppose a New Yorker feels about the same when you ask him if he comes from Chicago as a bloomin' Londoner does when you ask if he's from Regina!"

"Oh, I don't know that there's any peculiar virtue in coming from the city with the largest number of idiots!"

"Maybe not, but I find that in this life—which is the only life I know much about yet—a man isn't just stuck on his virtues. Oh, Lord, here I am philosophizing again! You see, couple of years ago I pinched a copy of some magazine off the *Emily C. Just* at Kittiko, and there was a piece in it about a fellow they called a 'backwoods philosopher.' That's me, I says! Two years ago, and I ain't hardly got over it yet! Every time I buy mushrats cheap and sell 'em high, I put it down to my giant brain, and every time I get stung on 'em, why, that's because I'm too good for this mean world. Sure! But it's funny to watch me trying to show off when I meet an educated fellow, eh?"

Joe Easter was red with laughter. Ralph relaxed. He talked shyly but honestly of his difficulty in mastering the wilds; he was edging toward his real worries when, like a cyclone on the prairie, they were smitten by the appearance of Woodbury, roaring ill-naturedly, "Hello."

He stood by their shelter, dripping, brave with many fish, feeling abused at not having been greeted as a martyr hero.

"Hello," Joe Easter said, equably.

"Don't believe I know you, my friend!" snorted Woodbury.

Ralph saw Easter's eyes, much less candid and friendly now, as he remarked to Woodbury: "Hope you fellows don't mind my butting in. This is kind of a favorite camp-site for me. My name's Easter—got a trading-post at Mantrap Landing—"

Then did the sales-manager (and vice-president) of the Twinkletoe Stocking Company excel himself in cordiality and worthy salutations, as between two strong men met face to face though they came from the ends of the earth:

"Well, well, well! Joe Easter! Put her there, old-timer! I've heard of you a thousand times. I was up here three years ago; didn't get as far as Lac Qui Rêve, but planned to. Why, I was figuring on buy-

ing grub at your store when we got there. My name's
Woodbury, Wes Woodbury, Joe. Introduced yourself to—Prescott? His first time up here. . . . His
first time anywhere away from the nursery, by God!
. . . Say, what do you think! He wanted to wear rubber sneakers instead of boots! Course you got on rubbers and moccasins, day like it is today, but I explained
to him—"

Into the rapids of Woodbury's confidences Joe
Easter's voice cut like the stem of a canoe:

"I never wear boots in summer. Always moccasins
in the canoe, and rubbers over 'em ashore."

(Ralph was remembering that he had paid thirty-
five dollars for the noble boots recommended by Woodbury.)

Woodbury gurgled: "Well, well. I'll have to try
moccasins and rubbers, Joe. But say, this'll give you
a laugh. The boy here—he's beginning to feel his
oats today and figure out he's become a sure-enough
old-timer, but when he started he lugged a *pillow* along,
and he wanted to undress all over at night and put on
pajamas! Up here! North of fifty-three!"

"Is that a *fact!*"

Easter stared at Ralph; Woodbury glared at him;
he was reduced to the position of the bright boy who
has thought that he was entertaining sister's suitor, but
who is now sent up to bed with smothered adult giggles.
Easter turned away his edged glance, looked patiently

up at Woodbury, who stood stooped with his head just under the canvas shelter, and drawled:

"Let's see. I'm forty-six. I was born in New Brunswick. Son of a shoemaker. Worked in a wagon factory quite some time. So I've only been in the woods for twenty-five years or so. When I come here first, a real eastern swell with an extra shirt, I started teaming, then trapping, before I got into the wicked wiles of trading. Well, at first I certainly did want to be a real, hard-boiled, dyed-in-the-wool roughneck. So I used to sleep in my pants, even on hot nights. But— well—tell you—here's how it is: getting old and rich— often got several dollars left after I pay my year's bills—and now, when I'm off on the trail with the dogs in winter, buying furs, I sleep in everything I own, except my reading spectacles. But—"

He stopped abruptly. His eyes were fixed on Woodbury. His voice was frozen.

"*But,* my friend, summer nights I wear pajamas, especial' when I'm out on the hike. And they're silk pajamas, friend, and I'd rather give up my bow-man— Lawrence Jackfish, who's stealing your tomaties over there—than give up the nice pillow I've lugged around these five years! Of course for a smart city man like you—traveling salesman, ain't ye, Woodbury?—it's fine to enjoy hardship while you're hiking through here; but for me it's business, and I travel just as soft as I can, and if I could bum another cigarette off you, Mr. Prescott, I'd be real obliged."

There fell a Niagara of silence, and Easter smoked and Ralph smoked and Woodbury sought for words and found them not.

Woodbury, after a suitable time of indignation over this betrayal and levity, dragged another box beneath the shelter, and Woodbury—he smoked also. Save for the giggles of the four Indians over the latest Whitewater scandal, related by Lawrence Jackfish, the snap of pine-cones in the fire, the dispiriting rattle of rain, the protesting gulp of Mantrap River, there was nothing to be heard.

Ralph broke the unkind silence with a thin voice:

"Joe, my first name is Ralph. I want to retain you in this case. May I put something up to you?"

"Sure, Ralph."

"I'm a piker. I'm thin-blooded. I couldn't paddle a nineteen-foot canoe for half a mile. I couldn't carry a hundred pounds on the portage. I couldn't shoot a rapids, by myself. I couldn't—"

Dryly (and it was at Woodbury that the arbitrator stared, not at Ralph), Joe Easter suggested: "Why should you? Why should anybody but a fool expect you to? Which are you—doctor, professor, lawyer?"

"Lawyer."

"I guess you could lose me in five minutes on Broad-

way. I guess the band wouldn't care much what I
thought about it if I went to the Opera. I guess you
could handle a case in court better than I could. Well,
then—it's only four-flushers, folks that need to stiffen
their wabbly feeling about themselves by making out
there's somebody they can look down on, that go round
telling a tenderfoot how bad he is. Course you can't
carry big on the portage. Why should you? Ain't
going into the trucking business, are ye? Nobody
slave-driving—" Joe's voice was curiously menacing:
"Nobody slave-driving and bullying ye, is there—in
my country?"

Another vast and uneasy silence. Ralph fumbled
for the words which should break his imprisonment in
this bleak land, in the torturing gabble of Woodbury.
Joe Easter would know a way of escape. But he hesitated before pouring out the words which might change
life as swiftly as a colorless and powerless-seeming vial
of poison.

The surprise, when it came, was not from Ralph
nor Joe but from Woodbury.

He leaned forward under the canvas shelter, holding
out his pipe, looking down at it in a hurt and puzzled
way, speaking with the kindness which in an irate man
is always touching:

"Ralph, I guess I *have* been riding you pretty hard.
Prob'ly Joe thinks so too. Prob'ly you're both right.
I'm sorry, Ralph, old-timer; I'm really awfully sorry.

I didn't mean to. I go off half-cocked too easy. Let's shake and call it quits."

His hand was held out, flabby in the firelight; he was looking at Ralph trustingly.

Against rage, Ralph had been steeled, but to be dragged back into slavery by the man's decency was intolerable. He did not at once answer. Woodbury's hand dropped, unsaluted. The river vanished in the early, rain-shrouded darkness. The huge fire of pine-logs seemed brighter, as its glare quivered along the slanting canvas behind and over them. The four guides, with Easter's man, were preparing supper in the communism of the wilds, and Lawrence Jackfish was agreeably tasting the tinned pimento-cheese of the tenderfeet.

When Ralph let himself speak, he was no longer hysterical. He might have been summing up in a lawsuit:

"Wes, it's too late. You're not a bad fellow, essentially. You're merely an ignoramus who's been elevated to prosperity by this amazing modern system of the sanctity of salesmanship, and—"

"Well, let me tell you that—"

"*Please!* But I can't travel another foot with you."

"You'll have to! And from now on, you'll do your share—"

"Wes, it isn't so much your insulting me as your boring me. And if Joe can think of any way for me

to do it, I'll leave you—yes, leave you flat! Yes, quit!
Be a quitter! And right now! Why, I'd rather starve
by myself than have a feast to the sound of your yam-
mering. My God, man, I was so tired, and I struggled
to— Hell! Never mind that; that's over; and now—
Joe, can you help me?"

"Why—" said Joe, and stopped.

Desperately, wondering if he had misjudged the
baronial integrity of Joe Easter, aghast at being again
delivered to the rack of Woodbury's tongue, Ralph
pleaded: "I don't want comfort, Joe. I can live on
bacon—or just bannock. I don't mind rain or rapids.
But to have to waste what ought to be a holiday with
this stuffed shirt, this after-dinner speaker, this—"

"Whoa-up! Whoa-oa!" Joe was clucking patiently.
"I wasn't thinking of any difficulties. I was just wondering whether you'd prefer sleeping on the screened
porch or in the spare room, my place at Mantrap
Landing. Why, sure, Ralph. If you'd like to come,
I'll give you some fishing round home, and see you
get back to railhead. And I certainly would like to
show you a kind of picnic place I found one—"

Then the great Woodbury burst.

He burst, he exploded, he gushed lava all over the
lean-to:

"Now that you fellows have settled on a nice summer, including a lovely picnic, let me tell you a few
things! This man Prescott, Easter—I picked him up

in New York when he was so damn' badly shot that
his hand was shaky. Maybe drugs, maybe secret drinking, *I* don't know! I gave him a chance to come in,
at cost, on an expedition I'd spent months preparing—
telegrams and personal planning, to say nothing of the
money—what do I care for money! And then—"

"I'm paying my half"—ineffectually from Ralph.

"And then he lets me down. Well, if you think,
Mr. Prescott, that it's any skin off my nose to lose the
pleasures of your company—and if there ever was a
more scared, whimpering, grousing bird on a wilderness trip, I just want to know who he is, that's all, I
just want to know who he was; and if you think I'm
going to sit up nights worrying over losing the pleasure of your highbrow company, well, you got another
think coming, that's all, you certainly got a good long
think coming! Go on! I'm not stopping you! Not
for one second! But let me tell you this, my boy—you
sniveling little social climber!—these are my Indians.
I hired 'em! These are my canoes. I bought 'em!
You're supposed to pay for your canoe later—for
what's left of it, after you smash it in a few more
rapids! But how do I know you will? How do I know
but what you quit on your debts like you do on roughing it? I've never had a poker I O U of yours yet—
thank God!"

"Splendid," said Ralph.

"So," said Woodbury, "if dear Mr. Easter thinks

you're such a great little social entertainer that he wants to take you along, why, all right. But when I get to Mantrap Landing, I'm going to have a few words with the other white men there—I mean, with the *real* white men there—and when I get through telling 'em what I know, I don't think Mr. Ralph E. Prescott will be so blame' welcome!"

Joe Easter had, this while, been more silent than the tall spruce behind their shelter, for at least the spruce sighed in the steady wind, the unrelenting rain. Once Ralph had, unasked, handed him another cigarette. He had lighted it from a stick thrust into the fire. The blazing branch turned the wrinkles of his dry face into folds like valleys of red earth. Now he spoke, indifferently:

"Woodbury, you are not going to Mantrap Landing."

"Oh, I ain't, ain't I! Well, I'd damn' well like to see who's going to stop me!"

"Nope. You're not going. Not that I mind your spreading the news—among folks like Pop Buck and George!—about Ralph's general crookedness, or me kidnaping him. But I just naturally don't like your boots, Wes, or this dirty habit of sleeping in your clothes. So you ain't coming to Mantrap Landing. You're going to—"

"And who's to prevent me?"

"Me. I'm a magistrate. And I'd have to pinch you

and send you to Bearpaw on trial, for shooting moose out of season."

"Don't be a fool. I never shot a moose in my life!"

It is to Ralph's credit that he did not protest, "Why, you told me you shot half a dozen of them, three years ago!"

Joe Easter was droning on: "No, probably you never have. Wonder how many you've tried to shoot. But there's another thing I can pinch you for—and that I will and do pinch you for—and that is the carrying of liquor into Indian territory. Shut up, you fool! For once in your life, shut up and listen! You have a flask of hooch in your back pocket right now, and when I made my landing here, I saw you sucking it, up round the bend. Well, that's that, as the missionary at Mantrap says. Now, Wes, we don't want you here. And so if you'll hike East—"

Then for a second Ralph admired E. Wesson Woodbury as much as he had despised him. Woodbury was retorting, vigorous but no longer pretentious; he retorted as the fat boy who by some magic had become a forty-thousand-dollar sales-manager:

"Joe, you've got a lot of interesting conversation. Maybe you could arrest me for bootlegging, but you're not going to. For some fool reason (God help you later!) you like Prescott here, and he'd be dragged into any case against me. . . . Have some tobacco? You must be a little tired of cheap cigarettes by now!"

"Thanks," said Joe. He filled his pipe, and let it gurgle as he meditated, while Ralph felt more abandoned and desolate than in all his life before.

"Yes, maybe," said Joe. "Might have some trouble convicting you, besides. But— Look here, Wes." He spoke appealingly. "Me and Ralph are going to fish Lac Qui Rêve and the other waters around Mantrap Landing. If you and your two nice canoes was to go back and try Lake Solferino, you'd have a lot better fishing."

"Thanks so much; so thoughtful of you; only I'm not going!" said Woodbury, with a placidity beautiful to behold.

"Yuh, it is thoughtful of me—not many pants-salesmen or bootleggers have a chance at Lake Solferino—but you are going. *Charley!*"

To the innocent word "Charley" were added others in Cree—crackling, bitter, raging, enticing Cree. Woodbury's Indians leaped up by the fire. They dropped bannock-pan and teakettle; they stood in horror, listening.

"I just told 'em," explained Joe, "what would happen to 'em if they came to Mantrap with a bootlegger. They'll start guiding you to Solferino tomorrow—or otherwise, you'll walk!" He raised his voice again in indecipherable sounds, and the Indians crouched in the firelight. "Now, Wes," said Joe, "let's all have some of your supper. You start at four tomorrow morning."

CHAPTER NINE

ONLY for a moment, that next day when the sun
beamed on placid river and rejoicing pines, was
Ralph unhappy, and that was at parting with Woodbury, who said: "I don't know what it's all about,
Ralph. I hate to go off alone like this. Do you think
you're treating me very square, old man? Remember
when I found you shaken to pieces in New York?
Think you can face me when you come back there,
after deserting me like this?"

That moment was forgotten as Joe Easter cheerily
shouted: "Try the middle of the canoe, Ralph. Think
you'll be more comfortable there. Unless you'd like
to run the motor?"

Incredulously Ralph looked back and watched
Woodbury's caravan, his own caravan, his own canoe,
Wes and the familiar Crees, dropping down the Mantrap River, while he himself chugged up it with a man
he had never seen till last night, into a land unknown
and improbable.

He was aware of a difference in the manner in which
Joe conducted his expedition. With only one Indian
and himself for crew, this lanky man in sweater and
blue overalls never fretted, never shouted, gave his
orders only as suggestions. And where Woodbury
had watched his outboard motor as though he were

making an etching, Joe Easter twiddled screws and adjusted the carburetor uninterestedly, and for him it sang valiantly.

In his new canoe home, with his bed-roll and suit-case, his gun and fishing-tackle again tucked in front of him, Ralph sat between the strange Joe Easter and the stranger Lawrence Jackfish, that slender and sly-eyed Cree with the bead hatband on his cowpuncher hat. It was all incredible. He was not here. He couldn't be, possibly.

Woodbury had maintained—often—that the noise of his motor made it impossible to hear the suggestions of Charley. He must have had a good deal of pleasure out of impatiently stopping the motor and complaining, "Oh, what the deuce are you trying to say?" But Joe seemed able to hear through the motor's hum. As they swept up the clear glistening spaces of the river, he set Ralph talking with an innocent question or two —and Ralph did talk!

Normally not a chatty man, today he was like a small boy whose important questions and theories have for a week been dammed up by an impatient parent. He turned round in his place amidships, and poured out all the fancies and memories which had so bored Wood-bury.

London—had Joe ever been abroad? Never? Lon-don! The library of the Inner Temple, turrets across ancient lawns. . . . Trafalgar Square on Armistice

Day, with ten thousand people hypnotized into a unity of silence. . . . Side street shop-windows with the chocolate signs which are more English than Westminster. . . . The black oak fireplace at the Cock Tavern. . . . Berkeley Square on a spring afternoon, and pretty women whirring up for tea at the bleak tall house of a duchess. . . . Piccadilly Circus in a pea-soup fog, the red-faced policeman shining as with inner flame. . . . Then the Dover cliffs as you saw them returning from France; and the stout and jolly porters, after the little shrill facteurs at Calais.

What did Joe think—what would happen when this vast land had no more fur for trapping; when agriculture came, and the rumored gold mines were opened?

Religion—how did prayer seem to a man like Joe, alone for day after day on the winter trails—prayer and the hand of Omnipotence in the wilds?

Music—the theater—pictures—did Joe care for them when he went to Winnipeg to buy goods? Did he miss them at Mantrap Landing?

All this while, Ralph was thinking aloud, letting his mind, after these weeks of sluggishness, course through the complexities and contradictions he loved. Joe was apparently not bored. For a time there seemed to Ralph nothing absurd in rhapsodizing under the looming indifference of the rolling clouds. But in late afternoon the spirit of the hour and place enchanted him, and he was contentedly silent. The Mantrap

River had widened into a lake. The gold-green light lay on pale poplar trunks, on gray rocks, on water like a polished shield, with the shadows meditative and long. Their wake was in two long curves, unbroken and unrippling, carven in crystal; and behind them rose in a calm beauty almost intolerable the great full moon.

In awed quiet they swept ashore and boiled the evening kettle; serenely they sat smoking.

"This is what I came for!" said Ralph.

"Fine!" That grave gentleness of Joe Easter belonged to the stilled hour. They watched a fish leap from the water. The widening rings were of orange fire. Joe reflected:

"The woods can be pretty nice, if you don't nag 'em. But I've had some good times in the cities, too. I don't go much to these concerts you tell about. Heard Sousa's band once, though! In Minneapolis that was. Yes, I been clear down there. And I saw a dandy billiard match. But the funniest thing that happened to me there— Say, did you ever get your finger-nails manicured?"

"Why, yes, sometimes."

Ralph marveled. Certainly Joe's nails, cracked with carrying fur-pack and fire-log, did not suggest any especial interest in manicuring.

"So did I, once. Peculiar thing it was. It was when I was in Minneapolis, as I said, about a year ago.

Thought I'd blow myself to a society shave and hair-cut, and I took a chance on their throwing me out and went to the Ranleagh Hotel. Swell place—marble and gold all over everywhere. Girls sitting waiting for their fellows, I guess, in a place off the lobby, all plush and everything. Peaches! Barber-shop down in the cellar, but what a barber-shop! All white tiles, with gold doodads along the ceiling, and a great big enormous table with magazines, and morris chairs to sit in while you're waiting, and a couple darkies to brush you off and sneak your hat away from you and just when you're looking around and figuring out they've stole it, there they are, handing it to you with a bow like you were the Duke of York!

"Well, sir, my barber, he was a skinny little wop—but say, some barber that boy was; he shaved this rough old map of mine like velvet! And what he didn't do to me besides that! Sprayed me with perfume! Massaged my face—guaranteed to give me a complexion like Lilian Russell, only it didn't take. Washed my head—I found out then what become of that plug of tobacco I lost four summers ago. But—here was the big show:

"When I sits down he says to me, 'Shine?'

" 'Sure,' I says.

" '*Shine!*' he hollers, like he'd banged his thumbnail, and a darky boy jumps like he was shot, and slid clean across the floor and tackles my foot. I didn't dast look down at him to see what he thought about my shoes.

"'Shampoo?' the barber says.

"'All right,' I says.

"'Violet-ray treatment?' he says.

"'I don't know what it is,' I says, 'but I don't get to civilization very often, and I'll take a shot at it. Well, I'm stepping into society,' I says. 'When I go out of here, I expect they'll ask me to be president of some bank.'

"You could see he was kind of bothered. I'd called all his bluffs. He'd thought he had me stopped on the violet ray, but I'd took his dare. Then he gets a bright idea. He kind of snickers, and winks at the Julius Caesar barberin' at the next chair, and says, loving-like, 'Manicure?'

"'Sure,' I says, before I realized what he meant. And by golly, before I could stop him, out of the next room comes a girl—man! *the* prettiest girl you ever laid an eye on!—golden hair, all bobbed, cute as a picture, and peaches-and-cream cheeks and swell figure and lovely smile, and before I could think of anything to say, she'd set right down beside me and grabbed my rough old mitt in her tender little hand and—

"Well, I could of died of shame, making her work over my old paw—and anyway, Joe Easter getting a store nail-cut, and right out in public, wouldn't that knock you cold? Suppose Curly Evans (he's the Pro-

vincial Policeman up in this district—kind of wild
sometimes, and maybe a little thoughtless, but a great
pal of mine; real roughneck; you'll like him)—suppose
Curly had come in and seen me doing a stunt like that!
Never 'd of heard the last of it! And I didn't know
how long it would take the manicure to wear off.
Suppose when I got back to Mantrap I started playing
poker with Curly and Pop Buck and some of the
trappers, like Pete Renchoux, and suppose just when I
started dealing Curly would say, solemn—I can
hear him saying it, like reading the First Lesson in
church: 'Brethren, this dearly beloved dog-thief, Joe
Easter, has had a manicure while he was away from
us. On top of that—"

Curly Evans's putative suggestions as to Joe's further dissipations were improper.

"Well," Joe sighed on, "there I was, risking murder
and sudden death—risking it?—why, say, I was getting it! I was dying with embarrassment at having
that girl—about twenty-two, she was—look over my
mitt. Like a boiled ham!

"I says to her, 'I don't guess you want to tackle the
giraffe's hoof today,' I says, 'and I don't blame you.
You oughtn't to have to work in the zoo.'

"Well, sir, the smile she gave me—like a sunrise
on Lac Qui Rêve—and such a darn' nice *respectable*
smile, too, not like these Janes you see in the Junction

Restaurant at Bearpaw—and she says, 'Oh, it's so
much nicer to do a real strong he-man's hand—'

"I could feel my barber snickering, and I got kind
of sore, and I must of blushed clear down to my
watch-chain. And say—her voice—like a meadow
lark it was—say, I *do* sound like a damn' fool, but
honest, she was all them things, and already I was
gone for fair.

" 'So much nicer,' she says, 'to fix a real husky hand
for once, 'stead of all these fat traveling-men and'—
she let him have it straight—'and these sap-headed,
perfume-stinking barbers!'

"Zowie! You could feel my barber getting the electric current right through him, one million volts. Maybe he didn't stop his palavering for the rest of that
beauty-treatment! (And three dollars and sixty-five
cents it cost me!)

"Me, I couldn't think of anything to say to her.
Alverna (found out afterward that was her name—
pretty name, don't you think?—kind of fancy, maybe,
but nice-sounding, and kind of different—Al-ver-na!)
—she had me so scared by her elegant voice and her
quick come-backs and everything that I didn't any more
dast speak to her than I would to get up in church and
call the preacher a liar.

"When the barber'd finished doing all the things to
me that they had in the catalogue there, and couple new
ones I guess he just made up on the spot—I never

have figured out whether the time when he got the talcum powder up my nose was an accident or a treatment—well, when he was all through, she hadn't quite finished my claws. Guess she'd found 'em pretty tough. Gee, I was ashamed! But the barber trun me out and I had to go off with her to her table. And maybe I didn't feel like a fish that's just been heaved to a hungry dog-team when I had to get out of that safe chair and the nice big sheet they'd hid me with, and go chasing after her to the next room, across that slippery tile floor, before all them barbers and the swells getting shaves, haircuts, and singes and everybody, and sit down at that dinky little table. . . . There was a barber-supply calendar with a picture of two kittens in a basket, on the wall right behind it.

"Well, we got talking. She certainly was a great nand at getting a fellow over feeling shy. She'd look at you—not in no come-on way, but like she trusted you and thought you were a great guy—and, well sir, I found myself telling her all about fur-buying, and what a dandy little house I had at Mantrap Landing, and everything. And she told me she was an orphan —dad died when she was a kid, mother had just died this last year; she and couple other girls had a little flat. And told me how crazy she was about music and so on—like you are.

"She was getting the digging and blasting pretty well finished up now, and me—

"I was scared chilly. One thing in the world I wanted to do was to see her again. Couldn't come in for another manicure next day—that ain't something you can do every day, like getting drunk.

"I wanted to ask her could she go to supper or something with me, but I didn't dare. It was like the first swim in spring, up here, when the ice's just gone out, and you stand there and teeter on the bank, and make out like you're going to dive, and then you look around solemn, and walk back to the house as dignified as you can without never diving, like it's just a great habit of yours to go walking bare-naked.

"And she finished, and she says, 'I think that's all,' and I stands up, and I stands on one foot and then I stands on the other foot, and I wonders if she'll let me give her something for herself over 'n' above the amount of the check. But I was afraid she'd be offended if I made a break like that, and I guess I looked like a gawk generally, and then I said good-by.

"Well, she just smiled, like she liked me, and she says, so polite: 'I do hope I'm going to see you again before you go North. I'd like to hear some more about that lead-dog of yours.' And I blurts out, 'Kuk-kuk—come 'n' 'ave supper with me t'night!'

"Like a ten-year-old!

"But she came. Supper? Man, it was a banquet! It was nectar and what d'you call it. She showed me how to order—right to the Hotel Ranleagh we went—

great big enormous room all long red curtains and paintings on the wall, about history and so on—Alverna said it would be all right; didn't make any difference about me not having a dress-suit.

"And she taught me a lot of new stuff to eat. Joe Easter, shoveling in alligator-pear salad (ever try that? —it wasn't so good—kind of a damp taste it had), and lobster Newburg, and kidneys that the waiter—he fixed 'em right before your eyes, there on the table, in a chafing-dish!

"Well, I want to show you how unfair a fellow can be. You know, for a second, when she got me to order all this, I wondered if— She was even prettier'n I'd thought; she was wearing a dandy little dress, silk I think it was, just showed her neck a little—she was so pretty it scared you, and nice and refined and everything; but just for a minute I wondered if she wasn't trying to work me for a lot of expensive food. And, Ralph, that kind of hurt me; didn't care a bit about the cash, but I'd admired her so—

"Well, anyway, when she'd suggested all this junk for me to eat, and I said, 'And you'll take the same?' she just puts her hand on her breast, and she says, 'I will not! If I can have what I want, I want a great big man-sized steak and a cartload of French-fried potatoes! I'm so hungry I could scream! All I had for lunch was a napoleon and a cup of coffee. All I could afford. I don't make enough money to feed a gold-

fish. And I don't let many gents take me out—honest,
I don't!'

"Say! So frank and honest and everything—I just
loved her! Little Alverna!"

"What became of her?" asked Ralph, as Joe lapsed
into dreams. "Have you ever heard from her?"

"Oh, yes! I married her, next day. You'll see her
tomorrow."

CHAPTER TEN

TILTING to the sail, soaring among bright rocky
islands, they crossed Lac Qui Rêve and came to
the huddle of log cabins which was Mantrap Landing.

All day, though he had tried to be cheery and full of
wisdoms for Joe's benefit, Ralph had been uneasy.
Alverna, queen of the manicure table, was the fiend
who gnawed at him.

He was pestered by two contradictory pictures of
her and of her house. "Told how crazy she was about
music and so on." Yes, of course! She would be so
artistic that an artist would hate her; she would be so
primly ladylike in her new prosperity that she would
make a lady burst into obscenity. She would probably
snub him. She would describe her perfectly elegant
gen'leman-friends in undertaking parlors and express

offices. She would hint that Ralph couldn't get away
with no pretending to be a gent and a Yale man, not
with her he couldn't! And she would turn his easy
friendship with Joe into a horror of plush-covered gen-
tility.

Or, as bad, she would not be genteel, but have
turned slattern.

Ralph remembered the Bunger House at Whitewater; and at Warwick he had seen the trappers'
cabins. He knew how filthy a ménage could become
in these carefree wilds. He recalled a cabin at which
they had bought gasoline: a kitchen-dining-room where
the frying-pan lay, dripping grease, in the flour-barrel,
and the dish-towel had been used for cleaning boots;
where gummy dishes remained on the table from the
end of one meal till the beginning of the next, at
which moment they were cleansed by dipping them
into a boiling pot of soup apparently meant for eating.

The bed was a whirl of dirty blankets, black-streaked
pillow-slip, axes, guns, fish-scales, torn newspapers, and
injudicious dogs. Over and through and under everything was a heavy sour smell of wet clothes and ancient
food.

Would Joe's cabin be like that—only, added to these
masculine horrors, an odor of stale scent, of Alverna's
cold-cream and nail-paste? And, languidly slopping
through the mess, a peroxide blonde in a torn dressing-

gown, no longer trying to be attractive now that she had trapped her innocent and infatuated man of the wilds?

All day long Ralph looked cheerful and told Joe that he was a great man, and tried to enjoy these last hours of spacious freedom.

From across the lake the settlement of Mantrap Landing was a speck on a ragged green shore. As they buzzed through the glowing water it grew larger to their eyes. Ralph made it out as a straggly line of log cabins on a bluff by the mouth of the Mantrap River—which flowed through Lac Qui Rêve and on. Behind the cabins were shaggy hills of pine and disorderly brush, part burnt over, part lumbered off, more desolate in half-nudity than the gloomy forest. In a cluster halfway along the line of cabins, beside a frame church of peeling slaty paint and spire covered with rusted tin, were Cree wigwams of canvas and birch-bark.

Even close at hand, the settlement seemed to Ralph so impermanent, so little of a solid and civilized dwelling-place, that he compared it to the scattering of boxes and bales dumped in the reeds and long wild grass at the beginning of a portage.

A lonely place and sad it must be at sunset; no enduring shelter to warm the melancholy heart.

Instead of coming directly to the nearer cabins, Joe made a great sweep and approached the other end.

"Got to give old McGavity—the Hudson's Bay factor—his chance. My hated rival in business, all right, and Alverna thinks he's an old crab and pretty awful moral, but he's a fine old coot," said Joe. "He's a Scotsman—he *likes* porridge! Still homesick after thirty years in Canada. So I always give him a chance to fly the flag for me. I don't suppose it's hardly official, but I'm the Justice of the Peace—as much as there is one. That's how I could throw the fear of God into Woodbury about carrying hooch. . . . Kind of a dirty trick, too, considering I got a whole case of Scotch aboard!"

Lawrence Jackfish, at the bow, had taken their own flag from an oilskin case, and he attached it to the rough sapling mast, while Joe twice fired his shotgun.

They were sliding fast toward the Hudson's Bay post—the "fort," it was called, and once it had been a fort indeed, besieged by Indians. Now Ralph saw a trim log cabin, the ends of the logs squared as in a Swiss chalet, and across the front a glossy new sign "Hudson's Bay Company."

It meant to him the conquest of the wilds. . . . Indians of the old time in feather bonnets and fringed buckskin; the hawk-faced Governors, gentlemen adventurers with lace ruffles and cocked hats; canoes with eight lusty paddles; and, floating down unknown rivers, the songs of French voyageurs.

The space before the post was a prim lawn, with a shining flagpole propped with whitewashed stones. Out of the store rushed a man plump and apparently not young. He waved his hat; he held up a revolver and fired it twice in greeting; then broke out the flag.

Scarlet and bright in the sun, it flickered against the dull green hills. Ralph was not an Anglomaniac, but he felt the romance of that flag; saw it flying, felt it proclaiming British daring, not only here in the barren pines but round the world—over steaming Burmese river-ports, on ships rolling through icy seas, against gilded temples, on the Horse Guards' Parade in rumbling London. He thrilled to it; he saw in McGavity and Joe some sharing in a high tradition; and so he came to Mantrap Landing, no longer lonely and doubtful but with the pride of a man welcomed by resolute friends.

As they turned, slid by the Hudson's Bay post, by the church and Indian camp, other shots saluted them, answered by Joe's banging gun, and they approached a long wharf of logs and planking. On shore was a log store, Joe's store, labeled "Easter Trading Company," with a shambling log warehouse and a surprisingly neat cottage—log too, no doubt, but covered with clapboards painted in cheery green and white. A girl ran out of the cottage, down the bluff, and out on the wharf, waving to them, her hair bright in the sun.

"Alverna," said Joe.

He seemed to Ralph strangely noncommittal.

Ralph looked at her anxiously. As the motor was

shut off and they floated through the placid shallow
water, dark yet clear in the shadow of the wharf, he
saw that Alverna was surprisingly all that Joe had
painted her. She was young; she was slim and radiant.
There was no peroxide to that honey-colored fluff of
hair, bobbed and curly. Her white skirt and low linen
sailor-blouse were crisp. Her eyes were babyish, childish her straight little nose—very face of a child—and
her cheeks were unpainted; her voice was caressing
as she hailed them:

"Joe, I've been terribly lonely for you!"

As the canoe grazed the wharf and Ralph stood up
stiffly, she leaned down with her hand out in frank
welcome, and sang: "Hello! Pleased to see you, I'm
sure."

Ralph Prescott, the professional bachelor, was in
fact considerably more excited about the presence of
Alverna than he had been about fifteen-pound muskalonge, the prospect of seeing a moose, E. Wesson
Woodbury's travail with the outboard motor, or anything he had experienced in the Wild Northland save
the sturdy friendship of Joe Easter. He felt for the
first time since the death of his mother that he was
veritably coming home, as he crawled up on the wharf.

Not till he had peeped at Alverna for half an hour
did he decide that her eyes were not babyish but damp
and secretive with desire; and not till that night, when
he lay sleepless on the porch of the cottage, did it come

to him that it might be difficult to combine his friendship with Joe—a man whom he liked as well as any one he had ever encountered—with the incessantly feminine, the softly and inescapably alluring, the unconscious and illiterate and overwhelming sorcery, of Joe's moist-eyed wife.

As they trailed up the wharf, Alverna asked only: "Everything go all right? Oh, *did* you get me the crêpe de Chine? *And* the candy? Five pounds? *And* the fashion magazines?"

She flung out an aria of light, excitable chatter about all that had happened. Old Mag had had pups. Her biscuit dough had fallen. There had been a mosquito in her room last night. Curly Evans, the policeman, was on his way here—some Chippewyan Indians had passed him way up the Ghost Squaw River. And she had washed her hair, just this morning.

Ralph was curious about Joe's attitude, as he followed them. Himself, he would have been stirred by her, yet irritated by her twittering. Apparently Joe was neither; apparently he took her just as she was, as he took warm sun or hopeless rain, toil or feasting—gravely, peacefully, never seeking to change anything in life from what it inevitably was. His arm was about Alverna's shoulder, but he was not ardent; he bent his head to her exclamations, but he did not comment on them.

They made procession through the bare yard, beaten

by the moccasined feet of many Indians, a court surrounded on three sides by the store, the warehouse, and the cottage. They passed a gate, a garden with a few northern flowers, roses and tiger lilies, and entered the cottage.

To the neat-minded Ralph, after the filth of the other cabins, of tent and camp-fire, it was a linoleum-floored paradise. There were four rooms: two bedrooms, living-room, and kitchen-dining-room. Either Alverna or Joe was a born housekeeper, for the house was as fussily in order as a New England kitchen. The rooms were lined with artificial wallboard, painted in glossy blue. There was no litter of dirty dishes, and the woodstove shone black. On the polished sideboard was a row, luxurious to Ralph after weeks of greasy enamelware, of gilt-rimmed china plates, and by the sideboard a canary cheerful in a cage.

"I carried that damn' bird four hundred miles in a canoe!" said Joe.

The pictures were chromos of yearning maidens in rowboats, or of cavaliers in something like the costumes of 1500 bowing to young ladies of 1750.

Six weeks ago Ralph would have twinged with elaborate and cynical reflections to the effect that they were horrid pictures—so *crude*—but here they gave him a feeling of home, of cheerfulness, of security, of rest.

Beside the poison-green tufted velvet couch in the living-room was a parlor organ of the days of William

Dean Howells: a magnificent structure with diamond-shaped mirrors, potted geraniums on airy brackets, and red silk behind carved fretwork. (Both couch and organ had been carried by sled along the winter highway of frozen lake and river.) On a shelf was Joe's astonishing accretion of books: a paper-backed Bertha M. Clay novel beside "Pickwick Papers"; a Church of England prayer-book, "The New System of Accounting," and "Pollyanna" together; Wells's "Outline of History," a James Oliver Curwood novel, Longfellow, and "The Smoking Car Joke Book."

Ralph had small time to glance about. Alverna seized both his hands and cried: "I'm awfully happy you came along with Joe. Are you going to stay some time?"

"If you'll let me!"

"Oh, sure—oh, you bet! Be *awfully* glad. Are you up on business, or a vacation?"

"Just a little fishing."

"Say, I bet you come from Chicago."

"New York."

"Honest? Oh, that's grand! I've always been craaaazy to see New York! But I'm not a hick. I was born in Minneapolis—well, practically in Minneapolis —in Idella. Oh, we'll have some dandy good long talks, Ralph—you don't mind me calling you Ralph, do you?" She languished at him. And it is written that Ralph Prescott did not look on her so coldly as his stenographer would have expected. "You can call me Alverna, if you want to."

"Why—" said Ralph.

"Any of that ale left in the cellar?" said Joe.

"Sure. You bet," she caroled. "I'll get you boys lunch in a jiffy. I bet you're hungry, after all that horrid bannock. Say, Ralph, do you want to go and wash? Do you like perfumed soap? Lots of gen'le-men don't. But then lots do. Oh, say, Joey! We got to give Ralph a party tonight. We'll get Georgie Eagan and Pete Renchoux—they're trappers, Ralph; they're taking a loaf here before they go back to the woods for the winter; we'll get Pete and Georgie and Pop Buck, and maybe Nels Stromberg, and shake up some poker. We got plenty of gin, and Nels'll bring some of his new batch of white mule—it's awful nasty but oh, Bertram, maybe it don't pack a kick! Shall we, Joe? Come on, Joe! Aw, let's!"

"Why, sure—tomorrow, maybe," droned Joe. "Wouldn't mind a little poker and a drink myself. But tonight, Ralph bein' a New Yorker and a great hand at reading and music and all that, I think we ought to have the—the respectable folks—Mac and his wife and the Reverend Dillon."

"Oh, God!"

Alverna brought it out in a startling shriek.

"Honest, Ralph, Joe is the limit. Mac—that's McGavity, Hudson's Bay factor—he's as funny as a crutch. He's got neuralgia in the sense of humor, and Ma McGavity, she hates anybody having a good time. Reverend Dillon, he ain't so bad; I guess maybe he wouldn't mind a touch of hooch himself if he could get away with it, but still he's a missionary, and he's hired to crab the game. Oh, Joe—"

"We'll have them tonight—the Macs—and get it *over*. See how I mean, Alvy?" Joe said placidly.

"Damn you!" She flew into the tantrum of a four-year-old child. She stamped her foot. She seized his lapels and shook him. "I could kill you! You never listen to a word I say! I want a *party!* I don't want a funeral!"

"Get it over, Alvy, and then we'll throw a real party tomorrow evening." Joe had not even frowned at her explosion. "Got a surprise for the boys—whole case of real Scotch! And I'll tell 'em it's your present."

She hesitated, then she flew into ecstasy as she had into rage. She bussed him smackingly; she even hurled herself on Ralph and, to his embarrassment, kissed at his cheek.

"All right," she clamored. "Maybe you're right to get the old crows off our chests. Now I must find you boys something to eat."

She began to bustle about the kitchen, humming "I'm Just Wild About Harry" as amiably as though never in her life had she cared for anything more violent than cooking for the men-folks.

Ralph noticed that her nails still bore the unreal flush of manicurist's paste. He (who had always hated unduly rosy nails as he hated muckily perfumed hair) found himself admiring her for keeping up her poor attempts at refinement. And he meditated: "No wonder she's furious sometimes. Joe is the soul of kindness, but he's so sedate—like me, I suppose—and she must find it dull here sometimes."

She prepared for them coffee served in real china cups, real incredible ham between thin slices of real and more incredible bread, and whole ripe tomatoes from Joe's tiny greenhouse, with a clean linen napkin on the tray.

Ralph Prescott of New York would not have regarded china cups, cold ham, or white bread as epochal; certainly he would have refused a naked tomato; and he would have taken clean napkins for granted. But after weeks of bacon and bannock and tea, in a land whose season is so short that it is hard to grow vegetables, he had discovered food.

How luxurious not to squat on a tarpaulin, with knee-bones cracking, holding a tin cup fiery to the fingers and dribbling into his coffee condensed cream from the two holes punched in a tin can, but to sit righteous in a chair, his legs ecstatically stretched under a table with clean beautiful oilcloth, and pour the cream —though it was the same condensed cream—from a jolly little gilt and white pitcher! How delicious was

the ham, how exquisite every crumb of the fluffy
bread! And the incredible relish of a fresh tomato—
rarer in its crisp flavor than fruits of Araby; the love-
apple, very food of love, to be eaten to soft music
and fainting lights.

"By golly, that's good!" he shouted, in the tones of
a Wesson Woodbury, and Alverna's smile made his
feast the more joyous.

Never had he felt so intimately at home as with his
friends Joe and Alverna, over a red oilcloth chastely
depicting the burning of the capitol at Ottawa. . . .
Her bent elbows were white and sweet against its con-
flagration.

Before they had finished, the screen door creaked
open and, without knocking, in rolled an aged and
whiskered man, mighty of shoulder, huge of paunch,
wrinkled and hoar and very smiling.

"Oh, Pop, you old sweet thing!" screamed Alverna,
leaping up from the table and launching herself at his
chest.

"Hey, git off me!" he said casually, encircling her
with a grizzly-bear arm, lifting her, and dropping her
in a garish golden-oak rocker.

Joe explained: "Pop, here's a fellow we got to give
the keys of the city to—Ralph Prescott. Got to show
him some real fishing. Ralph, this is Pop Buck, the
toughest old scoundrel north of Dauphin—been in the
woods for sixty years—first man to team from Win-

nipeg to the Mackenzie River—seventy-five years old, and hasn't quit cussing yet."

"And," said Pop Buck, complacently, "can hold more liquor than any ten young men in the Mantrap River district, and win more pots on two deuces. Glad see yuh, Ralph!"

Ralph's hand was white and feeble in the grasp of that hairy paw. Pop seated himself cautiously in a kitchen chair. Alverna flew over to perch on his lap. He stroked her tinsel hair while he rumbled:

"Yep, sixty years since I hit Winnipeg. Just a fort and a mudhole then. But my days are over. Used to could kill an ox by twisting his head. But now I've retired on my pension—that's my polite name for the dough I make my boy send me, 'less'n I go bust his head in—and I'm no good no longer for anything but light amusements, like booze and love-making."

"Oh, Pop, you're just ter-rible!" crooned Alverna.

"Well, you ask any likely young squaw around here if she don't think Pop Buck is a better dancer 'n any of these young cusses! Ralph, glad see you up here. Take you out fishing any time Joe's too busy."

"Thank you very much."

"From Winnipeg or the Twin Cities? Or maybe Chicago."

"No, New York."

"New *York*, eh? Well, well, well! And you look perfectly human. Well, New York's got along pretty

well without me. I was born East myself—Fort
Wayne, Indiana—but I never could figure out why a
fellow that had plenty of damn' meanness and ugliness
right in his own self had to snuggle up to six-seven
million other fool humans to keep warm. Bad enough
here—all-year-round population of eight white men
and twenty Indians, and maybe fifty more crowding in
every summer between trapping seasons. That's
enough brands of foolishness for me. Only one sensible person here anyway—Joe Easter—fellow that can
take a drink or leave it alone, and usually shows enough
sense to take it. And even he's up and married this
toil and trouble with the goldilocks."

Alverna curled against his chest, purring, "You
know you're crazy about me."

"I am like hell! Well, yes, maybe I am. So am
I about liquor. But that's no sign I like to take it on
my porridge. You're a luxury, that's what you are,
Kitten, and a natural-born, hard-working, conscientious, able-bodied grafter, and there's nothing that
tickles you so much as to get all the young trappers and
storekeepers around here crazy about you and then
look innocent."

"I do not!"

Alverna flung away from him, almost indignant. "I
can't help it if a lot of idiots hang around. They
haven't anything else to do."

"That's as may be," Pop Buck snorted genially—

genial as an old pine tree in a June breeze. "Anyway, I'm glad Ralph comes from New York. *He* won't fall for you! There's chickens like you on every block in that burg, Kitten!"

She looked at Ralph. Her eyes demanded, "Are there many girls like me?" And reluctantly his eyes admitted, "No."

Winsomely, with soft insolence, like one who knew many secrets, she slipped from the room, glancing back with a look which seemed to be meant for each of them alone.

CHAPTER ELEVEN

"WHADYUH think, Pop?" mused Joe, when Alverna had left them to the freedom of masculine conference. "Alvy had a fit because I insisted we ought to have Mac and his frau and Reverend Dillon for supper tonight, and get 'em out of the way, and then do a little climbing among the mountain-tops with a real party tomorrow. . . . Ralph: Mac and the Reverend will be crazy to meet you and hear all the news about New York and Europe and everything. McGavity ain't so much on books, but he's traveled a lot —believe he went to France one time, 'fore he come over here from Scotland—and the Reverend, he's a holy terror—guess he's read about every high-class

book that was ever written. Why, he reads the Bible
in Greek! Way I figured it out, Pop, we ought to have
'em in tonight. Whadyuh think?"

Pop Buck shifted his corpulence in his chair, tugged
a pipe out of his mighty pockets—they were like wheat-
sacks sewn to the tent of his worn jacket—laboriously
filled the pipe, wheezed out a whiff of smoke, grunted,
tamped the pipe, lighted it again, and lumbered into
speech:

"Well—tell you—here's how I figger it. . . . Ain't
a professor, are you, Ralph?"

"No, a lawyer, Pop."

Alverna had slipped from Ralph's mind. He liked
Pop Buck. It was this he had come to seek, this refuge
from the fidgets of New York. . . . Yes, he was glad
that he had deserted Woodbury—

"Lawyer, eh? Well, that's some better than being
a professor. Professor takes boys and makes 'em into
fine moral young fellows, and a lawyer merely keeps
'em out of jail for acting that way. Hope you don't
mind my coughin' and snortin' and bein' blasphemous,
Ralph. Joe always makes me like that, him and his
dern' refined poetic feelings!"

"Anyway," said Joe placidly, "I've got you now so
you don't spit tobacco juice on my clean floor any more.
Now look here, Pop: was I right about the supper tonight?"

Pop Buck sucked mellifluously on his foul pipe and sighed:

"Well, I don't hold with George Eagan and all these fellows that insist missionaries is all devils. I'm kind of a radical about that. Way I figure it, a missionary is all right—long as he don't interfere with drinking and cussing. Now you take Reverend Dillon here. He's a pretty good coot, for a fellow that's spent all his life in college and so on. One time when he was out on the trail with me in January—and by golly it was cold, too; mittens almost froze to my nose when I blew it—Reverend Dillon, well, he thought about it a long time, and finally he figures out it's up to him to pass some observation, and he says, 'Pop,' he says, 'Pop, it's damn' cold!'

"Don't know's I'd go so far 's to say that it was a good Damn. Fact, between us, it wasn't more'n a boy-sized Damn. But it showed good will and hopes. So I'd have him tonight, I think. But—"

There was in Pop's voice a heavy anxiety.

"But I hope you won't waste any liquor on him, when there's so dern' little round here, and all us young fellows needing it to keep our health up."

"I won't," said Joe.

Pop Buck departed.

While Joe galloped out to invite his guests and Alverna began to prepare supper, Ralph lolled on the screened porch, looking across the wide glow of Lac

Qui Rêve. There was a cot on the porch, and he
had chosen it for bedroom as against the stuffy spare-
room with its small windows. He was at once content
and worried. He saw Joe Easter's little philosophies
drowned in the flood of Pop Buck's booming cynicism;
he saw Joe's fondness for Alverna rubbed raw by her
flirting and mincing and play-acting; he saw the man
lonely, and courageous in his loneliness; and Joe's life
and its problems were more to him than the puzzles
of any golden client, any fatuous acquaintance of the
club.

Then, "What a rotten useless bookworm I am!"
he sighed, and went out to try to help Alverna.

It amused her to create food. Her art of cooking
was the higher in that she had to depend on canned
things and make them seem fresh. Joe had brought
with him boxes of new luxuries, into which she dived
frenziedly, bubbling (she never stopped talking while
she worked) : "Isn't it a shame to waste all these viands
and everything on dubs like the Macs! Reverend
Dillon (I call him Ray, in private, and believe me, I
get away with it, too, but Joe would skin me alive if
he caught me being fresh with a Reverend)—Ray does
appreciate nice grub, but I guess old McGavity and
Mrs. Mac think it's kind of naughty to be caught eating anything but prunes and pork and beans."

Soup—canned vegetable soup—she prepared, but
she enlightened it with English sauce, and carrots and

parsley from their amateur greenhouse. The asparagus was canned as well, and so was the butter which formed the basis of the sauce, but with red pepper and slivers of onion and white of an egg (precariously fetched from Kittiko) she did cunning chemistry.

It was luxury to watch her slim fingers, to listen to the silver current of her voice, and presently Ralph forgot that her only adjectives were "cute," "swell," "dandy," and "nice."

The central dish was to be that moose-meat which, killed legally in season or illegally out, in the house of the Justice of the Peace or the missionary or the law-abiding McGavity quite as much as in the reckless shacks of the Crees, was the staple meat of the land. And it was, as usual, tough; it was extraordinarily tough; a knife rebounded from its rubbery mass, and forks fell beside it bent and weary.

"Just a matter of gumption and elbow-grease," said Alverna. "I made Joe get me that sausage-grinder— almost the only one north of Bearpaw, I guess. Here, you turn the handle."

Thrice she had Ralph grind the tenacious fibers of the moose-meat in the little aluminum mill, after she had belabored the cut with a steel hammer. This Hamburg steak she briskly mixed with sliced onions, garlic, and bamboo shoot—canned, from a Chinese shop at Winnipeg—sprinkled it with celery sauce, and set it slowly broiling over an even bank of birch coals.

"Watch it now, Ralph dear, and I'll scoot in and change my dress and show the lilies of the field a coupla tricks!"

She darted into the bedroom beyond the kitchen. He wished that she would shut the bedroom door completely. She was so innocently comradely, but he would have preferred her not taking quite so much innocence for granted. He tried to ignore her white-clad figure whisking about the next room as he stood solemnly guarding the moose-steak.

If she was still fussy about polished nails and a certain delicate use of rouge, Alverna was also admirably quick, and in ten minutes she had changed from sailor-blouse and white skirt to a frock of black moire with fantastic scarlet embroidery flaming at the hem. In its darkness she was the more slender and flexible; her hair, sleek now and demure, was the more luminous. For the first time he saw her not as a lively child, a "good sport," who was something of a nuisance and rather to be admired for keeping up her little airs and gayeties among the leathery white wives and greasy squaws of the barren land, but as a girl with whom one might walk proudly through a drawing-room.

She posed in the door, her hand held drooping before her shoulder, too obviously showing off to be offensive.

"Do you like me?" she murmured—clinging voice, eyes caressing, moist seeking eyes.

It was with almost the voice of Pop Buck that Ralph grumbled: "Oh, yes, I guess so. Come on now and watch your steak. Do you keep turning it over or not?"

She sidled toward him; she begged, like a white puppy with a blue neck-ribbon begging for bonbons: "You're an old grouch! Now isn't it a sweet little dress?"

"Of course it is," nervously. . . . Mr. Ralph Prescott, so calm to instruct Supreme Court justices, so full of abstractions and of succulent words all set end to end, reduced now to irritated vacuity.

He was glad when Joe lumbered in—his blue eyes lighting at the sight of his guest, resting happily on his pretty wife. Joe hemmed, "Well, if I've managed to stay away long enough so you children have most of the work done, I'll take a chance on sticking around. The Macs and the Reverend both coming, Alvy. Be right here. . . . I'll do you proud. I'll shave, and wash my neck, and I'll put on a clean white shirt. . . . Decided what you want to do, next few days, Ralph? Fish, or rest up a bit, or what?—that is, aside from flirting with Alverna. Course you couldn't keep from that; she'd feel insulted if you did."

"I do not flirt! I think you're horrid, the way you talk!" pouted Alverna.

"Why, you poor child!" Joe chuckled, casually removing his coat and disposing of it by the neat method

of firing it across the kitchen into the bedroom. "I'm
not bawling you out. As soon expect a calf to bear
kittens as expect you not to look come-hither at every
poor cuss that happens along. I'm just trying to protect Ralph."

There was, Ralph fancied, a wistful seriousness behind Joe's teasing as he went on:

"Besides, even if you weren't the lightweight flirting champion, Alvy, you'd want to grab Ralph off and
hear the latest about the shows and dance-steps and
everything. I'm a noble soul, and a great authority
on trap-bait and third-grade arithmetic, but not so
much on society. Only, don't bore Ralph to death!"

It was an implied compliment, perhaps, to be taken
quite so soon into the heart of a family quarrel, to be
made part of it, but Ralph felt it rather an irksome
compliment, when Alverna hurled a plate on the floor
and screamed: "Oh, you and your old Ralph and all
the rest of you men make me sick! Because I try to
be jolly, and have a little conversation besides just dirty
stories and swearing and how all-hellish smart you
birds are at shooting and fishing, and because I like
to have folks act like educated ladies and gen'lemen,
and maybe ask you to take a little time off from your
hard work at sitting and listening to your hair grow,
and clean up and look kind of nice and civilized— Oh,
you make me sick! Just because a girl is nice to people,

you all got such nasty minds that— The steak's burning!"

Her tirade ended in a shriek of domestic solicitude, and Ralph sneaked away to the front porch.

Three minutes later he could hear Joe's voice cheerful as he recounted the incidents of his trip Outside, while she amiably gurgled questions, and encouraged him with "That's swe-ell," or "Gee, that was fierce luck!"

"Oh, for the reticence of an E. Wesson Woodbury and the philosophical calm to be found in that golden presence!" Ralph sighed, in a rather flabby attempt to be sardonic. But he knew that he did not wish to escape Alverna's violences as he did those of Mr. Woodbury.

Family dissensions and family confidences were both interrupted by the appearance of Mr. McGavity, the Hudson's Bay factor, his good wife, and the Reverend Mr. Ray Dillon of the Church of England Mission, all walking as gravely as cats on eggs.

Mrs. McGavity had a double chin, gold spectacles, cheeks that were round but parchmentlike and adorned with liver-spots. She had a simpering, pious jocosity. Her converse was full of little personal jokes, little sly digs, which no one ought really to have minded and which caused the most amiable persons to choke with quick fury.

In another circle of society, she would have tapped people with fans. Very virtuous she was, never accused even by the most venomous of drug-taking, arson, worshiping heathen idols, robbing banks, or being often in the way of eloping; virtuous she was, and lush with ideals for others as well as for herself, and full of jolly rebukes which she presented in the kindest, sweetest, most matronly way, with a bright display of gold teeth. She had wonderful eyesight. She never missed a flirtatious look, nor a cobweb in the cabin of a neighbor.

The Reverend Mr. Dillon was a tall, thin young man with a high forehead and a remarkable Adam's apple. He was always forgiving the Indians for being Indians.

After their sweetness there was a certain relief in the heavy gruffness of Mr. McGavity. He was an anxious man, with a mustache and an abdomen. He said in a hesitating way the most lugubrious things about store-fixtures and the duty on furs.

Mrs. McGavity opened the merriment with a tenderly sighing "Good evening, Mrs. Easter. I do hope we're not putting you to much trouble, coming to supper sudden like this."

She peeped at Alverna's bouquet of roses in a marmalade jar on the table. She giggled slightly, in the direction of Joe.

"You know, Mr. Easter," she snickered, "we all love the dear child for being so young, and believing

she can just put it all over the old grannies like Aunty
McGavity, that've gotten so lazy and stupid after all
these years. It's darling, her being so dear and ambitious, and fussing so much over the way things look,
and I do hope she'll still be able to keep up some of it
when she's had children!"

Mrs. McGavity looked again at the table, and choked
a little in neighborly mirth. Ralph noticed that Alverna's mouth was drawn in a thin line.

His own turn came:

"How do you do, Mr. Prescott? I'm real pleased to
meet you, I'm sure. I hear you're from the States.
From—New York, Joe said. But you weren't *born*
there?"

Her really miraculous powers of observation were
devoted to his stained and greasy whipcords, his spotty
jacket, and at the end she smiled with faint fat amusement. He could feel his spine prickle as he labored
at politeness:

"No, I was born in Pittsfield, Massachusetts."

"Really? Massachusetts? It's so curious. You
look so much like a man I met that came from Okla-
homa—he kept a shoe-store. Massachusetts. Um.
You see, I come from the States, too. My husband's
from Scotland. You and I will have to stand together.
He thinks all Scotsmen are so superior, but I often
laugh and tell him—he doesn't mind my having my
joke, and rubbing it in now and then—life would be

so dull without a sense of humor, don't you think?
I tell the Reverend that humor is next to godliness
and— And I often say to my husband, 'Oh, you wild
Heelanders may think so well of yourself and all, but
I notice most of you are working for somebody else
over here!' "

Mr. McGavity's lips had the same tightness as Alverna's.

His helpmeet turned on the Reverend Mr. Dillon:

"Have you been trying to hold services in the Cree
language again, Mr. Dillon? . . . It's so dear and
good and sweet of the Reverend, Mr. Prescott; he tries
to preach in Cree, and I do admire him for it so, but—
he! he! he!—the Indians can't understand one word
he tries to say! Oh—soup!"

So, having put every one into a delightful humor, the
good lady leaped at her chair, tucked her napkin under
the folds of her shiny neck, and sucked in an ecstatic
mouthful.

Mr. Dillon was less jocund:

"Come among us for a little fishing, Mr. Prescott?"

His voice was surprisingly profound for one of so
thin a neck.

"Yes, a little."

"Your first visit in the North Country?"

(Would they never shut up, and let him enjoy the
rapture of soup? Real soup! Hot! With a flavor!
In china plates!)

But: "Yes, it's—uh—it's my first visit."

"Well, well, indeed! Your first visit here. So you come from New York. At first I thought it was from Chicago."

"Oh, come now, Reverend!" gleefully presented Mrs. McGavity. "You mustn't be making such terrible social breaks. These folks from New York are all so high and mighty, with their skyscrapers and banquets and everything, that if we don't guess they come from there when we first lay an eye on 'em, we just show ourselves up as awful rubes. Oh, yes! Yes. You can always tell 'em by their touch-me-not ways. . . . Don't mind Aunty McGavity having her little joke, Mr. Prescott! . . . This really is nice soup, Mrs. Easter."

As with dreadful neighborly mirth they made their way through soup, moose, asparagus, canned corn, wine-jelly out of gelatine and coconut biscuits out of a tin—each mouthful Ralph rolled over his tongue, with gratitude to the fat little gods of eating—Mrs. Mc-Gavity seized most of the conversation:

"Are you still having trouble with the cookstove, Mrs. Easter?"

"I didn't really have any trouble with it," said Alverna.

Her tone was, for a second, more hostile than a respectable person would have liked to hear from a young chit addressing a veteran of the frontier.

Mrs. McGavity shook a coy forefinger at her, and:

"Oh, come now, deary, 'fess up! Mustn't be afraid to admit—I've got such a *good* one on her, Mr. Prescott! When she first came here she thought she could keep a nice fire of coals, just as if this were the city, where you can get hickory wood instead of our pine and popple that burn up so quick and all. She told me that *she* wasn't going to use a frying-pan all the time, like the rest of us stupid old housewives! Oh, no, she was going to *broil!* And then, when she couldn't keep up a bed of coals, she said—she said—" Mrs. McGavity almost choked on her humor and her ample spoonful of corn. "She said it was the fault of the *stove!*"

"But," remarked Alverna, "I can keep a bed of coals now. With birch."

"But there's none near here—not for two miles."

"I know. I got some."

"Oh, now, dearie! You didn't make—"

For once Mrs. McGavity was not merry, but grieving, and hurt in her finer feelings:

"You didn't make poor Joe, with all he has to do, go way off in the woods and lug you some birch-wood!"

"No, Mrs. McGavity, I did not. I carried it myself. Two miles."

"Oh!"

For the moment Mrs. McGavity seemed robbed of material for wit, and she looked unhappy about it.

She discussed with Mr. Dillon the impiety of the Indian children who, unless absolutely driven, never seemed to care to go to Sabbath school. Then she thought of another one. She turned on Alverna:

"Were you much worried, with Joe away and all?"

"N-no."

"Mr. Prescott, it was such a joke on her when she first came. Why, whenever she heard a dog, just a plain team dog, sneaking around the bushes at night, she thought it was a bear or a wolf or maybe an Indian or Heaven knows what all! . . . Now didn't you, Mrs. Easter!"

Alverna confessed:

"Yes, I'm afraid I did. I was such a little idiot; oh, a regular nitwit!"

"I'm sure," said Mrs. McGavity, "you were real brave about it—for a girl that'd just worked in cities—in a barber-shop!"

Alverna had suddenly fled to the stove.

"Tea—boiling over—" she choked. She stood with her back to them.

Mrs. McGavity was continuing: "Of course it's hard for me to understand being scared. Maybe I just never had enough imagination. But I never could get myself to be afraid of anything. Why, when I first come into the woods—and it was just after the Riel rebellion, and the Indians were still real horstile; they scalped a woman a few miles away from me—and I said, 'I'm not going to let anything get the best of me!' And nothing ever did!"

To Alverna, still at the stove:

"Why, dearie, is that another new dress? My, you certainly do know how to handle your husband and make him buy things! You can make him bring you back a new dress every time he sticks his nose outside Mantrap, and my old man—why, he wouldn't get me anything if— Maybe he's afraid the young fellows would pay too much attention to me! And maybe he's so fond of all these nice quarters with his Majesty's head on them that he feels it wouldn't be patriotic to let 'em get away from him! There, there!"

She leaned past Ralph, to the considerable imperilment of a valuable dish of wine-jelly, and patted her husband's chunky red hand.

"Don't you mind my joking, Jimmy," she comforted her consort. "I'd rather have you than all the handsome fellas like Joe, even if you are a porridge-headed, nickel-pinching old Scottie!"

"Hell, woman, I don't mind ye!" Jimmy's accent was as thick as knitting. "But I wonder if Mrs. Easter always gets your pee-culiar sense of humor!"

Alverna whirled about at the stove. "It *isn't* new— my dress. It's the old thing that had the silver belt on it. I bought it myself, with the money I earned myself—in a barber-shop! And I put these red dinguses around the edge myself! I did!"

"Oh, there, there, dearie!" Mrs. McGavity ballooned up, stalked Alverna, embraced her with a vast smothering by shoulders and expansive bosom. Alverna could scarcely be seen in the eclipse. "There, there, there! I hope I didn't hurt your feelings! It was just Aunty McGavity's little joke."

"No—I know—I just meant—"

"It's all right, dearie. And you made a real pretty job of it, with the red embroidery."

Mrs. McGavity stepped back to admire the revamped dress. Alverna, displaying its charms, spread out her skirt like a ballet dancer. Mrs. McGavity whispered delicately and helpfully, with a whisper which could not have been understood much farther away than the lake-shore: "Be careful, dearie! You're showing your legs!"

And beaming forgivingly on one and all, Mrs. McGavity waddled back to the table, while Alverna's new smile stopped abruptly, and she dropped her spread-eagled hands and turned again to the stove.

Mrs. McGavity's moment of absence had perilously given the conversation over to the others.

Ralph had little to say and Joe Easter less, but the Reverend Mr. Dillon was full of plaintive anecdotes, and Mr. McGavity desired to talk business.

Mr. Dillon was no intellectual Titan, but he was kindly and serene. But then again he was no intellectual Titan. He had a thankless labor in this field, he

sighed. The Indians did not seem to have much spir-
itual outlook. They were obedient enough about at-
tending Morning and Evening Prayer, and they listened
to his sermons—and maybe Mrs. McGavity *was* right
about his poor attempts at Cree, but he *noticed* that
the Indians *seemed,* they certainly did *seem,* to understand what he was trying to *say!* But right after
Evening Prayer, the Indians would go off to Counselor
Three Foxes' cabin, and dance there; and he knew for
a positive fact that last Sunday evening five of the
younger Indian trappers had played poker, and played
for money, till nearly midnight, in the wigwam of a
very doubtful character named Tristram Dogteam.

Then, while Mr. Dillon was catching his breath, and
Mrs. McGavity was making up for her previous inat
tention to the wine-jelly and the tin of coconut biscuits.
her husband seized the scarlet thread of social joy:

"Did you see Tom Pinkford at Brandon, Joe?"

"No, I didn't see him, Mac," said Joe.

"Didn't you see him at all?"

"No, never saw him."

"That's funny. I thought he was there now."

"Don't know, Mac. I never saw him. Maybe he
was out of town—didn't lay an eye on him. . . .
Ralph, you must get Mac to tell you—"

"But, Joe," insisted Mr. McGavity, "I thought you
were going to talk over Tom's white-fox farm with
him."

"Yuh, I had kind of thought of it, Mac, but—I didn't happen to run into him."

"What do you think, Joe? Are you stocking Wishepagon woolen socks for next winter, or are you sticking to Hamilton socks?"

"I'm going to order Wishepagon."

"Ah, I told ye so!" Mr. McGavity shook his hand in triumph. He turned on Ralph; he made it all clear and fascinating: "But it was me that first told Joe about the Wishepagon socks! He used to carry nothing but the Hamilton socks. Every sock in his store —Hamilton! And the Wishepagon sock—it won't shrink, it won't run, the red border is just as fast as if it was gray—it's real honest Scotch wool! And what do ye think? What do ye *think?* Time and time and time again I've spoken to the Inspector and I've told him, I've warned him, I've explained to him— I've talked to him honest, Mr. Prescott, as man to man—I've told him I could sell twice as many Wishepagon socks as I can sell Hamilton socks—the Indians may be awful boobies in some ways, you know, but they know what socks they like—they know whether socks shrink or *don't* shrink—they know—the Indians know whether their feet are dry or their feet are not dry—and I've told that to the Inspector, and still I get Hamilton socks! And what do you think of that, Mr. Prescott?"

Mr. Prescott said that so far as he could see, it was at least unfortunate and ill-deserved.

Alverna urged Mr. Dillon: "You must have some more sauce on your asparagus. I made it myself. It's a kind of mayonnaise."

Mrs. McGavity pointed out: "Oh, did you hear her? 'It's a *kind* of mayonnaise.' Now isn't that cute?" She giggled three fat whiffling giggles, and smiled on Alverna condescendingly—as a spinster publicly quotes and smiles on a clever child.

Alverna scowled exactly as that child would scowl.

And this was the beginning of an evening which, save for Alverna's unfortunate crying later, was full of neighborly cheer and of brave frontier talk.

CHAPTER TWELVE

RALPH had never admired any one more than Alverna during that official feast. It is true that her phrasing lacked the scholarly charm which one expects in a female. "Oh, gee, that's dan-dy!" was the way in which she acclaimed the Reverend Mr. Dillon's portrayal of his efforts to interest Indian ladies in weaving; and at Mr. McGavity's moral references to the charms of her revealed throat she giggled, "Oh, say now, where do you get that stuff!" And once, as testified, she had broken under a reference to her

extravagance. But otherwise she was filially attentive to all of Mrs. McGavity's observations—and we
have considered here but an insignificant portion of that
lady's jolly and bustling and forward-looking observations of the evening.

When Mrs. McGavity told how she had driven
away a wolf by shooting blank cartridges, awed a
homicidal Indian by remarking, "Well sir, and what
do *you* want?" and made Mr. McGavity's pants last
two years extra by cunningly darning them, Alverna
cheerfully applauded: "That was great! I'll say it
was!"

When the Reverend Mr. Dillon explained the dif-
ferences between the government of the Church of
England and that of the Wesleyans, she listened like
a lady disciple, bending intently forward, her radiant
little face tight in her slender hand. And when Joe
yawned during Mr. McGavity's disclosure of the fact
that a net stretched from Two Pines Point to Sullivan
Island would be much more likely to catch whitefish
than one sunk in Island Channel, then Alverna covered it by crying: "Why, Joe, you poor old dear, you're
so tired after your hike that you can scarcely keep
your eyes open! . . . Ralph, it's just wonderful the
way Mr. Mac knows all the best fishing-grounds around
here!"

Between exclamations Alverna was forever gayly
hustling—leaping up from the table, waiting on all of

them, whisking away used plates, cleaning them with
a lively sound of scraping, and singing "Yes, We Have
No Bananas" as she wiped them. She divined that
Mr. Dillon wanted more of the asparagus (she herself
took none at all, Ralph noted) and that Mrs. McGavity
had a lecherous eye upon the platter of wine-jelly.

And thrice Ralph saw her affectionately slip her
hand across Joe's hair as she skipped back from the
stove and took her seat.

They were his family, he felt grimly; for Joe or Alverna he would zealously cut the throat of Mrs. Mc-
Gavity, and that would be no brief task nor pretty.

The last smears of the wine-jelly had been scraped
up with clashing spoons, and Mrs. McGavity had ab-
sent-mindedly fished all the coconut biscuits out of the
tin by her elbow. They had sipped the tea, served not
with condensed cream but with real lemon excitedly
produced by Alverna from the new treasure-chest
brought in Joe's canoe. For half an hour they sat in
the morris chairs in the living-room, sucking toothpicks
thoughtfully passed by Joe, while in the kitchen Alverna washed the dishes. She had refused Ralph's
aid: "Any other night; but those wild sports need
somebody new to show off to," she giggled. When
all these greenwood sports were over, Mr. and Mrs.
McGavity rose, solemnly hid yawns, solemnly gasped:
"Guess it's about time to think of hitting it for home,
Joe."

Mr. Dillon shot up from his chair with them.
"Why! My good gracious! It's half-past nine! I
hadn't any idea it was so late! Let me thank you
and your good lady, Mr. Easter, for a most delicious
feast. And I hope, Mr. Prescott, that you will have
a most delightful vacation here. Good night, all!
Good night!"

"Good night—such a *love*-ly supper, Mrs. Easter,"
said Mrs. McGavity.

"G'night, Joe. Night, Alverna. Pleased met you,
Prescott," said Mr. McGavity.

"Simply *love*-ly! I wish I had a husband that would
get me a lot of canned goods, instead of having to fix
up everything by myself. Good night—good night!"
said Mrs. McGavity.

And they were gone, and on the house fell a boun-
teous silence.

Ralph, teetering on the piano-stool at the parlor-
organ, revolving it a little with a faint squeaking,
watched Joe, gauntly relaxed in a morris chair, and
Joe watched the silent Alverna. She stood at a window,
her back to them, plucking at the tidy net curtains herself had washed and hung. She could not have seen
much; even in the late northern twilight there was
only the meshed and cloudy outline of the trees.

She turned toward them:

"Well, I hope you're satisfied, Joe."

"Yuh, yuh, sure, went fine! Got it over. That

McGavity woman does like to shoot her mouth off,
don't she! You handled her just right, Alvy. And
it's all over!"

"Yes, for you it is, Joe Easter. You'll forget about
it. You wouldn't think of making her apologize. You
wouldn't even apologize to me for her. You'd have
her here in this house again—over my dead body you
will!"

"Why, what's the matter?"

"You know good and plenty well what's the matter!
Aside from calling me a fool and a rotten housekeeper,
and saying I gold-dig you for all the money I can get
and blow it in on foolishness, and saying I was a dirty
little coward—after what I've gone through these last
few nights, alone in the house!—and hinting I was
a streetwalker—oh, otherwise she was mother's little sunbeam, the damn' neighing hyena! I've had
enough! I played fair. I stood it while she was our
guest. Now I'm going to start something. I'll run
her and her fat-head of a husband out of—"

"Eh, eh! Whoa—whoa-up!" Joe had risen; he
stood with his hands on her shoulders. "She was
mean, and you were a corker. But keep it up. Don't
do her stunt. Don't expect her to be something she
ain't. Got to take everybody in this world the way
they are. And don't make *us* pay for her being such
a stinker. You were so decent—don't spoil it."

"It's your turn! I've suffered—now you'll suffer!"

She threw his hands from her shoulders; she raced the floor.

Joe placidly stood with his hands in his pockets, droning: "It's all true. Mrs. Mac is a fool and a bad actor. She expects you to be a setting hen. But then, you expect her to be a hoppin' jaybird. Me, I expect nothing at all. And I'm the only one that gets what he expects! You got to think of Ralph and me, and how——"

With a frightful scream she interrupted him. She threw up her fists, clenching and unclenching her fingers like the tentacles of some huge white insect, her pointed nails jabbing her palms. She tossed her head back, hair flying insanely. She screamed again. She rushed at Joe and beat his chest, raging: "Oh, shut up, shut up, shut up! Just like you—you let that devil shame me, then go and be so calm about it—you cold-boiled potato, and you *are* a cold fish, too, I'll tell the world! You'll go right off to sleep tonight! You'll snore! You'll forget! And I'll lie awake and feel so darn' sick because I can't get my hands on her fat neck and choke her to death! I'll show her. . . . Where's that whisky you brought in?"

"It's— Why?"

She darted into the kitchen, snatched off the tarpaulin cover with which Joe had hidden from the pure eyes of Mrs. McGavity the new case of Scotch. She yanked out a bottle as though she were pulling a hated weed. She savagely drew the cork and, standing before them, in the door between kitchen and living-room, she tilted the bottle and drank with a long gurgle.

"Don't do that!" Joe said sharply.

"Go to the devil!" she observed, as she banged the bottle down on the ledge of her sewing-machine.

Ralph, longing to escape and feeling that this would only draw the more attention, almost skipped off the piano-stool as she brushed by him. She strode to the green couch, hysterically threw herself down.

"That drink makes me feel a little better. If I hadn't had a spot of something, I'd of gone crazy," she snarled. "Now you look here, Joe. Come down to cases. You brought me up here to the woods. You got to make it possible for me to stay here. Figure it out for yourself: Just one other white woman in the whole place, and she's that pious old fake that's bound and determined to make me wretched. Either she's got to go, or I have. I've never done one single thing to give her any excuse for panning me—"

Joe stepped lightly across the room and closed her mouth with his broad palm. She choked, struggled, bit, but he silenced her, and he remarked somewhat coldly:

"Aside from your making Ralph sick, you're— You fool, I know the McGavity woman is a mischief-maker. But it's because she *is* the only white woman around here that you've got to put up with her—have her to depend on. She doesn't get you, but then you don't get her. And you won't. You won't listen to what I say. And— You've never done anything to start her gossiping? What about your pulling the wildest parties from Herschel Island to Nipigon? What about encouraging Curly and George and the rest of the boys to play poker all night and drink a lot of rot-gut white mule and holler so they can be heard way up at Revillon Frères'?"

"You enjoy it just as much as—"

"Sure I do! But I don't expect a holy bird like Ma McGavity to think I'm a Sunday-school scholar because of it! Imagine what she must think of you."

"Well, what I think of her—"

"Yuh. You kind of gave us a hint about it! As I say: why, she hasn't even begun to spout all she thinks. Her spirit's probably willing, but she ain't strong on vocabulary! And you can figure out for yourself how Mac and she must talk about you when they see you throwing a come-on look at every doggone last thing in pants that happens along! And then you expect her to admire you for— And Lord only *knows* how you carry on with George Eagan and Curly when I'm away!"

She sat bolt up on the couch. Her voice was not hysteric now but stilled with shocked fury.

"Joe Easter! Are you hinting that I'm a bad woman?"

He did not answer. His eyes were steady. Something in him so dominated the room that the wretched Ralph could not stir.

"Are you? Go on! Say it! Don't you dare start making all these dirty insinuations unless you're ready to back them up! *Well?*"

Still he answered only with a look like a vise.

She shrugged uneasily; she turned her eyes from him; she said feebly: "Oh, you make me tired. All these silly suspicions—honest, just silly. Because I want to dance and kid folks along, the dubs that like to sit up late talking about their corns, they think I'm tough. And"—rather weakly—"you listen to 'em! Why, Joe Easter, you ought to be ashamed of yourself! . . . Hadn't he ought to, Ralph?"

Once addressed, Ralph was released from his unhappy trance. "Oh, I wish you'd both stop quarreling! It gets you nowhere. I'm going to bed."

"But honest, Ralph," she begged, "you got no idea how hard it is for me here, with nothing but these poker parties. I'd rather have nice dances—like we used to have in Minneapolis, at Lake Harriet—with a live bunch—but *you* know: respectable. Maybe I wasn't anything but a manicure girl in a barber-shop, like that old hellion hinted—how I hate her!—but I was brought up real nice. My papa was in the furniture business. He had his own store! And believe me, a manicure girl meets more swell birds and interesting people and everything than an old turkey-buzzard like Ma McGavity ever heard about. Didn't I meet my old Joe there!"

She tried to make it cheerful, affectionate, forgiving; but Joe, slouching on the arm of a morris chair, did not look at her.

She desperately swung back to Ralph. Her defenselessness touched him, and her pleading:

"Honest, I met some wonders—you see, it was at the Hotel Ranleagh, and all the important people stop there. And a manicure girl gets a chance to talk with 'em real intimate, like nobody else in the hotel would. And no matter what they tell you, if a manicure girl respects herself and don't let guys get fresh with her, most folks treat her like they would their sisters, practically. Why, the people that I've met—and talked to! Senators and bankers and automobile racers and bishops and big advertising-men— And then Joe expects me to settle down contented here! When he could just as well start a store in Winnipeg (I hear that's a dandy town) or some place like that, and see life! The people I've met! Why, Ralph—" She sprang up and ran to him, a radiant child. "Once, when he was in Minneapolis, touring, I did the nails of Jack Barrymore!"

Joe suddenly came to life. He rose, he seized her arm.

"Been thinking, Alvy. I know it isn't easy for you

here. Not that I'm blind, mind you! I know that— Oh, prob'ly it is dull here. But I don't see how I can get away. Got my investment. With what little I've made these last two years, all the big losses on my furs, I couldn't possibly start business Outside. But maybe I could a few years from now. If you could just wait, be a little steadier and not fly off the handle like you do! When Mrs. Mac thinks she's being so cute, why, laugh at her. That's why—that's one reason why I tolled Ralph here. Part because I liked him right off when I met him. You bet! But part because I wanted you to have a chance to talk to a fellow that can enjoy the North and still do a job of thinking sometimes, and not just raise Cain all the while. Am I right, Ralph? Oughtn't she to try to stick it? Or ought I to send her back to the cities?"

"Oh, gee, Joe, couldn't you maybe do that?" She pirouetted, a skirt dancer. "Just go down for this winter, and come back right after the break-up in May?"

"And do what?"

"Oh—I could stay with the girls at the flat again."

"And get your manicure job back?"

"I wouldn't want to do that. One thing I do like here—besides you, dearie. I like my own kitchen and my own house, and doing things in my own time. And I *am* a good housekeeper, *ain't* I! I couldn't stand going back and having to be in the shop exactly at eight-

thirty, and taking all the mean customers—the guys
that are so stuck on themselves they think they can
make you P.D.Q., even if they're old and fat, with
a breath like a brewery. And having to be there days
when you feel so sick and your head aches. And the
fly barbers that won't never let you alone. No. Why
couldn't I just sort of stick around and go to the
movies—"

"With your fondness for hell-raising? Mind you,
I'm not blaming you; guess wouldn't care much for a
barber-shop myself; but you'd absolutely go to pieces
if you didn't have a job of some kind to keep you busy
and steady. And then, as you know, I'm not flush
enough to keep up two homes—"

He explained to Ralph:

"Situation's like this. Fur-buying—and that's a
more important part of a trader's business than keeping
store—it's awful' speculative. This year the market
dropped right after I finished my buying, and I had to
sell every doggone mushrat skin for sixty cents less
than I'd paid for 'em—and I had seventeen thousand
of 'em! About wiped out my capital. And now—even
the store is doing almost nothing. The Hudson's Bay
and Revillons' and I, we all had to shut down on giving
credit to the Indians, because they wouldn't pay their
debts. They've gotten into a great habit lately of
running up as big a bill as they could, and then, when
they get some money—the Government treaty-money,

for instance—they won't come in and pay up, no matter how long we've carried 'em. They'll jump in a canoe and go clear down to Lake Warwick and spend the money there, where they haven't any bills to settle. Don't blame 'em entirely. Poor devils don't get much money. But I'm not rich. I can't go on supporting a hundred Cree families. And so the only business I'm doing is with the few that pay cash."

Alverna, now for several minutes the demure and wistful lady, was shrieking again:

"Yes! And what he didn't tell you— Joe's nerve, to bring you into all this danger! And to leave me alone here nights, while he was gone!"

"I *hope* you were alone!" Joe grunted.

"Damn you, I won't stand your insinuations! And I'm going to *tell* Ralph what you've let him in for! . . . Because we've shut down on credit, the Indians are crazy-sore. They say we're starving 'em. And we are. And they've sworn they'll burn all three stores here, and murder us in our beds! Any night now, they may be down on us—"

"That," said Joe, "is plumb idiotic, and you know it. If it were true, I'd have both you and Ralph out of here—and myself. I don't like being murdered more'n most folks, in my bed or anywhere else. The Indians are i-rate, but they're shiftless—these particular bands of Woods Crees around here, I mean. They're scared of us."

"A man can be awful' scared," said Alverna, "and still burn all of us in our beds or— God! Look!"

She was pointing at the darkened window.

Ralph's heart stopped.

"Oh, it's nothing," she said apologetically. "For a second I thought I saw an Injun's face at the window. And that, Mr. Joe Easter, is the lovely, happy, safe way I've felt almost every second while you've been gone!"

And that, felt Ralph, was probably how he would feel from now on.

They debated, Joe and Alverna, for another half-hour; the interminable grievances and recollections of a domestic squabble; the debaters sinking almost into sleep, then springing into wakeful rage; both of them right and both of them cruelly unjust. Certainly Joe was unjust, considered Ralph; certainly Alverna was pitiful. Yet with it all he sneakingly sided with Joe.

Joe belonged to a man's world. He was out of place in dealing with a hectic temperament. The kindness which carried Ralph or McGavity or the Reverend Mr. Dillon was shipwrecked when Joe tried to navigate Alverna's gay calms and squalls of fury and fogs of passion.

Ralph tried to escape, but both of them turned to him constantly and he was bound in this madhouse. At the end of the combat he was too sleepy to care which of them won, too sleepy to care whether all the

Indians in the Mantrap River country came burning and killing.

It was Joe who exclaimed: "Keeping poor old Ralph up all night, and not his scrap at that! Could you fix his cot on the porch?"

But it was Alverna who prepared his bed.

Men can, no doubt, make beds in a mechanical, heartless way: Jap servants, hospital orderlies, stewards, French *valets de chambre;* but which of them would ever end with the busy and cheery pat of the pillow which mystically lures to slumber? Thus busy and cheery was Alverna, proud of her deftness.

Joe had gone to see that the warehouse was locked. When she had finished she stood beside Ralph in the dim little room of the screened porch, with the lapping lake on one side, the door of the lighted sitting-room on the other. She mercurially dropped again from briskness into grief. She was so slim a child in the dusk, and her voice so young.

"What am I going to do, Ralph? I'm scared to stay here, and so bored! Joe won't support me Outside. And how could I stand going back to manicuring, or being on my feet all day long in a store, or maybe a hired girl getting bossed around?" She held out her hands to him.

He backed away. It seemed natural to put his arm about her in a brotherly way—too natural.

"I don't *know*," he complained, as though he were begging for release from her burdens.

"Anyway, you are a dear sweet lamb. And don't think I'm too bad. Please don't. I could—for heaven's sake don't ever dare tell Joe this, but there was a man came here, a trader, oh, a dandy fellow, and he wanted me to go away with him, and I wouldn't. But— To travel and see the world! Oh, well—good night."

In the luxury of clean pajamas, in the triple luxury of clean sheets and mattress and springs, he slid into drowsing. But always he started awake. The house was still; Joe and Alverna asleep; the rustle of little waves on the lake but a deeper silence; and in that quiet, every mysterious stirring was the sound of an Indian—creeping toward the house; brushing along the screen of the porch; trying to open the screen door; scratching a match to touch off kerosene-soaked rags; stealthily drawing a knife; creeping through the darkness . . .

He lay tense. Suddenly he was shooting upright, sitting rigid, his heart galloping. There were muted footsteps, there was—

Unmistakable. Brushing through the grass. Brushing against a rosebush.

"Wh-who's that?" he quavered.

Some one running softly, then the black stillness.

CHAPTER THIRTEEN

WITH all his panic, with all his irritated memories of Alverna's hands and eyes, he must have slept, since certainly he woke—and woke at eight, which for that land is almost noon. The sun was riotous on the little waves, the pines a serene splendor and, after drugged sleep, he did not know whether he had dreamed the sneaking footsteps or heard them.

"Anyway, I'll sort of keep guard, tonight," he vowed—and did not care for it in the least.

But perhaps now the Indians knew two men were in the house, strategically stationed, they would not dare attack. And perhaps it had been just a drunkard staggering home. And perhaps—

Oh, it was all nonsense!

Thus he comforted himself, like a child calculating that though the Blind Ghost is two steps down the hall, and the Shrouded Burglar two jumps beyond that, daddy and mother can be heard laughing downstairs and there is quite a good chance of safety.

It was a morning, that, of much fishing, after the first important and Woodbury-defying rite of providing Ralph with moccasins and rubbers from Joe's store. Joe—his own breakfast he had cooked and gobbled at six—came over to beam on Ralph while he luxuriously savored his coffee and flapjacks; he beamed at Alverna, too; and there was nothing but friendship and sun and kindliness apparent in the world.

Joe had to do his accounts, but with Ralph he sent Lawrence Jackfish, who seemed to combine the duties of sailor, teamster, janitor, gardener, and huntsman, in intervals between dancing with young squaws or lying drunken in the sun. Lawrence had sneaky and lecherous eyes, but he could smell out fish in twenty feet of water. Probably, had Ralph's ex-Indians, Jesse and Louey, been along, Lawrence would have been as maddeningly witty as they in hours of sailing. But now he was silent, though he spoke adequate English, and Ralph, grateful for the lightness and swiftness of a ten-foot canoe, grateful for this summery ease after the big cargo craft, slipped among the islands, proud of being the bow-man.

At his first cast in the cool golden water off Blue Nose Island, his reel sang and his pole arched as a big one ran away with the hook. He played it for a quarter of an hour, and brought to the side of the canoe a fifteen-pound lake trout, silver-sided and spotted with scarlet.

Radiantly he came in for twelve o'clock dinner, Indian prowlers and domestic squabbles forgotten; and Joe admired the trout as though never, in all waters and all ages, had any one caught quite such a fish. He insisted on photographing Ralph holding up the trout.

(That photograph, as piously preserved today, shows Ralph simpering like a young mother.)

Alverna sang as she served at dinner the same unfortunate trout, rolled in cornmeal and fried. Her music was erratic but pleasing; she managed to make all tunes sound curiously like "What'll I Do?" but her noises had the agreeable twitter of frogs in the twilight, of the cricket on the hearth.

That she could ever have felt martyred, that Joe could ever have been stern with her, was clearly absurd. Joe told immense legends of Pop Buck, who was reputed, when he could no longer find any one to match him in drinking Swedish aquavit, to have trained an amiable brown bear, and to have sat up with the bear all night, full of hilarity and wisdom and alcohol, in an ice-sheathed skin tent under the Northern Lights.

In the happiness of his friends, Ralph was blissful.

Before the dinner dishes were washed, the two white trappers who were loafing at Mantrap Landing by way of summer vacation came ambling in to greet the stranger: Pete Renchoux, a swart and bouncing Canuck of perhaps forty, a round man full of little shrill laughters, and the young Britisher (or he may have been Irish) George Eagan, whose silences about himself hinted that he had left home for reasons not too laudable. They brought with them two quarts of moonshine, a powerful, determined, single-minded explosive, colorless as water and effective as cholera. These they solemnly presented to Joe, with the casual explanation that they had stolen them from Chief Burberry of the Lake Midnight band of Crees when he was sore in liquor; and they indicated that it was their contribution to a party which they earnestly hoped and manfully expected to begin now and to last till all hours, at least.

The hosts did what they could to be obliging.

Ralph drank one glass of moonshine mercifully so cozened with ginger ale that it did not taste like vitriol but merely like gasoline.

It was proper that after the trappers' gift Joe should reciprocate by urging them to try his real Scotch. He was successful in his urging, remarkably so, and by three o'clock, when Pop Buck waddled in, bearing a gallon of dandelion wine and as full as the trappers of ideas about having a party, the festivity was begun.

Naturally, Alverna had to kiss "Uncle Pop," and naturally, she had to kiss Eagan and Renchoux then, to show that there was no discrimination.

By five, Nels Stromberg, assistant to McGavity at the Hudson's Bay Company, and Biermeier, the Revillon Frères factor, had heard telepathic tidings of the affair—and by five Ralph had had enough of it. He had never found that more than five whiskies and soda at a time were beneficial to law-practice.

He heard Joe whispering, "Let's sneak out to the store and have a little furlough."

Like a country general store with patent medicines of forgotten vintages and boots of a bygone bucolic age resting on dusty shelves in a dark interior scented with plug tobacco and hay—like a ship-chandler's shop romantic with binnacle-lights and ancient figureheads and tarry rope—such was the inside of the log-cabin store of the Easter Trading Company. It was neat enough, for Joe was as fussy a housekeeper as Alverna, and fussier was his solemn assistant, a Wesleyan half-breed who was painfully loyal to his chief but who would never enter the house because playing-cards and alcohol were to be seen there.

For all its sweptness and orderliness, the store was electric with every legend of the North. Here were mackinaws, scarlet and green and russet and ultramarine; pea-soup shirts striped and checked in unknown passionate hues; lumbermen's boots of leather and rubber; a caribou-hide parkee bought from the Eskimos who come trading to Brochet on Lake Reindeer; nets for whitefish and deadly rifles for moose; traps for beaver, huge traps for bear; poison for wolves; and rows of bright red cans of salmon, peaches, jam. One end of the counter displayed such hats as a Hottentot lady might have invented. If you had taken a pink straw hat, covered it with glue, dipped it first into a pile of many-colored feathers, then into a heap of brass buckles, then an assortment of all the velvet scraps from a very large dressmaker's shop, you would have created such a hat.

"Fierce, ain't they!" said Joe. "But the squaws love 'em. If you were here when they get their Treaty money, you'd see every other squaw hustling in to buy one of 'em, and parading out with it on, over a shawl and a calico skirt."

In a dark room at one side were bales of furs, tight-packed, the hideous fleshy wrong sides out. Ralph was disappointed. He had expected the furs to lie in glossy piles, as in the palace of a fabulous northern king. These bales were as poetic as bundles of bark, and ten times heavier. But he realized that when they had been borne, by canoe and portage, by train and steamer, to London, they would blossom again, and nestle on the shoulders of women on the Place Vendôme, flash from limousines whispering through fog-enchanted Mayfair.

Joe guided him to the office at the back of the store, a very businesslike office with golden-oak desk and letter-files of yellow-painted pine. Ralph might have found there an unfortunate suggestion of law-offices and work, but actually this sober peace was restful, after the clamor surging about Alverna.

"Do you mind the racket? They're good boys, Ralph," sighed Joe.

"I know—"

"Not one of 'em but what'd risk his life for you,

if a canoe upset or if you were out with 'em in the woods and busted a leg and had to be carried on their shoulders."

"I know."

"Ralph—tell me: Where will the tragedy strike?"

"Eh?"

"Alverna's going to get awful hurt, or I am, or some third chump, or all three of us. I'm sure of it."

And Ralph was sure of it, and not all his training in cooing to worried clients gave him anything to say.

They sat brooding. From the house they could hear Joe's phonograph rasping out a fox-trot, could hear heavy boots scraping, and Alverna screaming: "Quit now, George! Ah, gee, quit!"

Joe sighed.

There was another sound; the crack-crack-crack of a rifle.

"Wonder what that is?" Joe mused, not very excitedly.

They sauntered back through the store, from the low stoop looked over the lake. Ralph could make out only a distant canoe, a vaguely seen man standing in the stern. But Joe exclaimed:

"Now there *will* be a shindig! That's Curly Evans —the Provincial Policeman in this district—great card —fine fellow."

He dashed back to his office, returned with a revolver, and shot every chamber into the lake. Already

the other stores and the Indians in camp were firing
their salutes, and Curly Evans swooped up to Joe's
wharf with the tumult of an admiral's landing.

Evans was in uniform, with a broad military hat
bound up on one side, like an Australian trooper. He
was a sturdy youngster, his yellow hair kinky, his big
and good-humored mouth always grinning—especially
when it was a matter of sneaking, through brush and
stumps, on a murderer blockaded in a log-cabin. He
dashed up, shook hands with Joe and Ralph, and
chuckled:

"Spree on? Lemme at it. Glad meet you, Prescott. Heard you were here."

He ran off to the house, to be greeted at the door
by one of the kisses with which Alverna appeared always to be generous.

Ralph mused: "How could he know I was here?
There's no telegraph—"

"Nobody ever moves ten inches in the North without being seen," said Joe. "You may think— Suppose you'd committed a crime and thought you were
making a get-away. Some Indian would have watched
your canoe from shore, and told the next Indian he
saw. We're all of us being watched every second.
Wilds? Why, say, every burnt tree up here has ears
and eyes. I'll show you. Curly!"

Standing at the cottage door, still in ardent discourse
with Alverna, Curly bawled back, "Yeh?"

"Where's this bird Woodbury—the white man that Prescott was with?"

"Fellow in the Spirit River band of Chippewyans told me Woodbury was camped on the Little Moccasin River last night. He's headed for Lake Solferino."

Ralph had a feeling of hidden hateful eyes about him, sinister in the green and kindly forest; and uneasily he remembered the slinking anonymous footsteps of the night.

Then in the fury of what Alverna and Curly Evans and Pop Buck regarded as a "slick party," he forgot all insecurity and the secret watchers.

By six o'clock, supper-time, every one except Joe and Ralph was riotous. Alverna was decidedly not an exception, nor was Curly Evans. Neither of them had gulped down so much of the throat-clawing moonshine as had Pop Buck, Eagan, Renchoux, but they had had enough to rise to that state of ecstatic gloom which is the mark of the more poetic drunk. Alverna and Curly were solemnly waltzing, round and round and round the living-room to the tune of "It's Three o'Clock in the Morning," played so slowly on the phonograph that it resembled a funeral march. The others sat about the table in the kitchen, very earnest about nothing whatever, pounding the table and asserting, "I tell you—I tell you—say now, listen," and never by any chance explaining what was this priceless thing they desired to tell.

Joe lolled back, tilted in a chair, thoughtfully and slowly sipping a weak whisky and soda, and talking to Ralph. Through the clamor, like a gull seen through a pasty fog, Ralph perceived Joe's shy passion for the North and all it meant.

"I'd hate to leave this country and have to take a job Outside, and I may darn' well have to do it, if I go any broker," Joe sighed.

For the third time since they had met, Ralph tried to feel out a way of offering to pay for his board. He could not do it. He knew that it would be as great an insult to Joe as to the lordly host of some old southern plantation.

"Course," said Joe, "I might try to go back trapping, if I went bust. But the rheumatism gets me, after a few weeks in the snow. But— Gosh, Ralph! I wish you could come out with me in the winter, just for a week, buying furs."

Through Joe's halting stories, Ralph saw that great white unknown land. The crackle and shimmer of the Northern Lights in a vast darkness over dark vast forests. The savage stars of the winter night. The joy of a cabin's yellow lights seen far down a frozen and snowy river when a fur-buyer was numb with hunger. High noon, and the frozen tundras a field of diamonds under the roaring sun.

"I wish you could see it. Always did kind of hate to hog a pretty view," said Joe.

Ralph wondered if Joe noticed Alverna at all. It seemed improbable that he would ever miss anything, yet he went on with his stories of bears and moose, of Indians desperate with hunger, unmoved, while she flew into a hysteria of gayety. Evans, Stromberg, Eagan, Renchoux—they were all quarreling now for the privilege of dancing with her, and when these hearty young men quarreled, they cast most important doubts on the purity of one another's parentages, and they could be heard out on Blue Nose Island.

She compromised by dancing with two of them at a time, an arm about each, giggling at every solemn triple whirl, kissing both of her partners as another lusty pair seized her. And all the time the old phonograph dragged out lugubriously, "I've — been — daaaaancing — the — whollllllle — night — throuuuuuuugh."

It was seven before Joe hinted to her, "We better shake up a little supper now, eh, whadyuh say?"

There was great activity.

Alverna stood on a chair and shrieked that she would not cook supper. No. Not for a bunch of bums like this. She would go on dancing with Curly Evans. George and Biermeier and Nels could wash up afterwards; Pop Buck would be cook, Pete Renchoux waiter; and as for those old grouches Joe and Ralph Prescott, they could get t' hell out of the way, that's what they could do; and *she* was going to dance till

Three o'clock in the morrrrning
With Curly—come on now, kid!

Pop chuckled fatly: "Great girl. Pete! Lez show
'em what the old men can do."

"Fine! I'll be a lady waitress!" yelped Pete Renchoux.

Renchoux, mighty trapper, mighty drinker, mighty
squire of rather doubtful dames, was a plump mani-
kin, slightly greasy, very gay. He seized Alverna,
lifted her from the chair on which she had been standing, while she kicked wildly and screamed, and yelled,
"Come, you dress me nice now!"

He dragged her from the room, and returned coquettish in Alverna's red-bordered black frock, with
a frilly white apron. On his head was a kerchief for
cap.

Pop Buck was preparing supper: bacon, pork and
beans, baking-powder biscuits—Pop's highest concept
of a party supper. Now Pop was, by all camp standards, a good cook. In a blizzard, with moss for fuel
and flour and water for his only materials, he could
have produced eminent bread. But in his burly, jolly,
kindly, riotous soul, one thing was lacking: any preju-
dice whatever in favor of cleanliness. In five minutes
he had Alverna's prim kitchen looking like a dump-
heap.

As he frizzled the bacon, he spat on the floor, and

bellowed, "Say, Ralph, d'ever tell you about the time
I shot the jumping deer with a bownarrow?" He set
the frying-pan down on the shiny red oilcloth—it left
a filthy circle. And when he opened the can of beans,
he amiably kicked the can under the stove.

But the company enjoyed the banquet—all save Biermeier, who showed a longing to slumber amid the
beans, and was gravely guided by Joe to Ralph's couch
on the porch, where he went earnestly and sonorously
to sleep.

Renchoux, as capped and aproned waitress, was very
noisy even if he was not very funny.

"Oh," announced Alverna, "you're just too *darling,*
Pete!" and she skipped up from the table and saluted
Renchoux with a mighty hug.

She also kissed Pop for his excellence in cooking,
and that ancient seemed to relish the salute.

In the midst of all this merriment and sisterly love,
Ralph glanced at Joe, and it seemed to him that Joe
looked very old, very tired, nearly beaten.

However hectic she might be, Alverna loved expert-
ness in housework, and after supper she insisted on
washing the dishes, with Stromberg and Eagan as
wipers, and when she had gayly driven Pop out to
smoke his pipe in the court between cottage and store,
she removed the signs of his cheerful sloppiness. Ralph
had never seen any one more pleasantly energetic than
was Alverna, her sailor-blouse sleeves rolled up, dipping

the plates in the iridescent soap-suds, holding up the plates and calling, "Who's the next punk dish-wiper?"

"Let me help you," Ralph said ardently.

"No, dear," she crooned; and her voice was—Ralph believed just then—the tenderest voice of woman he had heard since his mother had left him. "No, you go look out for poor old Joe. He's out there digesting, with Pop Buck. Cheer him up, the old cunnin'."

Ralph discussed with Joe and Pop the important question as to whether a safety-razor blade will float if it is dropped on water, but he yearned for the clamor within the glow of the kitchen; he raged at being taken for one of the aged noncombatants who smoke and drone apart from dancing youth. He heard her calling, "Up on the top shelf, Nels dear," and: "Oh, wait a minute! Gee, wait a *min*-ute, can't you, Curly! I'll come in and dance as soon 's we get rid of these darn' dishes."

Ralph had tried to drink as little as possible. Certainly, in any investigation of the affair, it is known that he had always hated drunkenness as he hated split infinitives or the devil or white-edged black dinner-ties. But throughout supper Alverna had been a violent hostess. Whenever she had seen an empty glass she had leaped up, dashed to the drainboard of the sink, where moonshine and Scotch were displayed as in a frontier saloon, and filled the glass with a yelp of "Come on now, dearie, don't you go and die on us!"

Presumably Ralph had drunk much more than he had intended. He knew that across Lac Qui Rêve there was the stain of a forlorn sunset. He knew that Joe was talking with the quietude of an unhappy man. But he could not really see, not really hear. He walked as in a fog, he heard as in a delirium, and all the while he was sure of three things: Joe Easter was the best friend he had ever known; Joe's wife was to him sacred, set apart; and he longed to be in there, dancing with her.

When Pop and Joe and Ralph returned to the house, after adequately deciding that the name of the man who had held up those two bank-messengers in Montreal was Buller, not Butler, and that it certainly was a shame that people should go about holding up bank-messengers, Alverna was dancing dreamily with Curly Evans, and George Eagan and Pete Renchoux and Nels Stromberg were standing by, waiting.

Stromberg greeted them: "Say, Joe, I hear Ed Tudor is throwing a dance tonight. What say we all go?"

"Well," said Joe, and "Well, all right," said Joe.

They started as soon as Alverna had changed her sailor blouse and linen skirt for a frock of muslin, cornflower blue. While she was changing, quite an assortment of men stood about her bedroom door and explained with loud jollity that they would be willing to help her.

Joe smiled, Ralph noted, rather wearily.

When she came out, preening herself, airily thrusting her bobbed hair back from her temples, passing her coquettish smiles from man to man, Joe croaked: "Say, folks, if you don't mind—I've got to finish up my accounts. The clerk got 'em kind of balled up while I was away. So I'll appoint Ralph here to be chaperon for me at the dance."

Alverna flashed across the room and hung on his neck. "Oh, Joe, darling, I'd just *hate* to go unless you came along! Think of what Mrs. Mac and the Reverend—think of what all the killjoys would say!"

Ralph said, rather desperately, "Shall I stay with you, Joe?"

He caught Joe's eyes again—those pale and fiery blue eyes—and they were pleading. The celebrated counselor-at-law, who by ordinary was wont to take up every human problem as though it were a problem in dominoes, was altogether confused. He felt that Joe was too fond of these men to kick them out, yet knew them too well to leave them with Alverna, yet too sick of her madness to endure it, yet too proud to know what he knew.

Joe trusted him alone, felt Ralph. Did he deserve that trust? He would!

He nodded to Joe, uneasily, and went strutting forth as leader of the clamorous procession which filed down a forest path to the dance at Ed Tudor's. All the while he was conscious that Alverna, behind him, was singing "Tea for Two" with Curly Evans, and that his own mind was full of her.

"She's so gallant—trying to make a life for herself in this loneliness," he meditated; and, "Oh, dry up! Forget her!"

CHAPTER FOURTEEN

DESPITE his royal name, Ed Tudor, otherwise Edward Tudor, was no member of the British aristocracy. He was a three-quarters-breed Indian, squat and dark, and at least one-quarter in him was a stew of French, Portuguese, and probably Mexican. But Ed was the most successful trapper of the district, and the possessor of a magnificent log-cabin with two rooms.

Nor was Ed Tudor's dance really Ed Tudor's. It was paid for by Lawrence Jackfish, who, having received real money for his trip with Joe Easter, was itching to get rid of it, and successfully caring for that itch. He had already bought a new hat like a movie cowpuncher's, a new bead hatband for the same, and a sixth-hand shotgun, and he was devoting the remains of his wealth to hiring Ed's cabin and giving a dance free to all comers.

The main room of the cabin, wide and very low, was floored with knotty pine planks and lined with newspapers pasted on the inside of the logs. On the rafters were piled sledges, dog-harness, and snowshoes. One side had the fireplace and table, the other a bed covered with a dizzy crazy-quilt. Two chairs drifted in a general way about the floor, and on these sat the more venerable Indian squaws. The rest of the guests littered the bed, squatted on their heels along the wall, or stood waiting with a patience almost Chinese for improbable gayety.

It was not the rule in the Etiquette Book of Mantrap Landing for the young men to ask partners to dance with them. When, after half an hour of thinking it over, four males had decided that they might as well dance at this dance, they stood in the middle of the floor, their hats on, whispering to one another and giggling, till four squaws, frequently young, made the same difficult decision and voluntarily joined them. The men and girls spoke not one word. Small talk did not exist for them; they wanted to get to the business of dancing.

They waited till the octet was completed, then began to pound the floor in a diligent square-dance, the young men swinging the girls violently or being swung as heartily by the powerful wenches. Though few of them spoke English, all the calling of the figures was in that tongue. In Cree the calls would have been too dismayingly long even for Indian patience.

"Birdie in the cage and three hands round," bellowed Lawrence Jackfish, and an unsmiling squaw was surrounded by four unsmiling bucks. "Birdie flies out and hawk flies in; hawk flies out and gives birdie a swing."

. . . Bump, bump, bump of the moccasined feet. Shriek of the caller, "Hawk flies IN!" Prancing figures, dull in the lamplight, dim in the whirling tobacco smoke. Under and over and behind the dance, the starveling squeak of the hungry fiddle, the louder thumping of the fiddler's feet, keeping time to the jerky strains, the jerky strains of the old-time jigs, Turkey in the Haystack, Turkey in the Straw. . . . Turkey in the Haystack. . . . Turkey in the Straw. Bump. Bump. Bump. . . .

Thus the dance as Ralph and his procession saw it, heard it, from the door, as they thrust their way through the crowd watching from outside. He was conscious that the gathered Indians looked at them uncomfortably. They stared at Alverna (laughing, flushed of cheek, jiggling always with the excitement of having a party), and edged away from Curly Evans in his uniform.

"Do you think we better intrude?" Ralph muttered to Alverna.

"Oh, to thunder with 'em! Show 'em a good time. Show 'em how to really dance!"

Seizing Curly's arm, Alverna dragged him in with her. The quadrille stopped, the blatting fiddle stopped, the dancers gaped. To the host, her husband's servant, Alverna bubbled, "Are we invited, Lawrence?"

He did not look very happy about it, but sheepishly he said, "Yeh, I guess so."

"Then tell the fiddler to play something a little peppier. Is that all he can play, those punk old tunes? Well, all right then, I guess we can kind of one-step to 'em."

While the Indians peered, their party taken away from them, while the fiddler went on with his tune like a mechanical piano out of repair, she circled round the room with George Eagan.

Pete Renchoux and Curly Evans found two Indian girls who could move with somewhat more grace than ant-eaters, seized them despite their titters of shyness, and tried to teach them the one-step, which they took up with all the vigor of a galloping cow. Pop discussed esthetics and mink-trapping with Lawrence Jackfish's grandmother, a matriarchal lady of twenty stone and much bass laughter.

Ralph looked solemnly at the roomful of Indians and they looked solemnly at him; and neither seemed to enjoy the sight much, and it is doubtful which of them was the more uneasy. But one by one the young bucks were enticed into the white man's game, and with reluctant squaws they walked rapidly round and round the room, in what they fondly conceived to be a one-step and what more resembled a Swedish drill.

The air grew more dizzying with tobacco smoke. Through this fog came the scraping of feet, the ceaseless honk-a-tonk of the fiddle, and the fiddler's beating feet. But piercing the racket was one clear note— Alverna's laughter.

"She does enjoy it, poor kid. She turns it all from a surly mob into something young and really happy," reflected Ralph, and his heart expanded, he felt suddenly free—free from the incessant thought-mongering of Ralph Prescott, free from worry about Joe Easter.

Curly and Alverna came pushing past him, through the cabin door.

"So smoky—get a breath of fresh air," she murmured, but she looked instantly away from him, into the daring eyes of Curly.

He saw them standing in the outer border of light from the door, under a spruce tree. Curly was teasing her, holding her hand, pretending to read her palm, while she bounced with pleasure and tried to withdraw her hand—and seemingly did not try particularly hard. Suddenly Ralph hated Curly with a flood of black jealousy. When she was with Joe she was taboo; when she was with Curly Evans she was something to be fought for. He stopped his eternal pest of thinking and let himself feel. And his feeling toward Alverna was something deeper and tenderer and seemingly more free from baseness than any emotion he had ever known.

Pity for her forlorn gayeties, admiration for her pluckiness, solicitude for her madness, need of the comfortable softness of her slim hands.

He was a lonely man!

So he felt, without putting it into words. He was a lonely man, and he needed her, while Curly Evans was an unscrupulous and wandering light-o'-love against whom he must protect her. He found himself slashing through the crowd outside the door, stalking to her under the shadow of the spruce.

"Alverna!" he snapped. "You oughtn't to be standing here with these Indians watching you! If you're going to dance, dance! I— Will you dance with me?"

"*Can* you dance, dearie?"

"I can! Damned well!"

"Well, Mr. Ralph Prescott, there's always been one simply elegant way of getting to have the pre-rivilege of dancing with me, and that was to ask me. Why didn't you?"

"I'm asking you!"

Curly complained, "Look here—"

"You go soak your head," she said to Curly, perhaps not very elegantly. She seized Ralph's arm, and soared with him through the onlookers, into the fetid cabin, out on the puncheon floor.

"Now we'll see about that 'dancing damn' well!'" she said.

But she looked at him affectionately.

She did see about it. Ralph was certainly the only trained dancing-man in that amorphous land. But hitherto he had always danced with the cold and tutored perfection of the man who does proper things because they are proper. His dancing came to life now, as his spirits rose to her lightness and eagerness and living warmth. Forgetful of the foggy room, the jumpy *ta*-ta-*ta*-ta-*ta*-ta-*ta*-ta of the galumphing fiddle and the plunk of the fiddler's foot, he soared to a heaven of consciousness of being near her.

"Say, you certainly shake the old hoofs. Why didn't you ask me to dance before?" she demanded.

Sturdily: "Afraid to! Why, hang you, Alverna—"

"Golly! The man's alive, after all!"

"If it weren't for Joe, I'd have fallen for you even before this."

"Why, I think you're perfectly horrid! You have a nasty mind! As if our just dancing a little could hurt poor old Joe! I think you ought to apologize!"

"You don't think anything of the kind!"

She seemed to look at him not less kindly for his harshness. She sighed (he had, in that tumult, to catch her words by the movement of her childish lips): "There's Curly wanting another dance."

When he grumbled, "Oh, curse Curly!" she apparently could endure it without suffering.

While Ralph discovered her and forgot himself, the

dance also discovered itself and forgot its awkwardness. The room was clotted now with Indian couples, trying to reverse and walk backward, with much bumping and much stumbling and a great deal of joyous cackling. Curly, after watching Ralph and Alverna sulkily, was now contentedly whirling with the slimmest of the young squaws, and Pop Buck was panting in his effort to move the protesting and delighted grandmother of Lawrence Jackfish about the room.

The fiddler was stirred to more violent scrapings, more furious poundings of his foot. Outside the cabin, the onlookers were squawking their admiration. George Eagan, who spoke Cree and who had the remittance-man's delight in going Indian after his exile from Home, was staggering among them, giving the bucks sips from his bottle of white mule, and the young men began to dance with one another in front of the cabin, full of yelping laughter.

And through the leaping crowd Ralph glided with Alverna, unconscious of everything save her.

He came to with a jar. At the door was an irate voice, a voice thick with Scotch accent and thicker with wrath, rumbling: "You people must stop this racket. I won't have it! *I can't sleep!*"

The fiddler stopped playing. The shuffling feet were still. The dancers stared at McGavity of the Hudson's

Bay, McGavity of the Fort, standing in the doorway, red and glaring and afraid of no one.

When McGavity saw Ralph and Alverna and Curly Evans, his lips puckered with doubt, and he scratched his chin.

"Hello, Mac," said Curly genially.

"Hello, Evans," said McGavity, not at all genially.

"We making too much noise?" said Curly.

"Well—the Missus and I couldn't sleep. I thought this was an *Indian* dance!"

McGavity sounded as though he meant something by it.

Alverna was whispering to Ralph: "Oh, Lord, what an earful Mrs. Mac will get about this, and what'll happen to me afterwards! Joe is a dear, but, God, how he can jaw!" She sailed toward McGavity, twittering: "We just dropped in for a minute, to show them how to one-step. Joe was coming for me, but I guess the poor lamb must have fell asleep. We're about due to be on our way home. Good night, Lawrence. Good night, everybody. Come on, Ralph. Good night, Mr. Mac."

She took Ralph's arm and confidently pattered toward the door. The onlookers made way for her, and she flowed through them, bowing right and left, looking as much like the lady of the manor as was possible with the red and irate eye of Mr. James McGavity upon her.

Ralph felt the nervous pressure of her fingers on his arm, and that moment he would have killed McGavity with speed and zest.

He marched with her from the cabin light into the dimness of the forest trail, undefinably happy, inexplicably excited, conscious of the night, of the snoring lake, of being alone with her. All problems, worries, loyalties, were lost in her quivering vitality—this manicure girl who was also Helen and Iseult and Héloïse.

Then, abruptly, he was very much not alone with her.

Curly Evans had caught up with them, striding down the rivulet of path. He seized Alverna's other arm, with the playful friendliness of a young brown bear. He shouted: "Gee, old Mac is just as chummy as a bullfrog, ain't he! I wish a cop didn't have to go on being a guardian of law and order and a pincher of liquors and generally a perfect gent after six P.M.! Why, I might as well be a missionary! Golly, Ralph!" —with a brotherly affection which Ralph, just now, sniffily detested. "You cer'nly agitate a mean double-A at the one-step. . . . But nobody can touch Alvy!"

He was obviously squeezing her arm; he was obviously squeezing it with boyish heartiness. Ralph was sick with jealousy. Why couldn't this blatant young fool let them alone? He—he would have talked to her about good old Joe, and they would have walked so quietly and happily and decently through the breathing night.

The three of them headed the homeward straggling of the party, and as they came bumbling into the Easter cabin, they found Joe asleep, stretched out in one kitchen chair with his feet on another. What Curly saw, and Alverna, has not been recorded; but Ralph saw Joe defenseless, drooping, all his courage lost in abandonment to weariness.

Joe's head hung back, his cheeks gaunt, his neck corded; and his hand, drooping by his side, was lax and almost aged with its swelling veins. So, in a fiery moment, all of Ralph's wretched worrying quickened again. . . . Had he guarded Alverna as Joe had trusted him to do? Had he kept her sacred? Had they, by rousing the scandal-mongering McGavitys, hurt Joe forever as a proconsul?

But Alverna seemed admirably free of worry. She cuddled on Joe's lap, she laughed at him and tickled him and kissed him, and, as he woke with a snort of alarm, she chuckled, "Ah, de rosy posy Josey!" and he accepted it equably, he observed only, through portentous yawns: "Back again? Better see 'f the boys want 'nother drink."

The boys did want another drink. They were polite about it, but firm. Pop Buck, Eagan, Renchoux, Stromberg, as they came trailing in, and even Biermeier, as he awoke from his intoxicated sleep, spoke of it as a thing to do.

"Now the real party beginneth, with little game poker," said Pop Buck.

"Oh, swell, sure, you bet!" trilled Alverna.

"That'll be fine," said Joe.

If as a dancing-man Pop Buck was rather less than perfection, he had all the art of poker. He squinted at his cards most casually, he never pounded the table, he never bluffed—apparently—but whenever he called he seemed to have more aces than any one else in the hunched circle about the red oilcloth, under the hanging lamp. And Joe Easter awakened. He was tireless in shuffling, dealing, filling, raising, his face expressionless as the mummy of Rameses.

All of them drank steadily, and except for Pop and Joe and Ralph, all their voices rose—rose—grew shriller and more emphatic, and all of them became more hectically desirous of betting everything they had on the turn of a card.

Alverna had taken a hand, but she seemed to have no decent reverence for the sport. She diversified the grim routine of jackpots by singing, by pinching Joe, by throwing a glass of water at Pete Renchoux, by arguing with Curly Evans as to whether she would later kiss him good night—an argument at which Joe raised his brows, seemingly not very well pleased.

She was unanimously invited to "get out of this and hustle us a lil grub."

"I'll help you, Alverna," Ralph said hastily.

"Shake us up some bacon and eggs, Alvy," demanded Pete.

"These trappers," Alverna confided to Ralph, beside the stove, "haven't any good taste. Always bacon and eggs! I'll show 'em!"

And she did. With scrambled eggs and tinned tomatoes, she produced something with which a French cook would have been satisfied. As Ralph drained the can of tomatoes and Alverna whipped the eggs, shut off from the poker-players by the cloud of their rough grumbling, he insisted softly, "You like Curly, don't you?"

"Sure. You bet. He's a grand fellow!"

He wanted to moon at her, "Do you like him better than me?" but even in his growing insanity the question seemed a little too puerile. He drained the water from the tomatoes, sulkily and silently, and it was she who carried on:

"Ralph!"

"Eh?"

"You're such a baby!"

"Why?"

"Oh, I suppose you're dreadfully smart about books and the law and everything—and I will hand it to you, the Jane that taught you to dance cer'nly did know her job; but you don't—oh, you just don't know how to talk to a girl."

"Yes?"

"Yes! You're such a funny shy bird! Gee, if all of New York is like you, it must be as exciting as the morgue on Sunday afternoon! But, oh, *boy,* if you ever do get waked up! You came out and grabbed me off Curly like you were old Mr. Lancelot, or who-ever that fellow was that came riding out of the West that we used to read about in school—Old Doc Lance-lot himself. I bet if you ever take ten minutes off sometime and fall in love, you'll be a regular little volcano."

She peeped at him, under bright lashes; he sighed, and smiled with her, and was content to stand at a kitchen sink, in a log cabin, with a manicure girl—the wife of his loyalest friend.

"But you," he hesitated, as she poured out the coffee, "you care a lot for Curly."

"Him? Why, you're crazy! He's lots of fun, but he's just a fool kid."

Ralph was strangely comforted. He told himself that it was on behalf of Joe that he was making these deep researches.

Into the maws of the heroes intent on poker the scrambled eggs disappeared without comment, and whisky and water washed them down.

However quietly and earnestly, in the passion of

poker, a group of males may drink their whisky, it does sometime get its effect. The night glided tranquilly and dream-wise, with no more squawking from the aged phonograph, but it glided not without results. Biermeier rose in the midst of a full-house versus four treys, lived as far as the nearest bedroom, and passed out again. Pete Renchoux vanished and was not heard from until morning. He had gone to sleep on the floor of the front porch. Ralph and Alverna took the places of the deserters in the game till they both nodded at the table and staggered out to the porch for air.

When they had left Ed Tudor's cabin, a little after eleven, it had been milkily dark. Now the miracle of night had been performed, and Ralph realized, in a haze of sleepiness, that it was day again, gray secret day before the sunrise.

Alverna was drowsing as she sat on his cot. He put her head down on the pillow, tucked her in there, and himself lay on the floor, between the huddled Pete Renchoux and the cot. He was blindly conscious of lights and dull voices in the house, of some one blaring, "And raise you one bean!" Then he was conscious of nothing at all, neither of dawn nor of Alverna sleeping babylike near him, neither of poker nor of stealthy Indians nor of the leaden rustling lake.

He was awakened to a gasp of terror by long-drawn howling, the wailing of the hosts of hell.

He sat up to realize that he had been dreaming of E. Wesson Woodbury; that he saw Woodbury, mud-caked, his face bloody with briars and mosquitoes, stumbling through a swamp, lost and starving.

After a bewildered moment he knew what the howling was. It came from the team-dogs kept for the summer on Blue Nose Island, away from food-stores; melancholy dogs, passing the howl from one to another in the unhappy dawn. But the vision of Woodbury persisted; lonely Woodbury, perplexed and silent now, his vacation turned into a solitary horror.

"Why! I deserted him! I ruined all his outing for him! And he *meant* to be so decent! We had so much fun planning the trip, back in New York," Ralph thought miserably.

It had seemed natural and just to leave him, in the vexation of Woodbury's nagging. Now Ralph felt like a traitor.

The dogs were howling again, long, hopeless, quavering howls, the very voice of that sad land. Along the shore a burnt pine trunk stood against the colorless lake. Near Ralph were many people, but apparently they were all dead in sleep, dead as the ghost of sound in that unhappy howling, dead as the black ghost of the murdered tree.

He perceived that all the party must have been too far sunk to go home. George Eagan was snoring on the green couch in the living-room. Pop Buck and Nels

Stromberg had presumably taken the beds, for Joe
Easter had joined Ralph on the porch. He lay hunched
on a blanket, shivering in his sleep.

Alverna, still in her crumpled cornflower muslin,
partly covered with the blanket Ralph had drawn over
her on the cot, was so defenselessly young and unwise,
so pitifully young and helpless. Her lips drooped.
She slept with her hand between her cheek and the
pillow, as a kitten sleeps on its curled paw.

"She couldn't have gone very far with Curly Evans
and the rest of them. And I shan't lose my head. It'll
be all right. Good old Joe! Dear Alverna!" he sighed.

Their nearness solaced him, but as he went to sleep
the vision of forlorn Woodbury, no longer grotesque
in bawling energy but tragic in abandonment, hov-
ered over him, and he knew that he must do something about it.

And beyond the screen of the porch Lac Qui Rêve
stretched itself in the growing light.

CHAPTER FIFTEEN

THERE were many cracking heads that morning
in the residence of Joe Easter.

Indeed, but for Pop Buck, there was no one who did
not look blue and feeble. Pop was awake before any
of them, ferreting out the Scotch for his morning's

morning, and preparing ferocious black coffee to succor the rest of them.

"That was a nice little party," he reflected lovingly, to a rumpled and uninterested group at breakfast. "And that was a great story you told just before you passed out, Curly."

"Did I tell a story?" growled Curly.

"Why, yes! About the traveling man and the revolver that wasn't loaded. Nice story. And that was a swell hand you held—the four queens, George."

"Did I ever hold four queens? Say, who the devil won, last night, Pop?" groaned Eagan.

"Lookit here!" Pop was worried. "Don't know what the world's coming to. Folks can't hold their liquor any more. Me, I was just as happy as a hop-toad, last night. Why, say, every year till I'm a hundred—don't know but what I'll quit drinking then—every year I'm going to keep the anniversary of last night like it was my birthday—"

"Oh, quit being so blankety-blank cheerful!" screamed Curly, and the rest moaned in agreement, while Alverna wandered in from the porch, so gloomy that she was almost silent.

Curly had apparently given up dissipation and the vain ways of youth and taken to being official and generally unpleasant.

He urged, at breakfast: "Say, Joe, Mac and you and Biermeier have got to do something about this

fuss with the Crees over credit. I don't know but
what you ought to have a policeman stationed here
right along till the trouble blows over. They're terribly sore about you three not extending 'em any
more credit. I hear 'em talking out on the portages.
They're planning trouble. You don't want to get murdered in your beds."

"Oh—Joe!" wailed Alverna.

Joe laughed. "Rats! Those fellows'll never do
anything. Too shiftless."

"Even a shiftless bird can pull a trigger," insisted
Curly. "I'm going to have a talk with Mac this morning, right away, and don't know but what I'll have
you, as J.P., call a meeting of all the Crees camped
here, and we'll thrash it out. I'm worried, Joe, for
you"—he looked across the table at Alverna; their
glances met and clung—"and for your wife."

"Curly, you will make Joe do something!" begged
Alverna.

"You bet, honey! Watch me!"

Ralph felt the understanding in their voices. And
suddenly, shamelessly, he was angry at Curly, not on
Joe's behalf but for himself. And still the specter
of the lonely Woodbury fluttered round him. No one
at that breakfast of the morning-after was more quiet
or more desolate than Ralph.

While Curly was away at the Hudson's Bay Company, Ralph waylaid Joe and demanded, without hedging:

"Joe! How did that fellow Woodbury who was with me strike you? Did you like him?"

"No, I didn't. Awful blowhard!"

"Well, wouldn't you have left him flat, as I did, if you'd been in my place?"

"Well, that—I—"

"Go on. Tell me. Straight."

"N-no, don't guess I would have."

"Why?"

"Oh, it's just— Well, a fellow that's used to hiking much in the wilds, he sticks to his bunch, that's all, no matter if he always likes 'em or not. Kind of a habit. You figure: suppose the other fellow busted his leg or something."

"Do you blame me for quitting?"

"No—no—sure not. Man's got to decide these things for himself. That is, of course, if you were making a business of being up here, and taking things like they come. But I can see how you felt."

"Look: I got to dreaming about Woodbury. Felt I oughtn't to have left him. Look: Would it be possible, maybe, to send out Lawrence Jackfish to find him, if he can, and get him to come here? Probably he could rent a room from McGavity."

"No. I don't like the fellow. Don't want him

around. Once you left him— What's done's done.
I'd just forget it, Ralph. Well—got to skip over to
the store and get busy. Oo, my head! S'long. See
you later."

Ralph, alone on the porch, fell into a misery of
meditation. There was, then, no escape from the con-
viction that he had been shoddy in quitting Woodbury.

"But I wasn't! He deserved it! Been a fool to
let him spoil my vacation!"

His mind swore that he was right, but his emotions
croaked doggedly that he had been a deserter.

So he had to rejoin Woodbury? Well, he would
escape thus from the danger of falling in love with
Alverna! (Where was she now? The house, her
singing gone, was blank. He longed for the comfortable sound of her quick footsteps.) Yes! His
duty to Woodbury, his duty to Alverna, his duty to
Joe, his duty to himself! He would go.

But—oh, not for another day.

He would have a moment or two with Alverna and
from the serene height of this self-sacrificing virtue
he would plead with her to become another Mrs.
McGavity and generally virtuous and safe and dull.

He had gone no further with his meditations when
Curly came charging in to find Joe, for the meeting
with the Indians. Ralph accompanied them.

There were two groups of Indians in summer en-
campment at Mantrap Landing—the Lac Qui Rêve

band, under Chief Wapenaug, and a small part of the
Lake Midnight band, from the uncharted country to
the south, with a chief whose Indian name had somehow been Anglicized as Burberry.

The title of Chief, Ralph had discovered, was considerably less royal in real life than in fiction. It was
about as important as the title of President of the
Village Council in a hamlet of three hundred. The
Chief could call meetings, and he served as inter-
mediary between his wandering band and the Government, but he was elected by his people and he could
be removed without trial by the Indian agent. His
principal ducal prerogatives were receiving twenty-five
dollars a year instead of five, when the Government
paid the annual Treaty money to its wards, and wearing a vast gold band around his hat, a blue coat with
brass buttons and a gold armband, and a medal so huge
that it recalled a comic policeman in a burlesque show.

But the absolute splendor of titles and decorations
has nothing to do with the pride taken in them by
their possessors. The new recording secretary of the
Harriet Beecher Stowe Literary and Embroidery
League of South Wappington gets as much excitement out of her elevation to office as an Empress of
Austria; the tennis champion of the Rosedale Villas
Country Club hears the hoarse cheering of the nine
spectators with more beatitude than William Tilden
at Forest Hills.

Wapenaug and Burberry, marshaling their hundred
braves for a council with three storekeepers and a
policeman, strutted with a pomposity which would
have been absurd in the King at the opening of Par-
liament. Their rather dirty shirts were concealed by
their brave brass-buttoned coats, their decidedly dirty
faces were shaded by gold-banded hats, their enormous
medals thumped on their proud stomachs.

Mr. Dillon, the missionary, had lent the church for
the meeting. In front, below the altar, facing the
Indians, were Mr. Dillon, Curly Evans, Joe, McGavity,
Biermeier of Revillons', Ralph, Pete Renchoux, and
the chiefs. The chapel was almost filled with Indians.
They were swart, a little grim, expressionless as Ori-
entals, but to Ralph they seemed to have lost all the
spirit of the ancient Indians. As they used white
men's traps, paddled white men's canoes, and knew no
music save the cheaper ballads from Broadway, so
they wore white men's unromantic clothes: store shirts,
black coats, long black trousers.

With Pete Renchoux to prompt him now and then
as to a word, Curly Evans addressed them in Cree,
and Joe whispered the translation to Ralph.

He was grieved, he was shocked, indeed he was sore
astonished, Curly was, to hear that certain irrespon-
sible young Indians had been threatening the factors.
He could understand that loss of credit must have

inconvenienced the trappers who had had a bad season. But they themselves were to blame. In the old honest days, the Indians, who were carried on credit for as much as three years, came in and paid their accumulated bills the moment they had money.

And such patriarchs as Chief Wapenaug and Chief Burberry—Curly bowed to them, and they bowed back, like wrinkled gingerbread idols—would still do the same. But he knew positively, did Curly, that certain Indians, instead of paying up when in funds, had gone off to Lake Warwick and not only spent their money but bought things they did not need: outboard motors, for the sons of men who had once paddled fifty miles a day; cigarettes, where pipes had always been good enough; ten-dollar shoes to dance in. Then they expected the Mantrap factors to trust them for beans and rifle-shells!

And if they thought that what they did in Warwick was not known to the all-seeing eyes of the Government—

Chief Wapenaug nodded; Chief Wapenaug looked sadly at his wicked young. (Chief Wapenaug had owed Joe Easter three hundred dollars now for four years, and three weeks ago he had come back from Kittiko with a motor, a banjo, and silk stockings for his industrious but indiscreet granddaughter.)

Curly had gone thus far with high eloquence. He

stooped his shoulders now, and tried to make his voice creepy and his boyish eyes mysterious and sinister.

In the center of the chapel a tall young Indian rose, yawned, walked out. Other braves looked at one another, and followed.

Curly hinted how mighty was His Majesty's force, the Provincial Policemen. They could see as far as thunder could be heard. But his dramatics were shattered by the grave exit of twenty men in single file.

"Sit down!" he shouted at the last of the disturbers.

Some one in the back snickered. A giggle went through the room. Chief Wapenaug grinned. And before that tittering mass Curly tried to go on with injunctions that they must be good boys and pay their bills; then their loving foster-uncles, the storekeepers, would give them further credit.

He finished rather weakly, flushing.

In the pause, while everybody wondered who ought to powwow next, the whole audience rose and flowed away, perfectly orderly, perfectly cheerful, hatefully snickering.

They could be seen standing outside the church, standing stolidly or with leers, unimpressed, waiting, ready for anything.

"God help you now!" Curly muttered to Joe and McGavity. "This'll encourage the young fellows to start something. In ten minutes I'll be out of here.

I'll hit it up night and day, and in a week I'll be back from Whitewater with two constables to station here permanently. 'By!"

This was no longer the laughing, dancing young Curly. He was a soldier in action. Ralph saw him dash through the Indian wigwam village to Joe's house. He saw him lugging a sack of flour, a sack of beans, a side of bacon, a canister of tea, and a drum of gasoline to his canoe; heard him with sharp, unpleasant-sounding orders arouse his two Cree boat-men from their holiday slumbers against the log side of Joe's store.

In ten minutes from his promise he was outward-bound. The lake was rough, but he headed into the center of it, the canoe flinging itself up in leaps, the stout little motor beating like a watch.

Then Joe spoke.

"Good boy, Curly," he said. "But I figure he went off half-cocked. No danger from the Indians when they laugh like that."

"Maybe not," said McGavity, "so when I tell you I'm going home to oil and load all three of my guns, you'll know it's just for exercise."

"Um," said Ralph.

He could not return to Woodbury now, and desert the endangered Joe.

But suppose Woodbury were in danger, too, a lone white man unwarned?

"I've got to do *something*. And I will! And whatever it is, it'll probably be wrong," reflected Ralph.

CHAPTER SIXTEEN

IF secretly Joe worried over an Indian outbreak when Curly Evans dashed off for help, he kept all signs of it out of his nutcracker face.

"Nothing much to do at the store. Caught up on my accounts. What say Alvy and you and I stick a couple sandwiches in our pockets and hike over to the swamp along Ghost Squaw River, and see if we can't shoot us a duck?" he proposed.

Alverna was, she chattered, when they entered the house, delighted. She was, she said virtuously, tired of all these fellows like George and Curly and everybody, that wanted to dance and drink hooch and make a lot of noise all the time. She was, she cooed, enchanted to have a nice beneficial quiet day in the open with her friend Ralph and her dear Joe.

Alverna had more costumes than were to be expected in a northern cabin. She donned a very practicable khaki skirt with a dun flannel shirt and high laced boots. But Ralph noticed that they were the boots of a heroine in a Wild West melodrama. They were so narrow, their heels so high, that she could not have walked over rocky ground without stumbling.

And she carried a blue velvet bag patterned with scarlet beads.

"Good Lord, what you dragging that thing along for?" complained Joe.

She rose to indignant shrillness. "Well, upon my *word!* I guess I got a right to take a handkerchief and a little powder, ain't I!"

"You got pockets in your shirt, ain't you?"

"And crush my nice little powder box? Fat chance! Wrong number! Ring off!"

"Oh, all right!" sighed Joe, while Ralph, who a few drowsy hours before had admired her gallantry, found himself listening to an inner voice protesting, "What a confounded nuisance she is!"

She minced beside them, complaining of the narrowness, the mossy slipperiness, the rockiness, the darkness of the trail through the pines. But Ralph almost forgot her as he listened to Joe, who read to him the signs of the forest. Where by himself Ralph would have seen only the alligator bark of the pines, the brown needles and lichen-splashed rocks, Joe revealed to him the spoor of a jumping deer, the track of a wolf, the den of a porcupine, the glory of tiger-lilies and the demure blossoms of the sarsaparilla. Alverna skipped characteristically from her injured mood into a contentment with their mild adventure. She even had, for as much as half an hour, the genius to keep still.

The world of dancing and of sulky Indians forgot, they brushed through the hot pines, edged round a slew exclamatory with red-winged blackbirds and agitated jack-snipe, and made themselves comfortable on a piny rock ridge between the slew and a pond, awaiting a flight of teal.

Ralph was unconsciously playing soldier and very proud and happy about it.

He sat with his light shotgun across his knees, feeling virile, as though he were about to slay something and show himself extremely heroic in so doing. He did not know it—he would have denied it—but unconsciously he was telling himself a story:

"His powerful shoulders revealed a careless confidence. Those mighty hands rested so lightly on his shooting-iron, those hawk eyes seemed so veiled in thought, that a creeping enemy would never have guessed how swiftly our hero could have leaped into action."

Alverna sat outlined against the gold-green of the reedy slew. She interestedly opened her little velvet bag, and humming "Oh, How Do They Get That Way!" she powdered her nose, reddened her lips, fluffed up her hair with little backward flips of her hand, and settled down to polishing her nails.

Ralph noted that Joe looked at her with irritation, but himself he was admiring: "She's awfully cute!"

He to whom, a month ago, the word "cute" had been more abominable than all obscenities.

Black, orange, and gray, the lichens on their rocky ridge made Japanese prints—little bridges and silver mountain cones. Through a screen of trees, the lake beyond them twinkled. The slew at their back was a simmer of drowsy warmth, with shiny patches of still water among the reeds. A blackbird caroled, swaying on a willow bush, and round them the wild bees hummed. The hour was full of comfort and of dreams.

Then Alverna shattered it:

"Oh, gee! This ol' place is so hot. I could go right off to sleep. Where do you get that stuff about ducks flying over here? I haven't seen a one-legged sparrow yet. Wasn't that a great party last night, Ralph—wasn't it, Joe? Wasn't it— Gee, I thought it was a dandy party, even if Pete did get lit and talk so fierce, he ought to be ashamed of himself, but of course he didn't really mean nothing by it, and I told Pop if he told that story about the elevator-man again I'd bust him one. Gee, wasn't he funny, wasn't Pop funny, when he put on my apron and tried to dance the Highland fling and— Curly was crazy—darn him, who does he think he's talking to, like he could run me and everybody—he was just crazy when he said I hadn't ought to of laid down with my bobtailed flush. I knew George had a full house; here's how I could tell: I was watching him, and I saw him get his first four cards, and he kind of put two of 'em together, and then another two, and I said to myself, 'I'll bet he's got two pairs,' and then when he got his fifth card, he licked his lips like a pussy-cat, and I says to myself, 'Oh, all right, Mr. Smarty,' I says, 'I'll bet you've turned one of those dear little twins into triplets, that's what you've done!' "

Her laughter echoed among the somber rocks.

"Say, for God's sake, Alvy, if there were any ducks, you'd scare 'em fourteen miles off," sighed Joe.

"Oh, you make me tired!"

She yelped out the word "tired." Three ducks had that second come into sight, darting above the blind of trees. At her shriek they swooped upward, and before Joe could fire, before Ralph could quite remember which end of his shotgun should preferably be set against his shoulder, they were gone.

Ralph said nothing. Joe said nothing. Alverna looked the angrier that she had nothing to say.

There was half an hour of ducklessness.

"I suppose we better be getting back. Poor time of day for ducks anyway. Maybe we'll try 'em again tomorrow afternoon. This evening we're going to Biermeier's—Revillons'—to feed," said Joe.

Then he exploded:

"And be*sides,* Alvy— Maybe I'm unreasonable,

but it makes me so doggone *sick* to see you here, outdoors in the woods, making up your face like you were in a bathroom!"

"Oh, of course! You'd like me to look as sloppy as Ma McGavity! You just want me to look nasty, so nobody will ever look at me! Well, let me tell you, Mr. Joseph Easter, I'm not going to turn into a fright for you or anybody else! All you want is a housekeeper, but there *are* people who think I'm not so bad!"

"Yuh, I'm sure of it!"

"Now what d'you mean by that? What d'you mean by that? Just what're you trying to insinuate?"

"Oh, Alvy"—very wearily—"do shut up, and let's go home."

She had brought, for sole burden besides her velvet bag, a twenty-gauge shotgun, light as a target rifle, and for all her apparent slimness Alverna was as sturdy as a washerwoman. But like most young female athletes, she yearned now and then to be treated as a fading lily.

"Oh, Joe, this gun is so heavy!" she whined, as they trod the rut of path in Indian file.

Her husband shrugged.

"And it gets all tangled up with my legs."

Domes of silence.

She looked back at Ralph, her lips trembling, a tear actually on her lids. "It isn't that I care a damn whether he carries it, but I do think I might have a little attention!"

"I'll carry it for you," Ralph glowed. He knew that she was a pest, he knew that he ought to sympathize with Joe, but she was so pitiful, this alley kitten among the hound-pack—

No, he realized, he was lying to himself. It wasn't her pitifulness that drew him, but her unscrupulous feminineness, her professional girlishness, her devilish instinct for working up fond idiocy in every male. He was a traitor to Joe—whose back seemed so forlorn in his rough brown coat.

And her grateful eyes swept away these profound and edifying reflections like a sponge.

Now Ralph had brought not only his twelve-gauge shotgun but also a rifle, in the hope of practice; and three guns are no burden for a greenhorn to carry on a trail where at every yard you stumble on a root or a mud-hidden stone. The guns got themselves crosswise, they slipped, they banged his shins. He tried to carry them over his shoulder, then under his arm, in a dignified, accustomed-looking manner. He was reduced to lugging them in his two arms, like an armful of stove wood—while Alverna, glancing back tenderly, lisped:

"You're sure it isn't too much trouble?"

"No-uh."

"*Sure* now?"

"Oh, they're all right!"

"You'll let me know if they get too heavy for you?"

"Surely."

"Hadn't I better take mine now?"

"I can carry it all right."

"Oh, did you trip?"

"Well, sort of."

"Oh, I'm terribly sorry! Don't you want me to carry my gun now?"

"No, I'll manage it."

"Well, be sure and tell me when——"

Joe looked back at them.

Hitherto his expression had seemed to apologize to Ralph for letting him be pestered by this female gadfly. Now he seemed to lump them together as morons. Ralph had been annoyed enough by her commenting, but his annoyance turned toward Joe, his affection took in Alverna. So! That boor thought they were both—merely because they were aware of city courtesies, because they were interested in something besides poker and duck-hunting—he thought they were affected chatterboxes. All right! Joe might be a noble soul, but the way he failed to appreciate this poor, kind-hearted little——

Then, sharply: "I'm getting obsessed by this brat! I've got to do something about her. I've got to get out of this!"

They came back to the house and abruptly, gently as possible, Ralph urged of Joe:

"I ought to go join poor Woodbury, if I can find him. Enjoyed my stay here enormously, but—ought to start right off this afternoon."

Joe opened his eyes in slow wonder; he spoke with a friendliness that submerged Ralph in misery:

"Wish you could put it off till tomorrow, Ralph. You remember we promised Biermeier we'd go over to his place for supper tonight. He'd feel hurt if we laid down on him. He's an awful' nice fellow. I wish you'd try to stay."

Ralph stayed.

CHAPTER SEVENTEEN

FLOATING on a lake so smooth, so clear of depths, that he seemed to drift in a motorless airship between sky and valley, Ralph fished through the afternoon, and in this peace the conflicts of man and wife, of white man and Indian, seemed remoter and more absurd than the wàrs of ant-hills.

He shrank from, then happily forgot, the coming violent social engagement at the cabin of Mr. Biermeier. Rumor, flaunted by Pop Buck, predicted that the occasion would be as bibulous and sportive as last night's Bacchanalia at Joe's. It would, in fact, Pop rejoiced, be exactly the same party with the same conscientious drinkers and the same poker.

Ralph fumbled for excuses to get free, but when he returned to the house he found Alverna so ecstatically hopping with anticipation that he could say nothing.

Joe, according to the rules, should have preferred staying prosy and slippered at home. He should have labored at secret plans to keep his frivolous lamb away from the wolves. But when Ralph whispered, "Wouldn't you like to sneak back here right after supper, instead of playing cards?" Joe replied in wistful surprise, "Why, golly, I *like* a fist of poker and a little drink!"

He sounded as if his new toys were being taken away from him, and he were being sent to bed early.

"Oh, yes—yes—course—" said Ralph.

Alverna was dancing all by herself to the phonograph, her eyes brilliant. That afternoon she had busily made over her red-bordered frock. She had turned in the edges of the bodice and filled the V with cheap lace.

"Isn't it nice? Don't I look nice in it? I fixed it all by myself!" she exulted, coquettishly turning, peeping at Ralph over her charming shoulder.

"What a pair of children they are! Complications? Absurd!" reflected the mature Ralph, placid after his lazy voyaging.

He had not noticed that she wore a new pair of

slippers with high red heels, and had he noticed them he would not have divined that they might be important. With much good humor he dressed for dinner —that is, he washed his face and fetched out from his bag a deplorably wrinkled town coat.

The Revillon Frères post and Biermeier's cottage were a mile from the rest of Mantrap Landing, and away from the lake, on the Mantrap River at its junction with Ghost Squaw River. The path was a damp trail through swamp and scrub pine, and in one place it led across a morass on insecure logs laid end to end through the mud.

At the beginning of this bridge through the morass, Alverna stopped, and squeaked to Joe, "I *can't* get across!"

"Why not?"

"My new dancing slippers. The heels so high. I'd slip off the logs and ruin 'em in the mud. Oh, I can't, Joe, honest! I cannnnn't! You got to carry me! You got to!"

"Hell!" observed Joe. "Hard enough to balance myself. Why didn't you wear some regular shoes, and carry them darn' things in your pocket?"

"Well, I didn't, and you got to carry me!"

"Well, you ought to of, and I'm not going to carry you!"

Ralph would have liked to volunteer. She would

be an agreeable burden. But it seemed no time for friendly offers.

Joe grumpily wavered over the bridge, and she followed him, swaying on the teetering logs or inching along sidewise, pushing one foot ahead and drawing the other up to it, her arms an agitated windmill. Her face was a knot of unhappiness the while, and without ceasing she whimpered and gasped her fear.

Halfway over, where the bridge broke off for a moment in a patch of firm ground, Joe awaited her, and spoke apologetically:

"No reason at all, wearing those slippers. You knew what the path was like. If you couldn't remember to wear proper shoes, you ought to of taken off your shoes and stockings. Here—I'll try to carry you the rest of the way, if you don't choke me to death."

"If! But! Though! When! . . . I *will* take 'em off!" she screamed.

Ignoring Ralph, she flung herself on a stump, tore off her silk stockings and her little slippers and, with her skirts high, she furiously splashed through the mud that tarred her white legs.

Behind him Ralph heard George Eagan shouting: "Hey, Alvy! Having a fit?"

Not looking back, informing the world of her woes, she asserted, "Joe wanted me to ruin my clothes that

I worked so hard to make, but I'll show him he can't bully me!"

Ralph was suddenly very sick of it all, and of his own middle-aged fatuousness he was most weary. He was sicker afterward when their host, as Ralph helped him bring ice in from the sawdusty ice-house for whiskies and sodas, grunted: "Poor old Joe! I wonder if he knows Curly Evans is making love to Alverna."

"It isn't true!" insisted Ralph.

"Don't make me laugh!"

If ever Ralph had been grotesquely out of place among the men of the forests, it was at that evening's poker game. In fiction, all proper tenderfeet, particularly if they wear eyeglasses and weigh not over one hundred and thirty-seven pounds, after three weeks on a ranch, in a lumber-camp, or on a whaler become hardened and wise. Usually they beat the two-hundred-and-sixteen-pound bully and marry the boss's daughter. But Ralph was tonight rather more of a tenderfoot, and a bored tenderfoot, than when he had left Whitewater on the steamer.

The third time Biermeier boomed, "Well, I'll just whoop you wise-crackers one large quarter 'f a dollar, the fourth part of a dollar, gents"; the seventh time Pete Renchoux piped in what he considered a Swedish accent, "By me, by Yumpin' Yiminy"; the eleventh time Pop Buck rumbled, "And another little drink wouldn't do us any harm"—then Ralph had had enough of merriment.

He tilted back in his kitchen chair, which squeaked, and tried to be excited over a hand consisting of the deuce of clubs, the four of clubs, the seven of diamonds, the ace of hearts, and the queen of spades.

He was conscious that Biermeier's cabin smelled of damp clothes, stale condensed milk, and fried fish; that the insurance-calendar picture on the log wall was torn; and that Pete Renchoux was forever spitting on the cigarette-littered floor. He knew that by all canons of being virile and sporting and wildernessy, he ought to relish these splendors.

He didn't.

He was glad when, three hours after supper, Joe yawned, and proposed: "Kind of all in, after last night. Stand going home, Ralph—Alvy?"

She had a number of complex things to say to each of her admirers, but they started.

Biermeier's young Aberdeen assistant proposed to walk back with them. Alverna whispered to Ralph: "Let's get ahead. That Scotch kid is so serious he makes me tired."

When they came to the bridge of logs, she peeped at him, in the dusk, and without a word he picked her up and carried her across.

So light and dear a burden she was—at first. Before he had balanced his way across, he was panting, and desperate with swaying over abysses of mud, but extremely proud of himself for his might.

When he set her down, on firm earth, he patted her shoulder with quiet friendliness. Their petty adventure had brought them together, wiped out his fencing and her incessant fretful grasping for admiration. This honest embrace, free from the morbid and teetering infatuations of the dance, had contented them. She spoke no longer with the pretty saccharine voice of the woman demanding compliments, but as a comrade.

"You were nice, Ralph. And Joe was right. Ought to have put on regular shoes for that trail. I'm such a nitwit!"

"Alverna!"

"Yes?"

"You oughtn't to tease Joe as you do, and keep demanding things from him. He's so frightfully decent and straight and kind. *And* intelligent."

"I kn-ow it. Gee, don't be silly! I'm crazy about him! But—this is such a dumm place up here, it gets me nervous. Golly, if I could come back to life again for a couple months! And see a show! Maybe I don't envy you! Seeing all the New York shows that I read about. You must 'a' seen this 'What Price Glory.' Was it swell? I'd like to seen that. It must be a great show. I knew an A.E.F. sergeant that— Say, there was a fellow! He never took any lip off any girl—just as soon hit you as eat—but nice, oh, awful nice, and never vulgar or anything. And 'Rain.' I'd like to seen that. I used to go to the theater all the time, when I was in Minneapolis. You see, I knew some actors. I don't know as I ever told you, but I did Jack Barrymore's nails one time! Say, tell me about 'Rain.' What kind of a show was it?"

When Joe reached home he found them talking with vast propriety.

Her mention of the plays, just the names of them, had flung Ralph's imagination to the streets of New York. He would be glad to be there, when the brisk autumn came and he was rested.

He was there now! A little fed up with poker, Pete Renchoux, and the gulping of Biermeier, he thought of quiet friends, bright drawing-rooms with flowers, and the still excitement of legal problems.

When Joe had gone into the cabin, Ralph still talked. He held out life to her. The Berkeley case, and his argument before the robed pontifical Justices of the Supreme Court at Washington. His ambition to write an enduring book on the laws of water-power. His friends: the classmate who was now a diplomat, the doctor who had performed an operation in an aeroplane, the explorer who had been tortured to death in North China.

Ralph did not know it, but his inner self was boasting: "I'll show her! She may think I can't jig and make noisy jokes like Pete. And maybe I can't. Or face danger like Joe or Curly. But I'll show her I am somebody!"

Dinners—yes, he did "put on a dress-suit" for them —yes, quite often.

The opera, smart night-clubs, week-ends.

His European ambles. An autumn day in Rotterdam, the leaves of the plane-trees dropping into the canals. Midnight of Christmas Eve in Rome, and the shawled throng on the steps of the Ara Coeli. The red-and-white tablecloths of restaurants in Daubigny; and a Mass of beer at the Hofbräuhaus in Munich. Striped awnings and the click of frivolous heels at Monte Carlo.

"Gee, you certainly have traveled some!" she admired.

"Good night," he said to her warm hand.

He wandered from the porch to the lake-front, brooding.

The theory he had encountered in dinner-talk and such moral fiction as he had read (he meditated) was that for a man to be nobly fond of a friend, to admire him and trust him, and yet be intolerably lured by that man's wife, was in all decency impossible. That theory he perceived to be idiotic. He liked Joe Easter as well as any man in the world; he would do anything imaginable for him; and he hoped that all their lives they two—in difficult New York as well as in

Mantrap Landing—would be intimates. He understood Joe's miserable irritation at his wife's folly,
and shared it. Yet all the while he was as inescapably
absorbed by her as though Joe and all loyalty had
never existed. He could see every line of her cheeks
and shoulders, hear her voice and be stirred by it
to insatiable tenderness. A good thing (he sighed)
that he felt pity for her. Let him hold to it! For
too easily he could fall into a fascination where, blind
and bound, he would no longer see her as childish,
ignorant, vulgar, pawing at every soul, but as the
bright rose of all the world, veiled in her own radi-
ance.

But on the other hand (he outlined it, as to a jury)
it was equally a lie that a man could not fight against
such fascination. The honest friendship of two men
was worth more than all the enchantments of women.

He would fight.

No, he must flee!

This was not his world. He was lost here. There
was nothing from which he could draw strength. And
forever it would be a satisfaction to have played out
the game with Woodbury; it would be enduring
strength to find him again and to—well, no, not tolerate him, but fight his petulance, and fight openly.

He was in this high mood of self-approbation when,
on the path from the Indian settlement, he stumbled
upon a tree across the path. In the thin darkness he

made out that the tree had stood by the trail; it had been cut to fall across the way, and deliberately, during the few hours since they had used this path.

He returned swiftly to the cabin. He fancied footsteps among the trees.

Alverna had gone to bed, but he found Joe sitting in the kitchen, comfortable in stocking feet, smoking a corncob and reading the weekly edition of the *Montreal Star*.

Softly, to hide it from Alverna, Ralph told of his discovery.

Joe muttered: "Don't know what the idea is. Let's have a look."

He tugged on his shoes with a nervous swiftness unusual in him, and he took an electric torch. As they strode down the path together, Ralph rejoiced in feeling free of the embarrassment which, like a curtain, Alverna had hung between them.

"Um," Joe commented on the cut log. "Fool thing to do, but I guess some Indian figured out it would bother us. Maybe kind of a warning. Say, don't tell Alverna! I didn't say anything, but when we come back tonight I noticed some one's stolen that fourteen-foot canoe of mine—the gray one. Least it's missing from beside the wharf. Are they starting something? Well"—Joe chuckled—"it proves they don't dare do so awful' much, anyway, don't it! Well, how about bed? Gosh, I cer'nly am sleepy!"

Ralph certainly was not.

He started to undress; then resolutely he buttoned his shirt again and from beneath his cot on the porch drew out his rifle and quietly filled the magazine. For the first time in his life he faced danger for some one else—though whether it was for Joe or Alverna he was not quite sure. He let himself out of the screened door, and sat on the steps, waiting.

The forest night was full of moving shadows and cautious rustling. He drowsed, with the edge of the upper step a pain across his back; he nodded; then— it may have been half an hour later—he jerked awake.

There had been a sound, the more terrifying in its indistinctness. He was slow with sleep, and incredulous when he realized through drowsy blindness that he wasn't playing a game, that some one really was creeping toward him.

He sat rigid. His eyes felt like burning spotlights. He peered intently. It was a sound as of faint sweeping—brush, brush, brush—relentless. Then he made out a crouched figure between house and store, a figure on hands and knees—

A dog? He almost laughed, but his laughter was chilled with fear as the figure rose, fumbled at the wooden shutters of the store.

"Who's that?" he clamored shakily.

The figure started to run. Ralph fired, twice, in an astonishing, murderous, frightened fury. There was no cry; only silence in that courtyard of beaten earth.

Suddenly Joe was beside him, grotesque in an old torn cotton nightshirt, saying calmly enough, "What's the trouble?" Alverna, behind him, huddling a negligee about coquettish yellow silk pajamas, was wailing, "Oh, what was it, what was it?"

"Fellow trying to get into the store."

"Well," Joe said mildly, "guess he won't try it again. Guess you didn't hit him, though—I could see somebody running up the south trail when I looked out. Might as well turn in. Don't worry about 'em, Ralph. We'll lock the doors, and nobody can get in; and before they could pry open those shutters on the store, I'd hear 'em, sure. But much obliged for—"

"You could not! You didn't hear that fellow! Oh, I won't go back to bed! I'm too frightened!" protested Alverna.

"Well, you sit and read till you feel sleepy again," Joe yawned. "Wake me up if you get real scared. But it'll be all right. G' night."

Side by side Ralph and Alverna sat on the steps, their feet wet with dew, in sunken relaxation after the battle.

"Terrified. Just terrified. Frightened to death!" Alverna whispered. He touched her arm in reassurance. She clung to his hand fiercely. "Oh, Ralph, I was so bored here! I didn't think anything *could* be worse than being so bored. But there is: being so scared. I'm just never myself. I'm always waiting for something dreadful to happen. And I don't know from which way it might be coming. Oh—*terrified!* You mustn't leave us. Joe says you feel you have to go join this awful man you were with. Oh, don't, Ralph dear! I know Joe wants you to stay. He likes you so much."

"And you?"—softly.

"Oh, a lot! Maybe you think because I raise so much Cain and all, and I like to dance and holler and be the village cut-up—maybe you think that's all I care for. But I get sick and tired of it. *Hon*-est, I do appreciate folks that are elegant and cultured and everything. Like you. Or do you think I'm just a pinhead?"

"No, you baby!"

"I'm glad. You'd be s'prised if you knew how I read the magazines and everything. And books, too, when I get time—of course I'm terribly busy. I'm so glad you don't think I'm all cantaloupe above the neck!"

She let herself relax in purring contentment beside him, then roused again in panic fear:

"You won't desert us! You'll help us? You won't go off and join that pig you were with?"

"Of course. Poor scared kid!"

"I *am!* I'm just a sparrow in the cat's claws. And I'm so sleepy, too!"

So he sat, guarding her, as she drooped into little fitful naps. Himself he felt guarded and fearless in her presence. And the lake crept into visibility in the returning light.

CHAPTER EIGHTEEN

"I THINK perhaps I'd better stay around a few days, till Evans returns with his policemen. I'll let Woodbury enjoy the sweet fruits of solitude a while," Ralph said at breakfast.

"That's fine. Hope you will. But don't feel you have to on our account," droned Joe. "If Alvy's scared, I can get Pop and maybe George and Pete to sleep here. But we'd be real tickled to have you stay as long as you can. And I'd like to hear some more about this water-power stuff. What d'you say Alvy and me and you have a picnic over on Blue Nose Island today?"

It expanded Ralph's ego, it made him feel that he was not merely a weakling among these men valiant in canoe and portage, to have Joe listen noddingly while he showed the possibilities of water-power plants in the wilderness.

A little before noon they buzzed by motor-canoe over to Blue Nose Island. Alverna had been most brisk and calicoed in preparing the basket of food, but now she dramatized herself as a young lady boating, presumably on the Isis. In her newly pressed cornflower-blue muslin, with clocked white stockings and red-strapped white shoes, a slightly torn paper parasol (her only parasol) over her, she lay in the bow against two pillows, of which one flaunted a Princeton banner and the other showed in burnt-leather a feather-bonneted Indian strangely unlike Lawrence Jackfish or Chief Wapenaug.

"And, confound it," Ralph thought savagely, "with all her monkey-tricks and her pretentiousness and her ignorance, she is pretty. Horribly pretty. And she could learn— Give her three years of decent society, and she'd be snubbing me for my bad table manners. Oh, curse it! Can't I ever stop thinking about her?"

He turned to Joe and made high endeavor to discuss pickerel and literature, but the sound of an outboard motor is not advantageous to subtleties.

They landed on a flashing beach under pine-fringed bluffs. When they had brought the food—and Alverna's pillows—ashore, Joe climbed the bluff in search of firewood.

Alverna reclined on the beach, her cheek on her hand.

"If you did go, I'd make you take me with you and get me away from this terrible place," she murmured. "Or would you be scared of me, without a chaperon?"

"Afraid not very feasible."

"Wouldn't you— Don't you think it would be fun to have me along?"

"Oh—yes—but—"

"It was so nice, last night, snuggling up beside you and feeling so safe, and just going by-by and— I hope you didn't kiss me, when I'd dropped off to sleep."

"I did *not!*"—irately.

"Wouldn't you have liked to of? Just a teeny, weeny, butterfly kiss?" Her glance was itself a kiss.

He sprang up, with an irritation that was not entirely irritation.

"Hell, yes, probably I would! But I'm not going to. Ever! This is enough, Alverna. This afternoon I start off and join Woodbury. I'm through! I'm going! I don't trust myself with you, and as for you, you're a complete fool—and so cursedly lovely! Can't stand it. Enough. I'm going."

"But just this morning you said— Don't you ever know your own mind?"

"Apparently not!"

"Can't a person depend on you for more than five hours?"

"Apparently not!"

"And you'd desert us now, when we're threatened by the Indians?"

"I'm threatened by something much worse—losing my honor!"

"Whatever that may mean, Ralph dearie! I've heard that before! I go to bum melodramas myself! And you'd *desert* us, when—"

"You can get Pop and George Eagan to come stay in the house. Maybe they'll kiss you!"

"Oh, Ralph! Ralph! Oh! That was mean, that was pretty mean! That wasn't fair! When I was just joking! Maybe I was sort of silly, but— Oh, you weren't kind!"

"I didn't intend to be!"

When Joe returned, with a charred log and an armful of dry branches, he found Ralph looking expressionlessly over the lake, his back to Alverna, while she stared up at him pitifully.

Ralph swung toward him; he spoke curtly.

"Joe, I hate to annoy you by changing my mind all the time, but I've been thinking it over again and I've decided that if you could lend me Lawrence or some other Indian and a canoe and a tent, I'll start out—this afternoon!—and try to find Woodbury. It's been—uh—fretting me. Feel like a deserter. . . . Though I suppose I'll go on feeling that way, leaving you at a time like this."

"All right, Ralph. Darn' sorry to see you leave us, but just as you feel. You got to do what you think best. Sure: take Lawrence. I can get Saul Buckbright if I ever need a canoeman. Wish I could lend

you my canoe-motor, but I don't guess Lawrence or
you could run it. Can you help him paddle?"

Ralph caught Alverna's lips, silently forming:
"Don't go! Please!" He ignored her.

And that was all.

It was twelve-thirty now. And at three that afternoon, his borrowed canoe stocked from Joe's store
and from Joe's private camp equipment, with Lawrence Jackfish at the stern, imperturbable as though
he were merely going to a dance, Ralph started out
across Lac Qui Rêve, bound for Lake Solferino.

He unhappily said good-by to Joe, Pop Buck,
George Eagan, Pete Renchoux, McGavity, the Reverend Mr. Dillon—and most of these good friends,
who might have been his intimates forever, vanished
from life as though they had been but printed symbols
in a book read at midnight.

Alverna was not there to say good-by.

"I guess she hated to see you go. Don't know as
you realized it, but Alvy is really awful' fond of you,"
Joe said gravely, while Ralph felt like a pickpocket.
"She slipped away right after we come back here.
Guess she's out in the woods somewheres, crying.
Poor kid! Now don't worry about the Indians. I'll
have George Eagan come stay here. God bless you,
Ralph! Come back to us whenever you can!"

As the canoe slowly crept out on the lake and Ralph,
in the bow, looked back at the knot of men standing

on the log wharf and waving to him, it was the saddest farewell he had ever known, save for that moment when his mother had taken his hand and sighed and closed her eyes.

His mind curdled with manifold regret. Was he deserting Joe? Had it not been the fault of his own flabbiness that Alverna had been flirtatious? Could he never, even in this land of brave forest and unsullied lakes, be direct and of inflexible purpose?

Were tragedy and confusion and hurt involved in all human contacts, save with such men as Joe Easter, who were ungnawed by Self?

And he would never see Alverna again. But he *had* to. He ached for her.

And, to drop far below the plane of honor and passion and righteousness, was he not a plain fool to subject himself once more to the blatting of Wes Woodbury?

And could he possibly keep up this shoulder-aching labor of paddling?

He had not, in his stormy complex-mongering, considered how hard it would be to paddle even two hours a day. Why hadn't he taken another Indian? He couldn't go back now and admit his weakness and say good-by all over again. But could he keep up?

Already—in fifteen minutes—each dip of the paddle was agony. His shoulders were cramped, the back of his neck was in a vise. His uncalloused hands stung.

And he could not, he snarled, avoid dripping water on his lap every time he swung the paddle from one side to the other.

Well—grimly—he'd have to get hardened.

If their food did not run out; if they did not starve meantime . . .

The invariable route for one heading toward Lake Solferino or Lake Warwick was past a long sliver of sand and jack-pine called Windy Point. It was per- haps two miles from Mantrap Landing by water, and three by land, if one should go over a scraggly hill known as Moose Mountain.

"When we reach the Point, I'll rest a little," Ralph promised himself. "Lawrence Jackfish will snicker at me. Well, Lawrence Jackfish can go to the devil!"

As they labored past the sandy spit at the end of the Point, out of sight of Mantrap Landing and its cabins on the bluff, Ralph was aware of a figure run- ning along the far side of the Point, a figure in skirts, bearing a pack, a light swift figure.

It was Alverna.

She was gesturing to them. She staggered a little as she came to the soft sand of the beach.

Lawrence, without orders, turned the canoe toward her. Ralph could see that her face was creased and old with unhappy stubbornness. She wore her sailor- blouse, her white skirt, and white canvas shoes—the same costume in which, so happily, she had welcomed him three days ago. But her hat was an aged felt, black streaked with rusty gray, belonging to Joe.

She carried a bundle, seemingly of clothes, tucked into a pillow-slip, and at her waist was a revolver.

As the canoe touched shore, Ralph leaped out, as forgetful of wetting his moccasins as an Indian.

"Good Lord, what are you up to?" he implored. "Come along up the beach and—"

"*I* don't care if Lawrence hears me! I don't care if the whole world hears me!"

"Well, I do!"

"Yeh, you would!"

But she plodded along the beach with him.

They sat on a rough hummock at the edge of the jack-pine. She dropped her bundle, wiped her wet forehead, sighed with weariness. His own sweat-stinging shoulders Ralph had nearly forgotten.

She plunged into it fiercely:

"I'm going with you."

"You can't! Impossible! Don't be insane. You can't!"

"Well—I am! You've got to take me. Listen: It isn't just being scared of the Indians. It's— To have to live there the rest of my life, with nothing but a cookstove and duck-hunting—and I *hate* duck-hunting!—till I'm old and wrinkled and bad-tempered and as much of a fiend as Ma McGavity—the devil curse her! I won't!"

"But you owe something to Joe."

"Not a thing! Man, can't you talk honestly, just once? Are you New York swells as hog-tied by a lot of words as a trapper or a barber? 'Owe something'? I've given him a year of sweetness. Oh, I know he found it sweet! He's had me, body and soul, and I'm *not* ugly, I'm *not* stupid, no matter what you think, no matter how much of a fool I am! And I play the fool mostly because otherwise I'd go crazy with the monotony.

"I've given him love. And I've cooked for him, I've swept for him, I've sung for him. And now he doesn't love me any longer. I know. A woman does know! He thinks I'm a fly-by-night. Oh, he's fond of me, but he doesn't like me the way he does you or Pop Buck. And I never did sure-enough love him. He's a peach—he's so brave and straight and everything— but he's just a regular old school-teacher, that's what he is! *Don't argue, man!* I guess I know pretty near as much about Joe and me as you do, even if you do think you invented law!"

"I don't think—"

"Well, you can if you want to. It wouldn't hurt you any! Oh, I didn't mean to be mean. Honestly, I think you're terribly smart." Her passionate integrity turned with the dismaying swiftness of a motor collision into unscrupulous luring. "I was just kidding. I think you got a swell brain. Wouldn't I like to wake you up once!"

"I'm sure that's most gratifying, my dear child, but you simply cannot go with me. Now do have some sense! Go back to Joe, and talk to him straight. I have no doubt he'll see that you get to Minneapolis or some place, if—"

"You have no doubt! Oh, you damned fish! Excuse me, Ralph. But would it be too hard for you to be a little bit human for a few minutes? Dear, I'm not like the skirts you know in New York. I haven't got anybody to turn to—except you. Listen, dear. I can't do it. If I was in the cities, Joe'd feel he had to have me watched or something. He'd prob'ly make me live with a skinny-necked old aunt he's got in Iowa. Nag me to death. Honor of his name or something. Oh, you men, with your Honor! How you do like to chain up your women-folks with it!"

"But you'll have to—"

"I won't! Now look here! You listen to me, Ralph Prescott. If you don't take me with you— And I mean it, d'you hear, I *mean* it! Don't I sound as if I did? If you don't take me with you, then I'll start off for Kittiko on foot, through the woods."

"You couldn't. It's absurd!"

"I kno-o-o-ow it's absurd! But I'll do it. I'd rather die in the woods than go back and be murdered in my bed—or jawed to death by McGavitys. You don't know it, but last night Joe laid down the law to me, and he says I've got to see more of that old hell-cat. I got to make myself love her. Sure. And I'm to be influenced by her and not by bad eggs like Curly Evans. I will like hell! I'll starve first!"

"I suppose you do mean it. But, good Lord, how would you get anything to eat, if you tried to walk—"

"I've got a side of bacon and some flour cached back in the woods here. Enough to last me a few days. And I got a fish-line and a trolling-hook here in my bundle. (Oh, Ralph, I just couldn't leave that sweet little black dress behind, or my new red-heeled slippers. I did love them so!) And I'll try to shoot some ducks with this revolver. Oh, I'll get along— maybe. I'll get a lift in a canoe from some trapper or some Injun."

"And be— Would you like to be picked up by some unknown roughneck, and camp with him, and find out he's a scoundrel?"

"Certainly I wouldn't! But you, when you're all nice and cozy in your camp, and feeling so fine and proud because you were a good little man—with a heart like a stone!—you can think of Alverna begging help from some son of evil, and paying him for it!"

"Oh, curse it! I do wish you'd—"

"Well, I won't! Ralph! Dear Ralph! Listen, dear. I won't be in your way. Honestly I won't. I

MANTRAP

couldn't make it walking, and I couldn't paddle all the way, if I stole a canoe. But I'm ever so much stronger than I look. I won't be a fool, like I was when we went duck-hunting. That was just to tease you. Why, I could of carried all three of those guns, and then six more! I'll paddle—you got an extra paddle in the canoe, haven't you? I'll do all the cooking. I'll carry—oh, I'll carry a terrible lot on the portage."

"It isn't that."

"Am I so ugly? Am I so cranky? Is it so stupid to be with me—when I sing for you, and crack little fool jokes, and try to jazz it up and make all my men-folks happy? Am I so hideous?"

"Wish you were!"

"Don't you like me?"

"Too well. That's it. You sneer at my talking about a sense of honor, but it's just that. Precisely that. Toward you and toward Joe and toward myself."

"Oh"—hopelessly—"I know! . . . I wonder if there ever was a man of honor who had so much honor that he could sacrifice it for a woman? Oh, my little man, God pity you for your honor! Good-by, my Ralph."

She rose, she plodded away, not heeding his protests. Her shoulders, so airy once to express every hilarious childishness, were stooped under her pack and old as a beaten squaw's.

He ran after her; he seized her arm; he took her hand. She let it lie listlessly in his.

"It's no use," she croaked. "I'm going. I really am. Joe is a dear, but he made one mistake. He oughtn't to of ever brought me up here. I'm going to be free, or I'm going to leave my bones in some swamp."

Her threat broke him more than all her gibes. Yes, she really would do it. He could see those frail bones found years afterward in some horror of slime; fragile white bones and leering skull once veiled and joyous with rosy flesh.

"But——"

He was no longer senile and intelligent, full of advice and of elderly amusement. He was youthful and rather terrified. "Suppose I did take you with me. Joe would guess we were together. He'd follow us."

"Are you afraid of Joe?"

"I am!"

"Golly, so am I!"

She grinned, for the first time. Then she spoke eagerly, outlining a map on the palm of her little hand:

"Look here. There's two ways to Whitewater and the railroad. There's the way you came—the way you're supposed to be going now—the Mantrap River and Lake Warwick and steamer to Whitewater. But there's another route. You sneak along back of Mantrap Landing, the other side of Moose Mountain, and

you hit the Ghost Squaw River, then up that a little
way, and right straight south to Whitewater, by way
of Lost River and Goose Lake and Weeping River
and Lake Midnight and Bulldog Lake. It's shorter,
as the crow flies, but there are a terrible lot of portages, they tell me, and some mean little creeks where
you got to pole or line. Almost nobody goes that
way, but you *can* do it. Curly did once. Joe's never
been through there, nor Lawrence."

"But if Lawrence is to guide us and he doesn't
know—"

"Oh, I've got a map of it. Took it off Joe's chart."

"When? When did you decide—"

"Oh, this afternoon, when you were getting ready
to run away from me, or maybe from yourself, and
I made up my mind we were going together. Joe will
never in the world guess we've gone that way. If he
did try to follow us—only I don't believe he would;
he's really an old corker at letting you have your own
way if you plank your foot down hard enough—but
if he did chase us, he'd go the other way, by Lake
Warwick."

"Well—"

"Ralph! Ralph dear! Can't you ever take a vacation from being the swell Mr. Prescott? Have you
always got to go around admiring your conscience?
Feeling you just had to go off and resurrect that boob
Woodbury! The idea! Pfui!

"We're not going to hurt Joe, not the least bit. I'll
be as good as a mouse—probably! And, oh, Ralph,
I will work so hard! I'll help carry the canoe on the
portages. Honest, dear, I'm terribly strong. Listen!
Stop talking! You know you're going to take me
with you! You are! Ralph! Wouldn't it be kind
of nice to have Alverna along, with no horrible people
to make things ugly?"

He tried to answer judiciously . . .

CHAPTER NINETEEN

IT had taken them all one day to make the three-
mile portage behind Mantrap Landing, behind
Moose Mountain, to the Ghost Squaw River.

Lawrence Jackfish had at first refused to go with
them. He had been won by a promise of two dollars
extra a day, and for two dollars a day, which meant
ever so many red shirts and red silk handkerchiefs
and cigarettes and mouth-organs, Lawrence would
have committed murder—several murders.

But if he continued as their guide, he was not their
servant; and his yellowish eyes peeped at them, his
crooked teeth leered at them, till Ralph thought with
relish of using an ax when Lawrence's back was
turned.

All afternoon they panted on the hot secret trail.

It was a foot-wide path through pine thickets. The air was lifeless as in a shuttered and abandoned house on an August afternoon.

Following Lawrence, who carried the upturned canoe on his shoulders, Ralph toiled with such a load of flour and bacon and blankets as he would never have believed himself able to lift. He was not walking—he was merely putting one foot before the other, endlessly, forever, with a separate effort of his will at each step. He was not alive. All of him was dead save scorching shoulders, wrenched small of his back, and plodding feet. He was a quarter aware that behind him, carrying almost as large a load as his own, Alverna was panting. But it was only when he had laboriously revolved the thought in his cloudy brain for ten minutes that he came to life sufficiently to suggest: "You've got too much to carry, child. Put down part of it, and we'll pick it up later."

"No," she said, breathlessly but stoutly. "I'm going to do my share."

He pitied her, the white and golden moth fluttering in a cobweb, but he was too paralyzed with fatigue to do anything about it. The most spirited part of his cerebration was the fear that some one, crossing over the mountain from Mantrap Landing, should see them and bring a raging Joe down upon them.

As to whether he was virtuous in rescuing Alverna, or vile in treachery to Joe, or maddeningly both at once—such frail philosophies could not make themselves heard in the torment of his toil.

If they could but get this portage done, if they could be joyfully away, in the freedom of the racing rivers, the wide and desolate lakes—

He learned to trot the back trail burdenless, like Lawrence, when he returned for another load, and behind him he heard Alverna forlornly pattering through the dry pine needles. He did not look at her, but he felt her comradeship.

They labored till the late dusk. Then only they boiled the kettle and, with fingers stiffened into hooks, devoured their bacon and bannock. Lawrence withdrew a little, and Ralph was happy in sitting with her by a low fire, coals glowing in a hollow of glittering quartz sand. He had never supposed that she could display such brilliant and lucid and endearing silence. And treacherously that silence drifted into sleep.

Ralph woke bewildered. The spell of slumber was like an eiderdown quilt over his head, and fumblingly he thrust it aside. In the light of ash-filmed coals, under the thin mistiness of northern midnight, Alverna was curled in stillness and Lawrence was snoring in his blankets, under a mosquito-bar. Mosquitoes. Ralph realized dully that it had been nothing more romantic than a mosquito which had roused him. . . . Then he perceived that Alverna was looking at him. Though her cuddling childish body had not moved, it seemed to him that her eyes were open. She was very near him, they two alone.

She peered at him drowsily and rolled into his arms.

His hands gripped her sides, then remained cramped and unmoving, not daring to move. A thousand times he had wondered, a thousand times pictured himself gallant in love. Now he worried, over and over, "What does she expect me to do?"

Terror, sheer terror and incapacity for life, began to shadow his embarrassment. He wanted to escape from her.

The fire was low. He had more imagined than seen her. But her shoulders were close to his eyes now; her sailor blouse was gaping, and torn with toil on the portage. Terror and anxiety vanished from him as he irresolutely kissed the hollow beside her collar-bone. He awaited for a second her indignation but she sighed and moved closer. She said nothing save a slow sighing "Oh, my dear!" and he forgot all the world of Ralph Prescott.

They were on the portage again at dawn; and by noon, with relief so profound that their panting was like the sob of wailing women, they teetered into the canoe and slowly paddled up the Ghost Squaw River.

There were two more portages, immediately, but they were short; they were almost luxurious. And then for the first time Ralph took his share in shooting rapids.

Though their general direction was up-river, they had cut across the curves of an S in the current, and for two miles they went downstream. Thus it was that the Ralph who a few days ago had shivered before rapids found himself shooting them and depending not on guides but on his own muscle, his own nerve.

They came to Ghost Rapids, silently, ignoring their peril.

Lawrence took the bow. He stood there, pointing with his paddle at the one inevitable way through the welter of rapids. Where Ralph would have steered to the right through an apparently even current, Lawrence read the cryptic manuscript of the water and directed him to a crazy zigzag left, then right, left again, and straight ahead, almost grazing a fanged rock.

It was Ralph's hour of test. Without for a moment ceasing to be afraid, he was steady at the steering paddle, abrupt at wrenching the canoe from side to side, all the while cursing hideously under his breath.

Suddenly they were in the last gush of the water, the bow of the canoe leaping five feet in the air, while Ralph chewed his lip. As suddenly they shot into the calm water beyond the rapids, and in relief Ralph sighed above his lifted paddle, so that Alverna looked back in wonder, and Lawrence loosed his hissing snicker.

CHAPTER TWENTY

FOR a week there was a nightmare of portages and snaky creeks up which they had to pole, of mosquitoes and the inferno of endless paddling; and Ralph's only solace was the unbroken gallantry, the smiling kindness of Alverna, as she took her turn at the paddle, as she plodded on the portage, as she sat by the camp-fire, her lacerated little hands twined about her knees, in a mud-smeared garment which had once been a white linen skirt.

He had courage because she believed that he had courage. When she slipped a trusting hand into his and murmured, "You've been so wonderfully good to me!" he was rewarded for his labor.

As he watched her sleeping, under wretched and insufficient blankets, in the cold nights which swooped down after the panting sun-drenched days, his dry heart blossomed in tenderness. . . . To think that he had once esteemed people because they understood Goossens's music or James Joyce's fiction, because they wore sleek clothes and were clever at the use of forks, because they could set up wooden words as a barricade against roaring life!

Tenderly he covered her with his own blanket, and lay shivering under a tarpaulin. And in the morning when side by side they washed their streaky faces in the chill water of a northern lake and their cheeks stung with sudden life, they smiled at each other and intelligently said nothing at all, and Ralph Prescott was no longer a cautious forty-odd, but twenty and aware of all romance.

Now this was their route, set down for any lunatic who shall of his own will leave wife and lawn and sheltered porch and stagger from Whitewater by the back way to Mantrap Landing, or from Mantrap dolorously to Whitewater.

By the Ghost Squaw River and Ghost Rapids and Bucking Rapids, up which they poled, with that chastening feeling of leaning out over the side of the canoe and wondering how soon the pole will slip and you will flop into the river, then by portage to Lost River, a portage half of sun-broiling rocks that were torturing to moccasined feet and half of swamp reeking with vast mosquitoes poisonous to sweaty neck and straining wrist, they came on Pike Lake. For five miles they sailed there more luxuriously than Cleopatra and Antony in scarlet-pinioned caravels.

Ralph marveled that he could ever have felt uneasy in a sailing canoe. By contrast with portages and the ache of paddling, to loll in the shadow of the bending sail, to feel the breeze on his scorching cheeks, to hear Alverna softly singing, yet all the time to be on their way, each moment safer from the menace of

Joe Easter's fury—this was a heaven he had never known.

Another portage, a reeling madness of five miles through thickets, and they came again to the openness of Thunder Bird Lake. But there was no breeze; they had to paddle all the shoreless and blistering plain of that dead expanse. And then, slowly, they perceived and acknowledged a danger.

Ralph had wondered at the persistent fogginess of the air in full sunshine. The shore was indistinct; the sun was a red ball at which he could stare undazzled; and the sun's reflection was a necklace of rubies on the pallid ripples of the pearl-gray water.

He looked back from the bow. "Getting foggy," he suggested.

"Yeh. Forest fire some place—smoke," said Lawrence.

"Forest fire? Near us?"

"Don't know. Maybe."

"I noticed it quite a while ago. But I guess it's pretty far off," Alverna made pretense. "Smoke will carry hundreds of miles."

Ralph had forgotten his fear of Joe's pursuit. But new danger stirs the imagination, and now to the travail of sixteen toiling hours a day was added a desperate wonder as to where the forest fire might be, and when they would burst out in a horror of arching flame.

And there was nothing he could do about it. He must go on. He was as helpless as though he were on a steamer in mid-ocean.

Where once he would have thought only of saving his own hide, he thought now of Alverna. Lawrence Jackfish might burn like a pitch-pine torch, and welcome; but if they should be caught by the fire (he pictured it, slowly, painfully, his mind dulled by paddling) he would protect her; he would cover her with his jacket, souse her in the lake . . .

Their chart showed that they were to pass from Thunder Bird Lake to Lake Midnight—the largest body of water on their route—by way of Weeping River. Here the streams turned southward. They would go downstream, and Ralph hoped for swift and easy passage to Lake Midnight.

They camped at the beginning of the Weeping River, in a sunset of crimson clouds murky with the impalpable smoke. The sun was red-eyed and irate as it set; the dusk was thick; and over the whole world was a sense of brooding fate.

They were wearily silent when they rose next dawn. There was no freshness in the air, and somberly they started down Weeping River.

It started out promisingly enough, with a gush of brown water between sandy banks monotonously lined with low willows. But the river became so shallow that the canoe scraped the sandy bottom. Presently they had but three inches of water, littered everywhere with rocks over which the canoe had to be lifted, in terror lest it be slashed beyond repair and leave them abandoned, starving, in the wilderness.

Instead of darting down a pleasant stream, they made less than a mile an hour, wading in slippery pools, tugging at the canoe. Alverna was still plucky, but her face was drawn, and Ralph bore all her suffering with his.

Mosquitoes joyously clouded round them, more portentous in their venomous insignificance than the black-winged fates.

"We'll have to give it up and hit cross-country for Lake Midnight. Looks here on the map as if we could get across to Mudhen Creek, which flows into Midnight. . . . Course map may not be right. So much of this country unexplored," said Ralph.

"All right. Let's," said Alverna, listlessly.

But Lawrence Jackfish said nothing at all, and Lawrence scowled, and Ralph wondered: "What's he thinking? What's he planning to do? How long can I make him take orders?"

They did, in fact, reach Mudhen Creek, and so came at last on the open waters of huge Lake Midnight. But the history of that passage would be a confused and unchroniclable nightmare. Ralph could never put it together; never determine whether they took three and a half days or four and a half from

Weeping River to Lake Midnight. The portage to Mudhen Creek was a delirium of quaking muskeg which let them down to drenched knees, of swamps crawling with scum, of brush which slashed their unprotected faces as they staggered with their loads, of airy mosquitoes singing their contempt, of persistent bulldog flies circling round and round their eyes, lighting and circling again, with a *zizz* which made the lords of creation shriek like lunatics, broken as they were with weariness.

And the cloud of smoke from the forest fires was over them always, but that menace had become as distant as Joe's possible pursuit.

They began to admit their shortage of food. It was Alverna who had the courage to speak of it.

Not always had Ralph plodded beside her in ecstasy. Before breakfast coffee and in the strain of the portage, he had often been irritated by her humming, her trick of pushing back her hair, the cruelty with which she split infinitives, and her bland supposition that everything which was not fierce or awful was either cute or nice. But these annoyances scarce rose to perception in his mind. For her strength and patient courage he had such affectionate admiration as he had once given to Joe.

"We got to start starving ourselves," she blurted. "Hardly enough grub to last us down Lake Midnight. The map says there's a trading-station near the south end of the lake. Once we hit it, I guess we'll be on a real good trail, and we can get some grub there. But our stuff has to last— Maybe we better cut it down to two meals a day now, and one a day pretty soon."

"I suppose so," sighed Ralph.

Bacon thrice daily had come to be all of his concept of heaven that was not comprised in Alverna.

"Hey, you, Lawrence, don't hog so much bannock! We got to go slow," Alverna observed, as sweetly as possible, but the Indian scowled.

To piece out the larder, they stopped at every swamp which promised a pickerel. But there were few fish, and the long delays made the fear of approaching forest fire more lively.

So hour by day-long hour they lumbered through swamp and muskeg and thicket, blind and mute, and when at last they came through a cool birch grove and found Mudhen Creek, Alverna stood weeping with relief, her face smeary as a muddy child's, and Ralph was too frayed to feel relief, too tired even to comfort her.

But after an hour of swift paddling down the Mudhen, helped by the current, on their way to Lake Midnight now, on their way to sailing and sacred food, his spirits rose and they two smiled again.

But they were so hungry!

At a pool below shallow rapids in the Mudhen,

Ralph flung in his trolling-hook and drew in, hand over hand, a ten-pound muskalonge more beautiful than the silver doe of heaven. They lit a fire, but scarce waited for the fish to broil; they tore at it half-cooked, black-handed savages, and when Ralph gave Alverna his bit of better-cooked fish, it was his one heroism in life.

He was sure now that their toil was over—but he was not quite sure that he was sure. When the Mud-hen flowed into the magnificent stretches of Lake Midnight, apprehension once more gathered round him.

There was a sinister look to those cruel waters. He understood the name of Lake Midnight when he saw that vasty stretch, the color of a bottomless spring. The lake was smooth enough; it reached out in a floor of black marble. But to venture on that frowning immensity in a canoe was like risking open ocean.

"Looks tricky, somehow. And no islands for shelter. Wonder if there's many squalls on it?" Ralph meditated. He kept his worry from Alverna.

There were squalls.

A breeze lifted before they had paddled half a mile. But it was a fair wind and they had to use it. Ralph was relieved that Lawrence kept as close to the east shore as possible, but that was not particularly close, for the shore-line was broken by many indentations. They were never more than a mile from land, Ralph calculated, yet they might as well have been a hundred. Neither he nor Alverna could swim half a mile, if they capsized, and the chicken-faced Lawrence would not try to save them.

Was it really only a mile to those distant trees, that secure beach? Ralph gazed to south, to west—a hundred and twenty miles it was to the south end of the lake, and to the west shore, forty. From the low plane of their canoe, the swart vastness of Lake Midnight was more engulfing than the round of desert.

He played with these thoughts and put them from him. He could not afford now the luxury of being timid; and when Lawrence suggested that they land and boil the kettle, though being ashore would provide half an hour of surcease from the feeling of danger he snapped: "No, go on. Wind may change."

They were, their map asserted, more than halfway to Whitewater and the high civilization of Bert Bunger's hotel when they camped that evening on the shore of Lake Midnight.

They had for supper only bacon and milkless tea.

When Ralph rose, a little after four, and came out rubbing his sandy eyes, the world was a mystery of fog. Only a patch of gray lake was visible, motionless except for faint etchings of ripples. He felt the vigor of the damp fog. The earth seemed new, re-created in a doubtful youth, and but for the specter of Joe, he would have rejoiced and felt ready for any venture.

He grew conscious that something was wrong with the scene, something very wrong, something missing. There was no canoe turned properly upside-down on the beach. There was no canoe anywhere. Nor was Lawrence Jackfish in sight, under his mosquito-bar.

"Lawrence! Lawrence!" Distress gave awe to his voice.

Alverna appeared at the flap of their tent, tousled and sleepy.

"What is it, Ralph?"

"Apparently Lawrence and the canoe are gone. Oh, probably he's out on the lake, to catchum fish for breakfast. You can't see far in this fog."

She stared; she hastened to the tarpaulin which covered their stores.

"No. He's skipped out for keeps," she said resolutely. "He's taken all our grub except a little flour and a quarter of a pail of lard and a teeny bit of tea. He's taken everything. He expects us to die here."

CHAPTER TWENTY-ONE

SHE neither wept nor scolded. They both lied about it; they assured each other that Lawrence would certainly be coming back. But their twined glances grew more intimate with common apprehension.

"Maybe we'd better wait half a day and see if he comes back," she said.

"Yes. . . . God! No canoe! Well, we'll try to walk to the trading-post. Wonder how far it is? What's it look like on the map, Al?"

"Must be eighty miles, anyway—providing we can come anywheres near following the shore; providing there aren't a lot of bluffs and thick woods that'll shove us back from the lake and maybe get us all lost. Anyway, dear—" She spoke cheerfully. "Thank Heaven, dear Lawrence didn't get away with the line and trolling-hook. And I've got enough matches. We can always catch some fish and broil 'em in their own blessed juice. And I've got the revolver and a box of shells. . . . Maybe we'll need the last two cartridges bad!"

They waited till noon, sitting on the beach, two babes in the woods, brave only in each other's presence. They were savages, both. Ralph had not shaved for four days. Once, with the noble Jesse and Louey to paddle for him, he had elegantly shaved daily in the canoe, his pocket mirror on his knees, dipping his brush over the side. But during these days of flight he never had the time. He showed a surprising stubble of black bristles; his nails were rimmed with dirt; his canvas jacket, once the pride of the polished young sporting-experts at Fulton & Hutchinson's, was foul with fish-scales, smeared with the blood of ducks and snipe, clotted with gray mud.

But his mouth had an angry steadiness. It no longer drooped and twisted in the duress of vain philosophizing.

Alverna had turned into a mad gypsy. As she sat beside him, quiet, undemanding, pouring pebbles from one hand into the other, she was a spirit of the forest. Her white blouse and skirt were torn, and patterned with waves of mud. Her pale bobbed hair she had combed sleekly, and she had conscientiously washed her face in the cold lake, but she had acquired a comic smut on one cheek as she had cooked the bannock that morning, and it gave her something of the impudent look of a fox terrier with a black jowl. One stocking was torn, the other had been discarded entirely, and along one of her canvas shoes was a long rip . . . the edges touched with blood. Yet there was confidence in the relaxed flow of her body, and confidently she whispered to him:

"I don't know if you can stand it, but I'm going to sing 'Three o'Clock in the Morning.' You've got to take me out to a dance when we hit Winnipeg— before you ship me off to Minneapolis and forget me —if we ever *do* get out of this."

She could not keep it up.

She whimpered, "I guess maybe we're going to die together, dear." She tried to smile. "Do you mind much?"

He lied sturdily.

She sprang up. "Might as well make-believe do something useful. I'm going to wash this awful skirt. Haven't got enough soap, but I can do something with sand. And you, Ralph, a shave wouldn't hurt your manly beauty one bit. Have a manicure, sir, and a violet-ray treatment?"

He did shave—with cold water and a film of lather from the bad little sliver of pink soap which was all they had. It hurt. She gaily washed not only her muddied sailor costume but also his proud and virile red cotton handkerchiefs, kneeling at the margin of the lake, stooped and singing and scrubbing like an Italian laundress by the Tiber.

They gave up waiting for Lawrence.

They were off at noon, after pretending to enjoy the last crumbs of the bannock and the one skinny jackfish which Ralph was able to catch by throwing out the trolling-hook from shore. Their packs were heavy, for a hundred-mile march, yet they had abandoned the tent, Alverna's beloved black frock and slippers; everything save blankets, flour, lard, fishing-tackle, the revolver, matches, mosquito netting and the one frying-pan which the good Lawrence had been so generous as to leave them.

But Ralph brought along Alverna's scarlet-beaded velvet bag, with rouge, lip-stick, powder, three absurd little embroidered handkerchiefs, and the priceless wafer of soap.

"Oh, let's leave that fool bag," she said regretfully.

"No. It's all there is of the old Alverna. . . . There's nothing of the old Ralph!"

She looked at him lingeringly. "There will be, when you get back to civilization. You'll hate me then!"

"Never! Look! We'll write to Joe, and we'll ask him for a divorce."

"Don't, dear. Please! Let's not make any plans. Let's not start thinking!"

She plodded down the shore, and he followed her.

For three miles they were able to keep to the beach of Lake Midnight. The yielding sand made dragging toil of every step, but at least they knew their way. Then the bluffs rose. For a time they scrambled between pine-trunks and the top of the bluff, high above the beachless water. Once they made fifty feet by edging along sidewise, holding by branches and bushes, hanging out over the sharp drop. They were forced into the forest, away from the lake, and at each step they looked in panic for the shine of water through the trees. They lost it, they lost themselves; and in a panic, running, glancing at each other with terror, they became snarled in a thicket of jack-pine. When they had struggled through and suddenly regained sight of the lake, Alverna deliberately sat down on the bristly earth and bawled, while he stood by her stroking her hair.

The bluffs dropped again, and they inched along hard shingle and muddy bog. When they quit, at darkness, in ten hours they had made fourteen miles —out of eighty, or a hundred, or, if they should find bays not recorded on their tentative map, perhaps twice a hundred miles—with food enough for scarce one day.

He was unable to catch a single fish for supper, and they supped on milkless and sugarless tea and a fragment of bannock before they rolled up in their blankets, with mosquito-bars clumsily hung over them on stakes.

All next morning, as they struggled on, Ralph was conscious of but four things in all the world: Alverna's uncomplaining pluck, the increased smokiness from the unknown forest fires, the fact that his moccasins and rubbers were wearing so thin that sharp stones were agony to his feet—and the absurd impossibility of the whole thing.

It was incredible that he, Mr. Prescott of Beaseley, Prescott, Braun and Braun, Ralph Prescott of the Yale Club, R. E. Prescott whose third cousin was a first secretary of embassy, should be starving and ragged in the northern wilderness; that what had been play should have become inescapable peril; and that an ex-manicure-girl should be to him the whole meaning of life.

When they stopped at noon, while Alverna sat on a slippery rock watching him throw out the hand-troller, she shrieked, without preface: "Ralph! I hear an airplane!"

"Why, honey, you're crazy! You'll be hearing Kreisler playing the violin next! You must— Say! I hear it! No, probably it's an outboard motor. Suppose it were Joe coming to— No! It is an aeroplane!"

Up the lake, a speck in the smoky atmosphere from the forest fires, swiftly growing larger, its humming momently more aggressive, he incredulously saw the air machine.

"They'll rescue us! Wave to 'em! *Safe!*" cried Alverna, prancing on the beach, running heedlessly out into the water to brandish her handkerchief.

Ralph joined her, flapping his dirty canvas hat.

In the rescue he felt a little sadness that their adventure should be over, that suddenly he was again merely Mr. Prescott of New York.

It was a hydro-aeroplane. The aviator was flying low. He saw them, swooped in an enormous circle, settled on the lake, and came taxiing toward them in a cascade of plowed-up water, a spectacle as strange in this barrenness of pineland and lifeless lake as a gondola with singing maidens.

The machine ran up to the beach, and Ralph and Alverna galloped over to lean against it, to gape at the occupants with faces almost idiotic in the unexpected bliss.

There were three men aboard. The aviator grumbled, "What's trouble?"

"My name is Prescott—New York. Been camping and fishing. This—uh—this is my wife. Our food got low, and our Indian guide deserted us. Took our canoe. We're almost starving, and I don't know whether we can make it to the next trading-post. Can you take us along?"

"Oh! I'm in the Canadian air force—these are two forest-fire rangers. Wish we could take you, but it's impossible. You see there's no room, not an inch."

The Alverna who for days had been all selfless devotion to Ralph was instantly titillated by the sight of three young men, especially by the flying officer— who, Ralph noted jealously, was damnably like Curly Evans. She was shining at them, preening herself, fluffing back her hair. In some incomprehensible way she had in the last two minutes contrived to rouge her lips.

She spoke teasingly:

"Oh, major, you wouldn't leave us here, would you? Oh gee now, have a heart! How d'you get that way! And I thought army officers were so awful' obliging and everything!"

The aviator was stern.

"But can't you see there's no room, madam? And I'm not a major! Perhaps one of the foresters could stay with your husband and give you his place, but we're hustling out to fight the forest fires—warn the settlers and organize fire-lines. Fact, we must buzz on immediately. And if you went with us, you might be burnt to death. We're going into the worst section. Though— Prescott, you better watch out along here, too. The fire's sweeping this way."

She wailed, a strange hopeless little ululation. Already she had lost her flirtatiousness. . . . She had kept it up just long enough to make Ralph forget all her loyalty and distrust her again.

The three men in the hydro-aeroplane looked at one another unhappily. One of the foresters suggested, "Guess we can leave 'em some grub and the folding boat and couple paddles."

"Right-o," agreed the others.

While the foresters were unloading the boat, and a side of bacon, a small sack of flour, a tin of lard, a really spectacularly beautiful can of corn, the aviator inquired:

"Deserted by your guide, eh? That happens very rarely. Which way have you been?"

"We—uh—we spent some time at Mantrap Landing," said Ralph.

"Oh, did you? Heard that Joe Easter—the forester

we stayed with last night said Joe Easter, the trader there, had his wife stolen by some sport, and Easter's after them. Never saw her, but they say she's an awfully pretty girl—"

As he spoke, the aviator's cheerful face was stilled with suspicion. He glanced from Ralph to Alverna.

They must have looked too expressionlessly innocent for innocence.

The aviator's voice became dry:

"And on Mudhen Creek, heading for the lake here, I saw a canoe with a fellow who looked, far as one could tell from five hundred feet up, as if he might be Easter. If I were the guilty laddie, I think I'd be making very active tracks. . . . All right, Kromer? Right. Good-by, people; watch out for the forest fire; camp close to the water."

One of the foresters had pushed out the machine and turned it a little; the other had twirled the propeller; and already the heavenly rescuer was dashing away in a gush of foam, an agony of roaring; it was lifting from the water and climbing.

In the silence Ralph stared at Alverna. He was not irritated and superior now at the flirtatiousness which she developed the second any male came into sight; he was pitiful, and he tried to persuade himself that she had yearned at the aviator only in order to insure their rescue.

"Gee, we better be making time! Cheer up," she

said. "Maybe Joe won't notice us. If we see him coming, we'll sneak ashore and hide."

To have to hide from Joe Easter, his friend, was to Ralph gutter-crawling. He was silent, robbed of all romance, as he looked over the folding boat and studied its nasty ways.

The boat, when it was opened out, was like a canvas soap-dish six feet long. The passengers had to squat on the floor. It was tippy and ghastly uncomfortable, but they hastened to load their small stores, and, forgetting hunger, they were off.

The lake was not too smooth. It grew rougher. Neither of them had yet learned the craft of paddling: how to meet a wave and breast it. Water gushed constantly into their canvas platter, and Alverna was busy bailing with a sod of moss, like a coarse sponge, while he tried to keep head up to the wind. Though they sought to hug the shore, they were constantly driven out, and Ralph was obsessed by a wonder as to whether, when they sank, his body would float across the lake and hang bobbing alongshore.

But another obsession was stronger. Now that he had been forced again out of his cozy illusions about Alverna, now that Joe was possibly on their trail, he began to think. He saw Joe—those naïve eyes, that steady kindness, that honest courage. For days he had been able to defy the vision, and joyously convince himself: "Joe was a fool. Good friend, but idiotic lover. He didn't understand her. I do! He couldn't hold her. I can! I don't feel guilty in the least."

Now he felt guilty enough; so guilty that no argument about having saved her from plunging out to starve in the forest was enough to strengthen him.

Yet all this while the power of thought, the pull of conscience, were feeble beside Alverna's youth. It was his first love; the first time in his life that he had been roused to throw away caution and dignity. Well! If fate was on him, for once he had lived!

Thus as he struggled with onrushing waves.

They were approaching a point thrust for miles out into the lake, out into rough open water where the canvas boat would never live. They crawled painfully along the point. As they came to the end of it, they looked fearfully beyond.

"We can't make it. I guess we're windbound, all right. We'll have to stay here till the gale goes down," he said despairingly.

But no fears, no regrets, could quench the Olympian delights of eating again—the richness of bacon, the reliability of bannock, the ecstasy of authentic corn out of a can raggedly opened with his sheath-knife.

Alverna had been silent and very industrious in their paddling, and she had made much of humming (only he caught her peeping at him, to see if he was impressed) while she boiled the bannock in the fiery lard. When they lolled back, gorgeously stuffed, she hinted: "But we don't *know* it was Joe he saw."

"No, that's so."

"So let's cheer up. Why, Joe'd *never* find out we'd gone this way! I feel like a fighting kitten, now we've got some grub and our lovely little boat that— Damn the thing!" Her effort at light laughter was excellent. "We'll make the trading-post, and get a real canoe there and another Indian to do the work. And *two* cans of corn! I'm going to swallow 'em both right down, like this—glup! Have you enough money?"

"Yes, I think so. Fierce how the wind keeps up."

"Oh, let's enjoy the rest. You really have enough?"

"Oh, yes!"

"Are you awfully rich?"

"No, I'm— Oh, I make a good living."

"What do you make, Ralph? I haven't got the least idea if you make four thou a year or four hundred thou."

"Well, say about forty."

"Forty—thousand—dollars—a—year! Gee! Well, I hope you've saved it, because when we get to Winnipeg you got to lend me my fare home, and enough to buy a dress and some shoes and stockings. Think of having clean silk stockings again!"

"I fancy we can manage that, and perhaps two pairs."

"Ralph!"

"Eh?"

"Dear! Please!"

"What is it, child?"

"You feel— You were cross because I jollied that aviator. I saw you."

"Oh, of course, you had to try to get him to take us—"

"No. Let's not lie. We haven't been lying, all these days, and gosh, I'm s'prised how I like it! I guess it's about the first time since I vamped the old school prof when I was in the sixth grade! You hated me for pulling the goo-goo eyes on that aviator and— Say, just listen at my 1900 model slang, will you! Don't know *how* I happened to think of that old one! . . . But I mean: You kind of looked sick when I tried to make him. You were wondering if I'd go back to that when we hit the pavements again. Weren't you, dear? *Honest!*"

"Well, a little."

"This'll hand you a surprise. So was I! Oh, I guess I'm an awful fly-paper. It looks like I just couldn't keep my hooks off any he-male that blows into town with the visiting firemen! But I had sort of thought I was off that, these last few days. . . . Oh, Ralph, Ralph dear, what are we going to do?"

"I don't know."

"Make it a double order! Suppose I did get a

divorce. Suppose you did feel you had to marry me—"

" 'Had to!' My God, don't you know how ghastly fond of you—"

"Oh, yes! Fond! But when you get back, when you're a smart lawyer again and awfully busy— Suppose you married me. Oh, I'd study like sixteen college profs, and I'd get so I could talk pussyfoot, but sometime when I'd had two cocktails, I'd bust loose and throw a gosh-awful shock into some of your doggy cousins (and I bet you got 'em by the truckload!) and they'd say, 'That Jane's a vulgar manicure girl, that's what *she* is,' and you'd get the toothache in your social standing. And you'd begin to feel you'd done Joe dirt, and—you'd hate me."

"What does it *matter?* Alverna! Child! But— can't you learn not to flirt? Don't you know—"

"Poor toy soldier! You haven't learned how to say, 'I love you.' Not even yet. I know. And I know— oh, after our starving together, and after I've learned what a real self-starting brain you have, I'll never— I guess I'll never fall for anybody else. But I won't have you ashamed of me. I couldn't stand it, dear. Just because I *do* like you! Hang it!"

She fled from him, along the point. He lay on the sand, his tired head on his arm, trying to think and completely not succeeding.

He was aroused by her shriek, above him: "Ralph! Ralph! I think Joe's coming! Oh, I'm terrified! Maybe it isn't Joe, but—"

He sat up abruptly. He could hear afar the tiny stutter of an engine; he could make out a speck in the lake to northward. Miles away he saw the bow of a canoe lifting to the rollers.

They were still windbound, hopelessly, and there was no use of fleeing along the shore, into the forest. There they would starve, if they were not first burnt to death by the forest fire. Better remain, and die swiftly.

For it came to Ralph that he was this moment in danger of being murdered. He remembered how relentlessly Joe's pale blue eyes had regarded that bounding ass, E. Wesson Woodbury.

He considered shooting Joe first. He could take Alverna's revolver—

No. Aside from the highly probable and ridiculous chance of missing, his whole training had been so conservative that he could not shoot at any man, particularly not at Joe Easter, whom he loved as much as he had injured him.

He felt Alverna rubbing kitten-wise against his arm. He kissed her one last time, and stood quietly, ragged and dirty, very proud and erect, and watched the coming of the unknown canoe.

CHAPTER TWENTY-TWO

THERE was no doubt of it. The gaunt man hunched over the tiller was Joe Easter.

His canoe was leaping half its length out of water with each singing comber, the spray glittering over the bow as it dipped again. When it turned to make a landing and wallowed through the trough, it rolled gunwales under, while the Indian at the bow fought with agitated plunges of his paddle to keep it from capsizing. But Joe rose to his feet as placidly as though he were ashore; he waved to them casually, and with his back to them he shut off the motor.

"I *could* have shot him," reflected Ralph.

The canoe was being swept along the point. Joe sprang into the water, dragged the canoe ashore, and stood considering the ragged forlorn pair, who waited hand in hand. There was no wrath about him; his eyes were expressionless, his lips unmoving; but he did not offer to shake hands; and Joe Easter usually shook hands when he did not shake a fist.

They waited—waited, with that red-granite face looming over them, till Ralph screamed:

"Oh, get it over! Shoot, if you're going to! I can't argue. We've been starving. Go on—shoot! Only let me tell you you did *not* treat her decently! Well, you've won. You've saved her from me."

Joe's eyes widened to mildness, and most mildly he said: "I didn't come to save her. I was aiming to save you!"

"I don't want to be saved!" Ralph was hysterical. "I won't be bullied! And you're not going to bully her any longer!"

"Why, Ralph, I couldn't bully you. I think a lot of you. Except maybe for Pop Buck, I guess I've come to like you better'n anybody I ever met. I was kind of looking forward to us being great friends all our lives. And—"

For the first time his glance particularized Alverna; dwelt on her with a brooding dislike. Then he turned again to Ralph, more warmly:

"I heard from the Indians which way you were heading, and I guessed she'd coaxed you to lug her along with you. I know you're strong on duty. I figured that once you were Outside, in New York, you'd feel you had to stick by her. And then there'd be hell to pay. That's what I been planning to save you from. You'd come to hate her. Oh, I was as bad as most, at first. Made me mad to think of my wife preferring some other fellow to a great noble guy like me. But I've got over that, and— No woman that ever lived is worth giving up a real friendship for. Especially not this girl, Ralph. She's sweet, but she's rotten. She's been going pretty far with Curly Evans, right along."

"That's a lie!" piped Alverna, but it was feeble, and Joe drowned her out:

"How many others, I don't know. But I know about Curly, all right. I hoped she'd come to her senses. I guess she never will. I'm through. But I'm not going to have her spoil your life, too, Ralph. I'm going to take you both to Winnipeg, and put her on the train for Minneapolis, and say good-by to you. Or maybe now you'd rather make another stab at joining your friend Woodbury."

Joe's voice was lifeless, and dreary and lifeless and futile Ralph felt in all this absurdly polite conference, this long-winded return to daily stupidity after the recklessness of his adventure.

He squatted on the sand, Alverna beside him, while Joe squatted facing them, stupidly scratching his chin as he droned, "Yes, you could outfit at the trading-post down here on the lake and go after Woodbury."

"Yes, I could," Ralph muttered. "But he doesn't seem awfully important now. And Alverna does! I think I could do something for her. You see, I thought I might take her to New York. I'm going to have her get an education and learn——"

"Nope; she's made trouble enough. She's going to stay with my aunt in Iowa," Joe asserted listlessly. "Then maybe if she learns to behave herself——"

"Hell!"

It was Alverna screaming. She sprang up, fists clenched.

"I've had enough of both of you! You men think you can dispose of me; you think you can buy and sell me and give me away, as if I were a dog. You could of, once. You can't now! Not after what I've gone through. Ralph! Did I whine once?"

"No."

"Did I lay down? Did I loaf? Was I scared?"

"Never."

"You bet I wasn't! As for you, Joe Easter, you can shoot or you can shut up. Kill me if you want to—I don't care an awful lot—but I'm tired of being a kept woman. You fool! Oh, you ignorant fool! I was just a crazy kid; I was a child. And you wanted me to turn into an old woman, like Ma Mc-Gavity—only better to sleep with. I am not going to stay with your dear aunty! And I am not going back and be a hired manicure girl. I may get a shop of my own. And I may go with Ralph to New York. But I'm going to do my own deciding, now, see?"

Joe began, "You'll do what I tell you—"

"Do I look it?"

Not the temperamental girl of Mantrap Landing, childish in fury, more childish in joy, looked down at them now, but a stern woman, arms akimbo. Her face was tanned black and torn with briars, her hands were hard and grimy, her voice was deadly, and her eyes were full of a scorn that feared nothing.

The two men glanced at each other uneasily, driven together in refuge from her anger.

"Well—I don't know. Gosh, I'm tired! Been traveling pretty hard myself. I— Anyway, I want to keep you from ruining Ralph's life, too." Ralph would never have conceived that Joe could sound so meek. "Let me go with you as far as Whitewater, and we'll talk over what we're all going to do."

"No, you might as well take yourself back to Mantrap—only lend us some of your grub," snarled Alverna. "I'll do all the talking about me that's necessary. Go on, shoot me, if you can't think of anything better."

"But—I haven't anything to go back to Mantrap for now," said Joe.

"How do you mean?"

"The Indians got me. Burned up the place."

"They *what?*"

"Yuh. I was asleep. I woke up and smelled smoke. I hustled out and the roof of the warehouse was blazing like all get-out. Funny the way it lighted up the lake, and the trees—they were brighter than in the sunshine, only the light was kind of on the *under* side of the leaves. Well, I had a lot of powder in there, in the warehouse, and some dynamite. It blew up. Threw a lot of burning timbers on our house and the store. They went like thunder, all but part of the log walls. Furnace. Didn't care so much about the store, but I did kind of hate to see our nice little house go. And I heard the canary begin to sing when the house caught fire, and then it gave an awful screech— I guess it choked on the smoke before the fire roasted it. And after the fire I found your new sewing-machine, Alvy. It was all twisted up, and the wood-work so charred— Everything gone. No insurance. The Indians must of done it, I guess. Maybe they figured these forest fires would hit Mantrap anyway, and nobody ever know what happened. So"—wearily —"that's all."

"But, good Lord," cried Ralph, "why did you come after us, then? Why didn't you stay and try to catch the man that did it?"

"What's the use? Too late now. It's done. Be-sides, Curly was back. He'll look into it. Besides— Oh, I guess I don't blame 'em much. I'd of done about the same thing, if I was an Injun and starving."

"But you're going back and rebuild?"

"No, I can't. My money's gone, after my fur losses. And I'm too much in debt to get any more credit. And after I've run my own show, don't know as I could stand it to stay up here and work for some other fellow that I used to beat at the game. No, I— Oh, I might as well go to Winnipeg and try to get a job there. I'm—honestly, I'm an awful good judge of furs, and I'm a good bookkeeper, and once I get

Alvy and you going right again, I'll just dig in and forget it—"

"Joe!" Alverna had been staring at him, radiant with pity. She dropped on her knees beside him as he sprawled on the sand; she stroked his hair, held his head between her palms.

"I'm going to stay with you! I'll scrub for you— I'll save money—I'll sing—I'll make you happy! I've got a real job now! Darling, I won't let 'em beat you! Old Joe! We'll show 'em! I'm going to stay —Winnipeg or wherever it is—Mantrap Landing or the North Pole!"

He drew away her hands, he held them while he looked at her with tired fondness.

"No. You were right. I'm too old for you, and too cranky, and now I can't even support you decently. You've made a start, Alvy; you're going on. But I'll take you as far as Winnipeg, and I can still raise enough money to run you awhile in Minneapolis while you look around. . . . So, Ralph, you can go look for Woodbury, and I'll take care of the kid."

"Never," from Ralph. "You need me. You're feeling a lot lower than I am. Now"—rather grandiloquently—"we'll all stick together, all three—"

Alverna skyrocketed with laughter:

"Oh, it's swell! Husband comes hiking to beat the band, to catch guilty city-feller and naughty wifie, and then all three sit around and jaw and have a love-feast! Excuse me, but it's getting too funny for me! Men are the talkingest idiots— Oh, and you thought I was a child! I'm the only grown-up in the bunch!"

The men stared at her with solemn disapproval, as she beat her little fists on the sand, shining with laughter.

"Well—gosh—better make camp till the wind goes down. Got any sugar, by the way? We'll have a lot to talk over," sighed Joe.

"Oh, we will! We will! Jiminy, how we'll talk! How men do talk!" whooped Alverna.

CHAPTER TWENTY-THREE

THEY had made camp; they had gorged on bacon; they had discussed Mr. Lawrence Jackfish and his lamentable disappearance.

Then Joe flashed with his one-time power of command: "We'll tend to him. Saul—this Indian I've brought with me—he'll stick. When he goes back to Mantrap, he'll look after it. Lawrence will never guide another party!"

By the fire they discussed, in a silence more prickly with vexatious complications than all their words, what was to become of them. Ralph broke it with:

"Joe, I think Alverna *is* coming with me to New York. I wonder if you know how fond I've become of her. Seems funny to say this to you, but since we've been so frank, I—"

Alverna interrupted pertly:

"I thought I'd kind of pointed out to you two birds that little Alvy has something to say about what's to—"

"Will you shut up! Both of you!"

The apologetic and broken Joe Easter had turned into the savage fighter.

"I'm gone. Ruined. And worse than that, I've done something I'd always swore I never would: I've tried to run other folks' lives. Always said I'd take people just as they are, and not expect Reverend Dillon to be a good conscientious drinker or Curly Evans a lay-reader. But I've tried to make you over into a decent woman, Alvy, and you, Ralph, I've tried to prevent you from making a fool of yourself over this girl. Yes, I've failed. But I couldn't help it. Say, I wonder if you know that all the time you two been talking so smart about 'Go on—shoot me,' I been thinking about doing by God just that?"

In the firelight, in the crimson of the northern afterglow, the barrel of a revolver shone as he held it with a corded hungry hand.

"I thought," he mused, "that I was one fellow that could kind of run his life philosophical. I was a fool. But it isn't fear of being hung that keeps me from killing both of you. It's just— Oh, God, I am so

lonely! I am so licked! Alvy, you've stole all my
friends from me—Pop, Curly, now Ralph. You've
made them all sneaks. And you've stole yourself from
me. And now you've made me realize that possibly
you do have some brains in your pretty fool head, so I
can't bully you any more. Only I am still going to do
a little dictating! I want to see what kind of guts there
are in Mr. Ralph Prescott!

"You or me, Alvy, one of us is going to New York
with him. He could find me a good job there—say
in some big fur business, or camping-goods or something. Or else you're going with him, and I'll just
disappear. I know that— A fellow learns a lot of
this fancy stuff that Ralph calls psychology when he
spends a few winters shut up in a cabin with just one
other guy, trapping. I know Ralph thinks I'm about
as good a friend, some ways, as he ever hit. He
thinks my table-manners are lousy, but I guess he'd
like to drop into my furnished room in New York
some evening, my hall-bedroom I guess it'd be, and
talk real he-talk, when he was tired of his Sassiety
friends. And he's going to choose—and right now!
—between sticking by me and sticking by you. Ralph,
which'll it be?"

Ralph looked from Joe's weathered face, real as a
storm, to Alverna's pretty lips—real as a skylark.
And there was no choice. There could be no choice.

But Alverna took that moment to toss back her

pale bright hair, with her old flirtatious gesture, and to giggle airily:

"Well, I'll just do the choosing! If dear old Ralphy or anybody else thinks I'm sitting around waiting to be told—"

"*Shut up, will you!*"

Both men had spoken at once, and both had spoken with the same intimidating harshness. Before their joint impatience she faltered and was still.

From all the risk and uncertainty of these mad improbable days, Ralph was suddenly delivered. It may be that he became sensible, it may be that he sank again into the cowardice of his old sheltered life. Certainly he fled from the turmoil of Alverna's allurement, and gratefully regained the security of Joe Easter's companionship.

"Would you really like to go to New York, Joe?"

"Yes. Sure."

Still more was the mild but sagacious Mr. Prescott returning to existence. After weeks of numbed distress and uselessness, his brain was clicking as once it had clicked over legal problems.

Yes, it would be pleasant to have Joe Easter somewhere about—oh, not make him miserable by having him in for dinners when there were supercilious golden women, with their pretty urgent trivialities, but have him as companion for long Sunday tramps on Staten Island, when they would remember how

virile and extraordinary they had once been in the romantic Far North—

"We could find something worth while for you,
Joe. For instance, Fulton & Hutchinson, where I got
my camping-kit—they always need sporting experts, I
fancy. And I have a friend who has a big fur-dealer
for client, and a chap that imports from Siberia and
North China. You know—sables. Surely. We'd find
something. Will you come?"

"All right," said Joe.

Alverna rose, slowly.

"So I'm out of it," she murmured. "The woman
gets about her usual deal. And you two birds—" She
made her voice defiantly gay. "Well, you can both
go to the devil!"

Quietly she huddled her blankets about her and
went, it seemed, to sleep. Ralph heard her sobbing
later.

CHAPTER TWENTY-FOUR

RALPH was conscious, in the night, that the wind
had shifted. It blew gustily under the edge of
his blankets, though at retiring it had merely ruffled
his hair. He was conscious, too, that the ceaseless
odor of smoke was stronger, but he was too fagged
to awaken completely.

Then Joe was twitching at his shoulder. He saw that in the vacuous last darkness Joe and Alverna and Saul, the Indian, were standing between him and the wan lake, and Joe was growling: "Get up. Quick! Forest fire headed this way."

The air was full of a subdued yet giant roaring; and all the sky to eastward was glowing with muddy crimson, surging with clouds of black smoke.

"Hustle!" Joe ordered them. "Get everything aboard!"

They fled to the pile of food; they pantingly rolled up blankets and chucked them into Joe's canoe. Now, burning branches were falling about them and hissing in the lake. The fire was nearer; they could see it as a curtain against which tall black pines were etched. In the creeping glare, Joe was a wild-haired maniac as he seized boxes, dumped them into the canoe. Saul was green with fear, and Alverna was an insane gypsy, her white throat blood-red.

"Ralph! You get in the canoe with Alverna," Joe shouted. "Saul can run the motor. He'll tow me, in your canvas boat."

Alverna whispered to Ralph in awe, "He's trying to get himself killed—for us!"

There was no self—though perhaps there was no great heroism—in the shaky voice with which Ralph urged: "No, you go in the canoe, Joe. I'm lighter. Waves are still high and—" It took an agonized wrench to say it; the waves *were* high, and he did not vastly care for them. "Canvas boat likely to swamp—"

Joe was running him toward the canoe, with cruel steel fingers at the back of his neck; Joe was bellowing: "Have I got to argue about *everything?* Do as I tell you, will yuh?"

Ralph was in the canoe, at the bow, which sickeningly rose to the abrupt waves. Alverna was behind him, and Saul was trying to start the motor, while Joe made fast the towrope to the folding boat and pushed the canoe out from shore. Then Ralph was too grimly dipping his paddle, urging the canoe away from that horror of thundering flame, to think of anything else in the world. He scarce knew when the motor started. He paddled as though the motor were not running, as though he alone could save them, while each second the lake was a more terrifying debauch of reflected flame.

Half a mile out, Saul stopped the motor. They looked back. The shore-line was a furnace, to the end of the point. As the blaze reached from bluff to bluff, sometimes fantastically skipping a hundred yards, the dry pines did not so much catch fire as explode like kindled celluloid, hurling up embers.

The fire traveled quickly. At dawn, though the mossy ground still smoldered, the curtain of flame was gone. But what had been a placid bank of green was now a stretch of tragic black skeletons of trees.

Just when Alverna had crawled forward in the canoe and piteously taken his hand, Ralph did not remember, but there she was, small and dirty-faced and dear.

He heard Joe call from the folding boat:

"That's over. Let's go ashore and boil the kettle." And Joe stood up, on the edge of the shallow boat—rather riskily, Ralph thought. With the greatest deliberation, so slowly that Ralph could not believe it, the boat turned over, and Joe disappeared in the waves.

They saw him go under. When he came up, snorting the water out of his nostrils, shaking his tousled head, he was thirty feet away. Had he been swimming under water? He went down again, came up, headed for the canoe, and seized the gunwale.

As Ralph and Alverna reached over to haul him aboard, he spoke:

"Just a minute. Ralph, here's a funny thing—what a fool a fellow can be! I'll bet this'll give you a laugh! I didn't mean to come up again, now I've helped get you out of the fire. Thought I could clear the way for you. Thought I could stay under water. But it hurt my nose"—pathetically—"and the water was so doggone cold! I'm a failure again—failure in everything. But I can still do it. If you want me to come aboard, you got to say so. Here's your chance to get rid of me!"

His head, raised just above the bobbing of the gunwale, out in that surly stretch of lake, was the gnawed and dripping head of a drowned man, and the eyes that once had blazed with such dry and incorruptible blue flame were red now and a little mad.

"Have I done this thing to this good man?" Ralph agonized. "Have I let him welcome me into his life and then hurt him like this? How I hate myself—and how I love her!"

Even as he meditated, he was raging aloud, "Joe, if you drown, I'll jump in after you—"

Alverna cut through the tragedy with a cool swift humanness: "Joe Easter, you quit being a chump! Crawl in here now, will you, or you'll catch your deathacold. Oh, shut *up!* And you too, Ralph. Here, give him a hand. Catch your foot up over the edge, Joe, *will* you!"

And, as Joe came meekly aboard: "Here's a pretty goings-on! Don't sit on that flour, Joe; you'll get it soaked. Put this blanket around you. Do what I *tell* you! Now you listen to me, you two brats! . . . Gaw, what babies all men are! Wanting to be heroes or some fool thing! . . . This is all the talking we're going to do. From here to Winnipeg we talk about the crops. And that ends it, see?"

They did talk of the crops—a hesitating Joe and a humble Ralph. But it was not the end.

CHAPTER TWENTY-FIVE

THE three who waited in the station at Winnipeg for the Minneapolis train had little resemblance to the charcoal-burners who had come staggering into the amazed settlement of Whitewater. Ralph was smug now in gray flannels and rather a neat thing in the way of a blue and white shirt. (He was a man who could always be fitted in ready-mades.) Joe Easter was shaggier, but all his wildness was gone in respectable brown garments which his wife had, without giving him a voice, chosen for him. And Alverna had—

She was a manicure girl, hard and glittering, too bright of cheek and much too bright of voice.

During their ten minutes of waiting they strove strenuously to avoid sincerity of speech. They scrambled for something jolly and interesting to say about the station and the passengers and the weather.

When the train was made up, Alverna mocked them in the voice of a parrot:

"Now don't let me keep you boys any longer. The red-cap will get my stuff aboard."

She gave a hand to each. They mooned at her like schoolboys.

"Gosh, better let us see you on the train," quacked Joe; and "Oh, we must take you to the sleeper!" said

Ralph; and there was not a pennyworth to choose between them for abashed awkwardness.

"All right, dearies. Gee, you certainly cheer me up a lot!" she said; and muffle-footed they followed her and her attendant luggage-carrier down the platform to the sleeping-car. Stupid-eyed, they watched her as she snappishly showed her coupon to the Pullman porter.

She stood staring at them.

"Good-by," she said.

Then, as the bemused males, sloths in a slothful nightmare, slowly moving and slowly rising to wretchedness, slowly revolving the matter of farewell kisses, opened their mouths to produce suitable sentiments, she turned human again for one instant:

"You poor kids! You talking children, that don't know anything about anything that matters! Don't you see? I can't play either of your games. I'm *me!* I'm going to be me! Oh, if you do love me a little, let me be me! Good-by. No! *Please!* Don't come in the car with me!"

They stood on the platform, gawping through the window at her as she settled in the tiny home of her Pullman seat. They saw her taking off her hat and daintily—too daintily, too airily—tucking it into the paper bag supplied by the admiring porter. They saw her fluffing back her hair with the familiar toss of her white wrists, her frail and shining hands. They saw her attentively observing her face in a pocket mirror and powdering her nose. And not once did she look out to find them.

"I can't stand it!" growled Joe.

"Neither can I," said Ralph.

And the two men prowled toward the end of the platform, hands in pockets, not glancing at each other, apparently uninterested in each other, yet closer bound by their common love for a flighty and worthless and altogether gallant wench than they could ever have been by facing death together.

They were standing at the end of the platform, trying to look as though they were looking intelligently at a pile of beams and rails, when the Minneapolis train started, gained speed, and passed them. Then they saw that Alverna was no longer airily making her toilet but sitting with her head bowed in trembling hands.

"Have men and women always got to hurt each other this way?" cried Ralph.

"Yes. Anybody that ain't content with being a peddler is going to hurt himself and everybody else, I guess," said Joe. "And now, Ralph—look here. We've been turned upside-down by things bigger than we are—enemies that sneak by night, friends we couldn't trust, fire and storm, and a woman. But now you go back and be a real fellow again, and I'll stay here and earn my living. You don't want to

drag me along to New York. Your being willing to
get me a job there is real nice, but I cussed you into
thinking of taking me, and of course it's all bunk. I
mean it. Hell, Ralph, I don't entirely blame you for
falling in love with Alvy. I did myself! But it's all
over, and now it's time for you to go back where you
belong, and forget me."

"But, Joe— Yes, you did suggest it first, my
starting you off in New York, but you were dead
right. Look here."

For Ralph to complete his proof that it would be
Joe's ultimate happiness to accompany him to New
York took two hours, during which (while the Minneapolis train clicked on the rails) they wandered
through Winnipeg and discovered a totally illegal
public house at which they had excellent Scotch.

Now that he was among city streets again, Ralph
was triumphant. He discovered that, to Joe, cities
and the roar thereof were more dismaying than any
rapids. In proportion as he waxed metropolitan and
eloquent, Joe grew meek; and as Joe had been his
lordly guide at Mantrap, so was he lordly in plans for
their joint future in New York. It may have been
the rediscovery of loyal friendship, it may have been
the loneliness that was inherent in the very air after
Alverna's going, and it may have been merely the
Scotch, but certainly he found himself outlining a
Manhattan future in which Joe and he would, at

considerable profit and enormous enjoyment, found a sports-shop of their own.

So in great discussion and amity they came to the hotel.

They had arrived from Whitewater in the morning, just in time to buy clothes. Ralph had not seen the hotel; he had merely sent his clothes there from the shops.

"Say, Ralph, you stay here, but I better go down to the Nipigon House, where I always stay," sighed Joe. "Gee, this place is too swell for me. Looks like a cathedral. *And* too expensive!"

"You're going to be my guest here, as I was yours at Mantrap," said Ralph, brightly, snappily, efficiently. "Honestly, Joe, I have plenty of cash—and right with me—travelers' checks. Listen, Joe: won't you give me the pleasure of entertaining you?"

"Well, all right, if you sure-enough want to."

The corridor of the hotel was a Gothic graystone aisle, with tall brocade chairs adorned with the royal arms and occupied by cynical flappers waiting for handsome men. Ralph strode the corridor haughtily. . . . He did not know it, but he was mutely saying to hovering bellboy and cynical flapper and handsome suitor, "I am not the greasy and tattered hobo who arrived in town this morning, but Mr. Ralph Prescott of the Yale Club, New York!"

His heels clicked aggressively on the shiny stone

pavement. But Joe Easter's footsteps were shuffling and afraid.

As he came to the long marble desk to register, Ralph heard:

"Well, Prescott! For heaven's sake! What are you doing out here?"

It was a robust and caviar-fed voice. Ralph peered at the owner of it, and discovered one James Worthington Virey, vice-president of the Dorcas Fidelity and Trust Company, of New York, and fellow-member of the Buckingham Moors Country Club.

They said, "Well, well!" They said, "Well, isn't this amazing!" Ralph modestly admitted that he had been doing rather heroic things in the perilous northern wilds. Mr. Virey let it be known that he was looking into a million-dollar estate of which his firm was executor.

Meanwhile Joe stood behind them, uncomfortably resting his weight now on one foot, now on the other.

Virey insisted: "Prescott, if you've just come to town—I do wish you'd do something for me. I have to go to a party here this evening—Scotch and bond-talk, I should think. I don't really know a soul who'll be there except for meeting them at business lunches—that sort of thing. Do come with me. I'll telephone the host and have him invite you."

"I—"

Ralph came to a full stop.

"I," he said, "am here with my friend Mr. Easter—head of the Easter Trading Company, you know. . . . Mr. Virey, Mr. Easter. . . . It would be very nice to go, after all these weeks in the wilds, but— If you think they might care to invite Mr. Easter, too—"

All the while he was chirping, Ralph was wretchedly conscious that he was lying; that there was no longer any Easter Trading Company; that in its heyday it had been but three log cabins; and that he was ashamed to say: "I am a poor weakling, by undeserved good fortune delivered from hell; and this is my friend Joe, a crude fellow who chews tobacco and believes in Dickens and who is altogether more gallant than you or I can ever be; and I'll see you farther before I'll go to a twittering party tonight."

But he heard Mr. Virey elaborately saluting the great Joseph Easter, president of the Easter Trading Company; he heard Joe muttering, "Pleased meetch." He registered for himself and Joe, and with acerbity demanded a suite of two bedrooms, two baths, and a sitting-room. He heard Mr. Virey chanting that indeed he would call up his host and discover whether his enchanting friends Mr. Prescott and Mr. Easter would be altogether welcome at the party; and that, so soon as he should have done so, he would inform Mr. Prescott.

They all did a great deal of cool but polite hand-shaking; and Ralph and Joe found themselves in their suite.

There was a bright, intimate little sitting-room with chintz armchairs, a magenta-shaded light on the table, a buffet with Montreal-Venetian cocktail glasses, and etchings on tapestry wall-paper. In the two bedrooms were blue silk comforters, very pleasant. And the bathrooms were of marble and nickel and tile.

Joe wandered through the suite. He stared at the etchings. With a shy red stubby finger he touched a silver and pale green table runner. He patted the springy beds, like a good housewife renting an apartment. But it was the glass and nickel enclosure of the shower-bath which made him halt.

He stood before it like a farmer in a Paris dressmaker's shop.

"Gosh, can you beat it, Ralph! Say, I wouldn't never dast strip down to my old hide and take a bath in that glass closet. Somebody might come in and snicker at me! And with that long looking-glass on the door— I must be getting modest! And the parlor with all those little lights and silk shades like shimmy-shirts— Ralph, there's no place where you can *spit* here! You better let me hoof it back to the Nipigon House."

"You'll get used to it in two days. Why, in a week you'll be kicking because the towels are too small."

Ralph unfolded a six-foot Turkish splendor.

Joe stared at it with dropping jaw. "That—a towel? I thought it was a carpet!" He touched it. "Say, a fellow could dry himself on that for two years! No sir, I just couldn't do it—I couldn't get it all dirty. I've done too much clothes-washing myself. Nope. It's too rich for me. And look, Ralph: I don't want to butt in on your party tonight. I'd just disgrace you. You go ahead and forget me. I'll chase myself out to a movie."

"Nonsense. Tell 'em some stories about the North. You'll give 'em a tremendous thrill. You'll be the hit of the evening."

Mr. James Worthington Virey arrived just then. Yes, indeed; oh, rather; his host for the evening, one Colonel Ackers, insisted that Mr. Prescott and Mr. Easter should come. A simple little gathering, with perhaps a drink. Colonel Ackers wanted to hear about their northern trip, about the forest fires, about the Indians' credit.

"We have no evening clothes with us," hinted Ralph.

"Doesn't matter. . . . And you'll come, Easter? Colonel Ackers will be horribly disappointed if you don't."

Thus besought, Joe could not refuse. But when Virey was gone he viewed his brown suit gloomily in the long mirror; he tried to turn his shock of gray-shot rusty hair into the sleekness of a movie actor by soaking it with water and assaulting it with a hair-brush till he grunted with the pain; and most pain-fully did he pare and scrape his nails with an enormous jackknife, despite the training of the manicure girl, Alverna.

It was with apprehension that he followed Ralph to the vast dining-room.

After weeks of squatting over a tin plate of bacon, Ralph frankly enjoyed the magnificence of the dining-room: the arched Caen-stone ceiling, the tapestries hung between cathedral windows, the gold and crimson chairs which would have been proper thrones for Spanish archbishops. But as he marched after the head-waiter, enjoying the cheap triumph of being recognized as probably a good patron, he glanced back at Joe and found him moving in agonized awe, rigidly keeping himself from looking at the pretty women while he risked the league-long passage to their table.

Joe permitted himself to be inserted into a chair by the head-waiter. Ralph saw that his forehead was shining wet. Joe held the menu off at arm's length and peered at its serried display incredulously. Some one at the next table tittered. Hastily Joe laid the menu down, thrust both hands into his trousers pockets, snatched them out again, dropped them on the table, then hid their red chunkiness in his lap.

"Find something you like, Joe? Or shall I order for you?"

"I guess—I guess maybe I'd like some bacon," said Joe wistfully.

"Haven't you had enough of it in the North?"

"Ye-eh—"

For a moment the head-waiter turned his head away, and Joe seized the second of safety to whisper: "That's the only human food I can see on the bill of fare! For Pete's sake, you order for me. Ralph, I can't do it! Too rich for me!"

"You wait. Why, man, you're just the person that *ought* to stay here, that *ought* to see New York. You'll have so much novelty out of it, once you get over being awed—"

"Yuh, plenty of novelty, but meantime I'll starve! Think I'd ever face this place alone? Only time I ever did go into a big hotel dining-room was with Alverna, like I told you about."

"It's going to be my business, old man, to see that you have the fun of beating the big cities. I'm making plans. Ten years from now you'll be a partner in Fulton & Hutchinson. And now let me order. Let's see if I can do as well as Alverna."

Ralph was tempted by terrapin soup, by squab in casserole, by mushrooms under glass, but he ordered, in a lively hope of convincing Joe that the environment of the rich was not without delights, a noble pea soup, steak with a whole harem of vegetables, and an ice like a puzzle.

They fell silent. Joe's mention of Alverna had brought her back. (Was she dining alone now on the train? *Was* she dining alone?) Here, in this jungle of velvet and cut-glass, he felt the clear quiet days on lake and barren foreshore; he ached for her smutted cheeks, her gayly cocked eye, her loud and joyous laugh.

He peered at Joe, and suddenly: "Hang it," he sighed, "I believe we're both lonely for her!"

"Yes. I am. I always will be. But for her sake, Ralph—me because I'm too poor and you because you're too rich—we got to stay away from her."

"Yes. Probably. Then— Joe, we must try to make something big and enduring out of friendship. You know, I probably need you growling at me, to keep from falling back into being a busy little lawyer."

"You don't need anybody."

"Anyway, you are coming to New York."

"Well— But let me warn you that I'm going to hunt me up a hash house, with sawdust on the floor and a waiter that wears sleeve-garters and no collar, and once a day I'm going in there and spit on the floor and holler, 'Hey, bring me some ham and beans and be damn' quick about it or I'll knock your block off!' Then—maybe—I can last through. Golly! What a steak!"

Ralph's cunning was successful. The sight of that lordly beef, decorated with peas, carrots, gaufrette potatoes, and crisp fried onions, gave Joe a new and in-

teresting prospect of the possibilities of life; and when
James Worthington Virey picked them up, at nine,
Joe was apparently convinced that New York might be
something besides an ambuscade of pretty women and
lofty waiters, all laughing at him.

Mr. Virey had acquired, by means unchronicled, a
temporary limousine. Joe settled into the upholstery,
gently patting a stomach glowing with beautiful food,
and beamed on the world. He looked almost idiotically
content. Ralph wondered, with slight alarm, if he
had had too much to drink, for Virey had produced a
bottle of Scotch in their suite. But he could remember Joe's taking only one mild whisky-soda; and he forgot his alarm as Virey chattered:

"Oh, by the way; forgot to tell you. You went
North with a fellow named Woodbury—member of
our country club—didn't you?"

"Yes."

"Did you two—um—uh—did you break up?"

"Yes, and I don't know but what I feel a little guilty
about it. I thought Woodbury was too talkative, in
fact I couldn't stand being with him any more; but I'm
not sure it wasn't a rotten thing to leave him."

"I understand. Personally, I've always regarded
him as a loud-mouthed charlatan. I was surprised
when you went with him, and I'm not surprised that
you left him. But here's the funny thing: He came
through Winnipeg the other day. I ran into him at

the hotel. He volunteered that *he* had chucked *you,*
deserted you, because you were so highbrow that he
was bored! He sounded fishy. Never did like him.
By the way, Prescott—you said Easter and you were
going to New York. I wonder if we couldn't go together. I'll have to leave tomorrow evening."

"Splendid! Let's," said Ralph.

He was exultant. Alverna would do something
vague, but admirable and enjoyable and highly cultural
in Minneapolis. He would make Joe a commercial
success in New York. Sometime, parentally and
philanthropically, he would reunite the transformed
Alverna to the gilded Joe. They would be his friends.
He would be godfather, uncle, and general benefactor
to their children. And now Woodbury had, by his
lying, excused Ralph's desertion.

Everything was beautifully straight and clear and
satisfactory.

So he came, full of nobility and lyrics, to the abode
of Colonel Ackers.

The Colonel was something in wheat, something in
railroads, something in banks, and he had built a residence roughly the size of Windsor Castle and considerably more modern. It had three drawing-rooms, a
library with several books, and a pipe-organ said by
the Chamber of Commerce guide-book to be the largest organ north of St. Louis.

The party was rather mild. Several industrious

couples danced to the radio, and a number of men applied themselves to a library table set forth with Scotch, gin, Grand Marnier, and Napoleon IV brandy. But mostly the party consisted of solid-bottomed men who stood before a fireplace adorned with elk heads, bear heads, mountain-goat heads, and stuffed fish, and discussed the rust in the wheat crop.

They made much of Joe Easter. They asked his opinion of Mantrap River muskalonge and the quality of muskrat hides.

Joe had entered rather shyly, craning up at the electrolier in the hallway and the cherubs which frothed along the ceiling. He merely gaped at the footman who held out a languid hand for his hat, and gave up that garment of virility with reluctance. When he was introduced to the golden hostess, to her silver daughter and a confusing host of other precious and metallic ladies, he sweated perceptibly, and he muttered, imperceptibly, "Pleased meet you—I didn't quite catch the name."

"It's going to be a job to teach him to be easy with strangers," reflected Ralph. "God, I am so lonely for Alverna! I should never have given her up—"

But Joe, when he was surrounded by men who, however portly with banking and the law, were yet conceivable as amateur fishermen, was only too easy. Ralph watched uncomfortably while he told hunting stories. Joe's voice became louder; more and more the damn's rollicked into his tales; and they were good lusty damn's, which could be heard in the room given over to dancing.

And once Joe backslapped a fidgety little millionaire with eyeglasses on a silk ribbon. That was before he began to drink.

Pendulum-like, Joe visited the whisky table, and while Ralph loyally kept away from him, loyally sat in the shade and tried not to spy, he could see that Joe was holding up the whisky bottle a long time whenever he poured a drink for himself.

The effect was dismaying.

Joe told of the missionary into whose church entered a bear, and that was a story delightful in bachelor log cabins but unexpected before the mahogany fireplace of Colonel Henry Tudor Ackers, with flappers listening from the doorway. He called the fidgety and silk-ribboned millionaire by his first name. And he offered to dance a Highland fling.

He made the offer after every drink, and he desisted only when Colonel Ackers said sharply, "I don't think you better, my friend."

All the while, Ralph perceived that Virey, who was responsible for their coming, was looking appealing. But he insisted to himself: "Oh, let 'em all go hang! If they don't appreciate Joe, they're fools. Even if he is lit, he's worth ten thousand of these fat money-grubbers. . . . Only I don't suppose I'd care much

for it if he acted like this some evening when I had
Conny and Dick and Mrs. Sandal at the flat. . . .
Curse it all! . . . I am so lonely for her!"

It was not till Ackers shot out his rebuke about the
Highland fling that Ralph took Joe aside and begged:
"Careful, old man. You're getting a little edged.
They might—uh—misjudge you. I don't believe I'd
tell all those stories, not with the ladies right in the
next room."

Joe looked at him dully, and grumbled: "Ah, t' hell
with 'em! I didn't wanna come. Now I—now I—
now got here, going have goo' time. Bunch of angle-
worms."

Virey indicated to Ralph, with a tilt of his head, that
they might well take leave, and with loud false cheerfulness Ralph announced to Colonel Ackers: "Afraid
we must be going. We had such a long train trip."

"I do' wanna go home!" protested Joe.

With shame burning him, with all the human owls
gloating over them, Ralph piped: "Oh, you must, Joe.
I'm so tired. Just dead tired!"

Joe came meekly enough. The only unfortunate in-
cident on the way out was that, as he shook hands
with their hostess, Joe stumbled a little and roared:
"G' night, Mrs. Ackerstein. Had hell of a good time!"

And the family Ackers were prominent enough in
Winnipeg, and Joe had been coming to Winnipeg long
enough, so that he should have known the name.

There were numerous and violent currents of thought in the limousine on their way home, but a total lack of words.

Joe got himself through the door of their suite, stupidly pawing at the door-handle, falling over the chairs inside, feeling his way along the wall, dropping fully dressed on his bed, and immediately snoring in his blind drunkenness. Ralph tried to lift himself to such heights as to help Joe undress and get him into the shower-bath, but he could not. He was so tired— so tired.

For hours Ralph tramped the floor of his bedroom, and the course of a fly circling in a hot room would have been more direct than a chart of his thoughts.

For all that he had been a lawyer dealing with every conflict and confusing shade of ethics, his own standards of conduct had been simple enough. A man was either a Good Fellow or a Rotter. A man did not make love to his friends' wives. A man did not, simply could not, be a stanch and dependable chap and still, after a few drinks, sink into smut and raucousness. And now—

He had admired Joe's integrity as greater than that of any man he had ever encountered. He had given him an unspoken pledge of loyalty. He had fled from what might have been healing peace to avoid making love to Joe's wife.

And he had taken Joe's wife with him on that flight!

And Joe—one to shoot first and talk afterward—had feebly talked first and failed to shoot at all; he had saved both their lives from starvation, perhaps from forest fire; and, by some twisted process not at all in accord with the straight cleavage of human motives to be found in the books, had given his friendship in exchange for his wife! And finally, after betraying himself as a hero in private, he had betrayed himself socially as a bumptious fool.

Ralph held his head; all the sterling principles which, he believed, had guided him through the complexities of New York, had been found shaky and meaningless in a log cabin, a foodless camp, a profiteer's drawing-room.

But whatever his confusion he held stubbornly to his plan that Joe should come with him to New York and find there, now that all his life of Mantrap Landing was broken and all his joy in Alverna ended, a new and solacing world.

"My friends have always done the right thing—and the uninteresting thing. Poor Joe! No wonder he was upset by that movie-lobby house tonight. I'll make up to him for Alverna.

"Only who's going to make up to me for Alverna?

"And if Joe wouldn't get drunk and make a fool of himself!

"So lonely for her, always—"

CHAPTER TWENTY-SIX

WHEN Ralph awoke, very late, he found Joe (slightly comic in new lavender pajamas) steadily smoking, and staring at him.

"Afraid I was kind of stewed, last night," said Joe.

"You were!"

"Too darn' bad. But you better get used to it, if I'm coming to New York. Only— Say, Ralph, no matter what I do, you got to remember that I've liked you a lot, a whale of a lot, and I've always made a stab at trying to treat people that I'm fond of—you or Alvy or Pop Buck or anybody—the way I think they'll like it best in the long run, not the way that shows off best in the store-window."

Before Ralph, a bit testy in want of morning coffee, could frame something neat to the effect that in the long run he would prefer Joe not to get drunk in public, the villain of the piece had paddled out of the room, on his raw red bare feet, and was to be heard screaming under his cold shower.

They were starting for New York that evening, with James Worthington Virey. The evening before, Ralph had telephoned to Virey, with apologies, and Virey had consented to giving Joe one more chance.

All day they drifted about Winnipeg. Joe refused to let Ralph further fill out his wardrobe, but he gave

to all of Ralph's remarks the meek interest of re-
pentance.

Once or twice Joe tried to hint that it would perhaps
be better if he did not go to New York. Ralph, determined to benefit Joe and to benefit him right, made
it clear that he would stay right here in Winnipeg till
Joe did consent to go. Thus at last he conquered.

In the afternoon, Joe insisted on taking all their
luggage to the train.

"No need of that. Bring our bags along with us in
the taxi."

"Well, I want to be sure everything will be aboard
when we get there," said Joe, and, nettled by this unexpected fussiness, Ralph snapped, "Oh, all right."

The train left at nine in the evening. Ralph and
Joe and Virey had a rather sulky dinner at the hotel,
and rather sulkily they drove to the train.

Joe had not only taken the baggage to the station
but, explaining that he distrusted the hotel porter, ob-
tained their Pullman accommodations: a compartment
for Ralph and Virey, a berth for himself. Aboard
the train, Ralph found his new suitcase safely stowed
in the compartment.

"Your berth all right? Your stuff there, Joe?" he
inquired.

"Sure, you bet."

"All right, let's all settle down comfortably here in
the compartment and perhaps have a game of cards."

"I want a little fresh air. Let's walk up and down till we start," complained Joe.

"Not for me. I stay put," said Virey.

It was because he was so irritated that he could not trust himself to discuss it that Ralph morosely followed Joe out of the Pullman, along the platform.

And Joe had the most inane things to say:

"Well, gosh, I hope you enjoyed some features about being in the North, Ralph."

"Certainly. Why not!"

"And I hope you'll forgive me for pinching Alvy off you."

"Don't be silly. Naturally, it was your right—"

"I don't know as I know much about what's right and what's wrong. But— Say, that first meal we had at Mantrap tasted pretty good, after being out on the trail, didn't it! Pretty good. Not that it was so much, I mean, but you know, after chawing bacon and so on— Eh, pretty good, eh?"

Ralph had no answer to these asinine recollections. He was dismally thinking of New York and of Joe's doubtful place there.

"All aboooooard!" sang the trainmen.

Joe motioned to Ralph to go first, and Ralph mechanically clumped up the car steps.

Suddenly the dull-eyed, drooping-shouldered, drawling Joe, with his observations about the joys of eating tomatoes, straightened up. His eyes were bright, his voice miserable yet alive:

"Just forget us! We'll pull through. You're free of us now. Keep free. Good luck, you old cuss!"

Ralph stared down from the vestibule as the train creaked into motion. Did Joe mean that he was not going—

He started to climb down the steps. The Pullman porter rudely dragged him back into the vestibule and slammed the door between him and the steps. And the train was really in motion. Joe was down on the platform, trotting beside them, waving his hat.

Having closed the door, the porter had darted away. Ralph leaped into the adjoining vestibule. That door was closed as well, and how to open it he had no notion. He ran violently through the next Pullman, startling the old ladies who were peeping into their straw suitcases, and found a door still open. He leaned out, holding by the steel door-jamb. But the train was going too fast for him to leap, and he saw Joe plodding along the station platform, his back turned—the dejected back of an old and hopeless man who in his day has borne great burdens without reward.

Utterly puzzled, wondering whether Joe had managed to get drunk again and conceal it till now, Ralph poked back to his compartment, to take counsel with Virey.

He encountered his Pullman porter, who besought: "Excuse me for slamming the door that way. The gentleman on the platform, he made me promise I wouldn't let you leave the train."

Ralph was too confused to answer. To Virey he worried: "Can't understand it. Joe wouldn't get on the train."

"Curious fellow," said Virey. "By the way, he asked me to give you this note after we started."

Ralph read, in Joe's neat storekeeper's hand:

"Friend Ralph: I don't seem to be able to persuade you am not a good person to take along no matter what I do & disgrace you etc. Am afraid you might persuade me to go, guess am not a very strong character and you're a great old persuader. So will just avoid argument, it might get us both sore & would not like that. Maybe I will be a little lonely but do not worry am a great hand at picking up friends. Come back to Canada some time. Good luck & God bless you. *God bless you!*   JOE."

While Ralph tapped his fingers on the note, in perplexity, Virey repeated, "Yes, a curious fellow."

"He certainly is. I don't get him at all," mused Ralph. "He's always been a man of some dignity and restraint. Yet the way he acted last evening— Why, it almost made me not want to take him to New York. But"—proudly—"I stuck by my resolution. But I can't understand how he could possibly have got so drunk."

"I wonder if he did"

"Didn't you see him—hear him!"

"Yes, but I sat farther down the room than you did, nearer the table with the booze. Did you notice what he did with the whisky bottle?"

"I certainly did! He poured out half a tumblerful, every drink!"

"Wasn't his back to you?"

"Yes, but I could see his arm."

"I could see his hand. The bottles, you may remember, were the non-refillable kind, with tiny little mouths. I noticed that Easter would first pour a lot of ginger ale into his glass, then take the whisky bottle —but he kept his finger over the mouth of the bottle all the time. I don't think he took one drop of liquor; I don't think he drank anything stronger than ginger ale, the whole evening. I wonder what he was up to, anyway. Maybe trying to persuade you that he was drunk or—"

"And this train," Ralph said savagely, "doesn't stop for miles, and then I'll be too confoundedly sane, after talking to *you,* to jump out and go back. . . . Just this second I've realized I'd been planning to go to Minneapolis—to see a girl. Now I never can. . . . I feel a little tired, Virey. Let's not talk. Shall we play some cards? . . . But the dear Lord help Wes Woodbury when he opens up on me!"

THE END

There's More to Follow!

More stories of the sort you like; more, probably, by the author of this one; more than 500 titles all told by writers of world-wide reputation, in the Authors' Alphabetical List which you will find on the *reverse side* of the wrapper of this book. Look it over before you lay it aside. There are books here you are sure to want—some, possibly, that you have *always* wanted.

It is a *selected* list; every book in it has achieved a certain measure of *success*.

The Grosset & Dunlap list is not only the greatest Index of Good Fiction available, it represents in addition a generally accepted Standard of Value. It will pay you to

Look on the Other Side of the Wrapper!

In case the wrapper is lost write to the publishers for a complete catalog

THE NOVELS OF TEMPLE BAILEY

May be had wherever books are sold.   Ask for Grosset & Dunlap's list.

THE BLUE WINDOW

The heroine, Hildegarde, finds herself transplanted from the middle western farm to the gay social whirl of the East.   She is almost swept off her feet, but in the end she proves true blue.

PEACOCK FEATHERS

The eternal conflict between wealth and love.   Jerry, the idealist who is poor, loves Mimi, a beautiful, spoiled society girl.

THE DIM LANTERN

The romance of little Jane Barnes who is loved by two men.

THE GAY COCKADE

Unusual short stories where Miss Bailey shows her keen knowledge of character and environment, and how romance comes to different people.

THE TRUMPETER SWAN

Randy Paine comes back from France to the monotony of every-day affairs.   But the girl he loves shows him the beauty in the common place.

THE TIN SOLDIER

A man who wishes to serve his country, but is bound by a tie he cannot in honor break—that's Derry.   A girl who loves him, shares his humiliation and helps him to win—that's Jean.   Their love is the story.

MISTRESS ANNE

A girl in Maryland teaches school, and believes that work is worthy service.   Two men come to the little community; one is weak, the other strong, and both need Anne.

CONTRARY MARY

An old-fashioned love story that is nevertheless modern.

GLORY OF YOUTH

A novel that deals with a question, old and yet ever new—how far should an engagement of marriage bind two persons who discover they no longer love.

GROSSET & DUNLAP, Publishers, NEW YORK

PETER B. KYNE'S NOVELS

THE ENCHANTED HILL

A gorgeous story with a thrilling mystery and a beautiful girl.

NEVER THE TWAIN SHALL MEET

A romance of California and the South Seas.

CAPPY RICKS RETIRES

Cappy retires, but the romance of the sea and business, keep calling him back, and he comes back strong.

THE PRIDE OF PALOMAR

When two strong men clash and the under-dog has Irish blood in his veins—there's a tale that Kyne can tell!

KINDRED OF THE DUST

Donald McKay, son of Hector McKay, millionaire lumber king, falls in love with " Nan of the sawdust pile," a charming girl who has been ostracized by her townsfolk.

THE VALLEY OF THE GIANTS

The fight of the Cardigans, father and son, to hold the Valley of the Giants against treachery.

CAPPY RICKS

Cappy Ricks gave Matt Peasley the acid test because he knew it was good for his soul.

WEBSTER: MAN'S MAN

A man and a woman hailing from the " States," met up with a revolution while in Central America. Adventures and excitement came so thick and fast that their love affair had to wait for a lull in the game.

CAPTAIN SCRAGGS

This sea yarn recounts the adventures of three rapscallion seafaring men.

THE LONG CHANCE

Harley P. Hennage is the best gambler, the best and worst man of San Pasqual and of lovely Donna.

GROSSET & DUNLAP, Publishers, NEW YORK

RAFAEL SABATINI'S NOVELS

Jesi, a diminutive city of the Italian Marches, was the birthplace of Rafael Sabatini, and here he spent his early youth.   The city is glamorous with those centuries the author makes live again in his novels with all their violence and beauty.

Mr. Sabatini first went to school in Switzerland and from there to Lycee of Oporto, Portugal, and like Joseph Conrad, he has never attended an English school. But English is hardly an adopted language for him, as he learned it from his mother, an English woman who married the Maestro-Cavaliere Vincenzo Sabatini.

Today Rafael Sabatini is regarded as "The Alexandre Dumas of Modern Fiction."

THE BANNER OF THE BULL

THE CAROLINIAN

SAINT MARTIN'S SUMMER

MISTRESS WILDING

FORTUNE'S FOOL

BARDELYS THE MAGNIFICENT

THE SNARE

CAPTAIN BLOOD

THE SEA-HAWK

SCARAMOUCHE

GROSSET & DUNLAP, *Publishers*, NEW YORK

RUBY M. AYRES' NOVELS

THE LITTL'ST LOVER

CANDLE LIGHT

THE MAN WITHOUT A HEART

THE ROMANCE OF A ROGUE

THE MATHERSON MARRIAGE

RICHARD CHATTERTON

A BACHELOR HUSBAND

THE SCAR

THE MARRIAGE OF BARRY WICKLOW

THE UPHILL ROAD

WINDS OF THE WORLD

THE SECOND HONEYMOON

THE PHANTOM LOVER

GROSSET & DUNLAP, Publishers, NEW YORK

ZANE GREY'S NOVELS

TAPPAN'S BURRO
THE VANISHING AMERICAN
THE THUNDERING HERD
THE CALL OF THE CANYON
WANDERER OF THE WASTELAND
TO THE LAST MAN
THE MYSTERIOUS RIDER
THE MAN OF THE FOREST
THE DESERT OF WHEAT
THE U. P. TRAIL
WILDFIRE
THE BORDER LEGION
THE RAINBOW TRAIL
THE HERITAGE OF THE DESERT
RIDERS OF THE PURPLE SAGE
THE LIGHT OF WESTERN STARS
THE LAST OF THE PLAINSMEN
THE LONE STAR RANGER
DESERT GOLD
BETTY ZANE
THE DAY OF THE BEAST

*   *   *   *   *   *   *

LAST OF THE GREAT SCOUTS
   The life story of "Buffalo Bill" by his sister Helen Cody Wetmore, with Foreword and conclusion by Zane Grey.

ZANE GREY'S BOOKS FOR BOYS

ROPING LIONS IN THE GRAND CANYON
KEN WARD IN THE JUNGLE
THE YOUNG LION HUNTER
THE YOUNG FORESTER
THE YOUNG PITCHER
THE SHORT STOP
THE RED-HEADED OUTFIELD AND OTHER
   BASEBALL STORIES

GROSSET & DUNLAP, *Publishers*, NEW YORK